EMBRACE MY DESIRES
MALCOLM & STARR PART II

STEELE INTERNATIONAL, INC. A BILLIONAIRES ROMANCE SERIES BOOK 8

CHARMAINE LOUISE SHELTON

CONTENTS

FREE BOOK

Get the start of the STEELE International, Inc. A Billionaires Romance Series with *Discover My Desires Sebastian & Lola Prequel* FREE!

Click Cover Below or visit **bit.ly/CLBooksNewsletter** to subscribe to my newsletter for latest news and launches, books from my author friends, and sizzling reads in book promotions. Plus, start reading the steamy billionaire romance *Series Prequel* of Sebastian Steele and Lola Lewis.

Their stories. Their discovery of unknown desires...

FREE BOOK!

EXCLUSIVE FOR SUBSCRIBERS!

A Trilogy of Desires Roger & Leonie Parts I-III

A Trilogy of Desires Malcolm & Starr Parts I-III

Series Extras

Series Playlist

STEELE INTERNATIONAL, INC. - JACKSON CORPORATION
A BILLIONAIRES ROMANCE SERIES CROSSOVER

Tempt My Desires Lachlan & Haley Part I

Tease My Desires Lachlan & Haley Part II

Grant My Desires Lachlan & Haley Part III

Intrigue My Desires Harris & Kat Part I

Decode My Desires Harris & Kat Part II

Honor My Desires Harris & Kat Patt III

A Trilogy of Desires Lachlan & Haley Parts I-III

A Trilogy of Desires Harris & Kat Parts I-III

Series Extras

Series Playlist

ABOUT STEELE INTERNATIONAL, INC. A BILLIONAIRES ROMANCE SERIES

Welcome to the titillating world of the multibillion-dollar global company and the love affairs of the family that controls it.

STEELE International, Inc. is a series of interconnecting Billionaire romance. Follow the Steele family as they fly around the world chasing the women they love and their happily ever afters. Get ready for glitz, glamour, and steamy romance books. What's better than that? The Jet-set Lifestyle has never been hotter...

The Desires Series is not for the tea set; it's for the top-shelf vodka straight up in a pretty crystal glass coterie!

Don't miss any of the sizzling romance books in the STEELE International, Inc. A Billionaires Romance Series:

Discover My Desires Sebastian & Lola Prequel
(Available Exclusively to Subscribers)

Fulfill My Desires Sebastian & Lola Part I

Heighten My Desires Sebastian & Lola Part II

Ignite My Desires Roger & Leonie Part I

Stoke My Desires Roger & Leonie Part II

Justify My Desires Roger & Leonie Part III

Deepen My Desires Sebastian & Lola Part III

Capture My Desires Malcolm & Starr Part I

Embrace My Desires Malcolm & Starr Part II

Cherish My Desires Malcolm & Starr Part III

A Trilogy of Desires Sebastian & Lola Parts I-III

A Trilogy of Desires Roger & Leonie Parts I-III

A Trilogy of Desires Malcolm & Starr Parts I-III

Series Extras

Series Playlist

ABOUT EMBRACE MY DESIRES
MALCOLM & STARR PART II

Malcolm

Come along with me—the second son; the rebel; the bad boy billionaire playboy of the family—as my brown-eyed beauty—laid-back LA girl who owns a luxury yoga and wellness center—and I embrace our true desires as our steamy love story continues.

Will my ex-psycho-playmate drag me back to my old ways? Or will My Earth Angel ground me for a second chance at our love?

Trip the light fantastic with us and see for yourself. If part one was enough for you, then it's been real.

Starr

All I can say is damn that man!

Join Malcolm on his journey of self-discovery and his quest for the ultimate thrill—Starr Knight—as they seek to rebuild their love in Bali, Mnemba Island, Monte Carlo, and wherever the sun takes this stellar pair in their sizzling second chance billionaire romance.

Their love story is a standalone romance trilogy in the series. Get a glimpse of their dynamism in other books.

Anthem: "Stop Dragging My Heart Around" Stevie Nicks featuring Tom Petty
https://www.youtube.com/watch?v=H5i7j0VhEHw

Playlist:
https://www.youtube.com/playlist?list=
PLXwYvn0e218DQDFhgWBlFO7mk8WakpGyA

Visit CharmaineLouiseBooks.com

MALCOLM

1 *Month Ago*

"I DON'T KNOW. She fucking ghosted me, bro... No, I have no idea what happened. One minute we're dancing at the STEELE St. Barth's beachfront club. The next, she's ignoring me. Not answering my calls, texts, emails. She even had her collars hand delivered by courier to my West Hollywood penthouse. So yeah, you tell me, Sebastian."

My frustration with my wayward sub-cum-girlfriend hits its limit after weeks of her MIA action—or lack thereof...

Starr Knight, my beautiful woman with the face of an angel and the body of a sinner. When she smiles, dimples dot her sculpted cheekbones the color of warm chestnuts and her wide, sorrel brown eyes shine. I smirk at the memory of fisting her long, curly dark brown hair as I lose myself in Starr's sexy AF body—five feet, six inches, fit, curvy. Her submissive behavior—after eight months of being together—trained to match my Dom needs. Perfect. For. Me.

As a multibillionaire bachelor, women flock to me with the goal to gain a hunk of ice on their left ring finger. Visions of dollar signs float before their eyes, right along with my striking visage. Arrogant, maybe, but true.

Starr? No.

My Angel is a boss. Stanford University undergraduate degree in economics then continued on to the B-School for her MBA. She earned multiple fitness certifications, including her specialty in yoga. Followed her passion for health and wellness combined with helping others and opened Starr Light Fitness and Wellness Beverly Hills seven years ago at 25 years old.

Her initial goal achieved lead to a partnership with STEELE International, Inc. to expand into worldwide fitness retreats at luxury resorts and to add a second center location in the Caribbean. Beautiful, bodacious, smart as hell, and a self-made multimillionaire. Boom.

Fortunately for me, I head STEELE's Entertainment Properties Division as the president and First VP of the Board. I oversee our casinos, hotels, and resorts. My division generates the most revenue for my family's multigenerational, multibillion-dollar luxury real estate development and management company based out of The STEELE Tower in New York City.

SLFW falls within my milieu.

Another stroke of luck came in the form of Lola Lewis,

now Steele. My sister-in-law met My Angel at her first international fitness retreat in Fiji on the private Laucala Island. Lola raved about her experience and how cool My Angel is as a yoga instructor. Then she acted as a match-maker. Well, that is for a business partnership...

Lola insisted I contact My Angel to discuss the opportunity. I agreed. But it was at Lola's wedding to my older brother Sebastian that I first met My Angel when she bumped into me. My eyes fell onto her gorgeous face, and sparks flew when my fingers brushed her soft skin as I balanced her on those fuck-me sandals.

Unbeknownst to me, the angel at my feet who shocked me to my core was Starr Knight, Lola's yoga teacher and close friend. It wasn't until the morning after the wedding I learned they were the same—Starr Knight, My Angel. Then she proved elusive.

After using my wiles to orchestrate a trip to STEELE St. Barths' instead of a boring conference room for potential partnership discussions, our mutual interest in the other led to us being in a Dominant/submissive relationship for the past eight months. A relationship I thought was on the cusp of a permanent situation.

Unlike my previous D/s relationships I had based on contracts for no longer than three months, the one with My Angel morphed into much more.

Within a month of being together, I took her to dinner with my parents, Morgan and Shelley. The Steele Matriarch knew My Angel from Lola and Sebastian's wedding preparations, then caught my interest in her at the festivities, naturally. My mother didn't disguise her pleasure in

My Angel being in our family as more than Lola's close friend.

My mother's expressive brown eyes lit up at the sight of My Angel approaching the restaurant's bar. She's a striking woman in her mid-fifties with shoulder-length, wavy black hair. Compared to my father from whom my siblings and I inherited various shades of his gray eyes, thick ebony hair, and six-foot-plus height. Except for our baby sister, Haley, who's two inches taller than our mother at five feet, eight inches.

She's the fraternal younger twin to Harris. Roger was the youngest until the twins were born—a double surprise for our parents. Then there's me with Sebastian as the eldest.

Each sibling works at STEELE International and has a board position: Sebastian recently took over the helm from our father as CEO and Chairman of the Board while he remains president of the Retail Properties Division; Roger, president of the Residential Properties Division and Second VP; Harris and Haley, fraternal twins, co-founders of the subsidiary STEELE Technology and Cyber Security and Members. Each of us head divisions best suited to our knowledge and interests.

I'm the most appropriate sibling to take on the Entertainment Properties Division. My wild ways of pushing the envelope and my love of the challenge extreme sports triggers prepared me for the role to lead our division focused on pleasure and thrills.

I thought cave diving and heli-skiing pumped my

adrenaline. But the pleasure and thrills My Angel gives to me beats them all. And I can't get enough.

It was on to the next level when we had dinner with her parents after being together for two months.

In their city, but on my ground at Spire 70 and Restaurant 69 in STEELE Rodeo Drive. Despite the initial annoyance of meeting Quinn Peters—her ex-boyfriend—unexpectedly My Angel and I had a good time with Peace and Sun.

Yeah, her father Peace Knight and mother Sun Knight—Jordan and Belinda originally.

They're brilliant environmental law attorneys who take on the most challenging cases against big businesses and win billions. The law firm—Knight & Knight LLP—her parents founded years ago after they met at a music festival while at Stanford Law School ranks in the top five of the United States. With offices in LA, Seattle, Denver, Chicago, Houston, New Orleans, Miami, New York City to represent cases in the top environmentally focused cities. They may be hippies, but they're sharks in the courtroom.

Needless to say, I succeeded in making a good impression on her parents.

Now, the big question: is Starr still My Angel?

My head spins as I rattle off the last few weeks of no contact with My Angel to Sebastian. I need Baz's advice as a fellow Alpha Dom for whom Lola is his sub and wife.

I know it's selfish of me, so absorbed in my life while Roger faces a crazy ass pretrial for sexual assault and harassment and STEELE International is the co-defendant. The baseless case brought forth by Delia Shaw, an intern at STEELE Paris and former classmate of Leonie at the Paris American Academy. Leonie *The Lion* Beaulieu gorgeous megamodel and then girlfriend of Roger, now fiancée and mother of his twin boys. He refused to pay Delia Shaw any attention, and now this bullshit.

Just as the pretrial judge was announcing his determination, Leonie cried out in the courtroom. Her water broke. The stress of the media frenzy and pretrial caused her to go into labor early.

Morgan, Shelley, Leonie's parents, Lola, Sebastian, and the rest of the Steele clan, the Jacksons, Joel Bailey and Hettie Fuchs, Norman and Anita Green, Luc Montaigne, Blair Thomas, Billie Chandler, Françoise Faucher, and some STEELE employees who gathered in support left the courtroom en masse.

Hours later, after Leonie gave birth, I caught up with My Angel, finally. She was so engrossed in her doula duties she didn't notice I followed her down the hallway as she headed back from the nurse's station. We hadn't spoken since the slight nod she gave to me when she entered the courtroom. Then she spent all of her time in the hospital at Leonie's side, so we didn't interact until the hallway encounter.

And what a dismal encounter…

"Hi, Angel," I say tentatively. "Crazy day, huh?"

She couldn't avoid me. So she nods and tries to go around my massive, six-foot-four-inch frame. I tower over her by ten inches.

I sidestep to block her path again.

We do a shuffling dance that Haley interrupts inadvertently.

As soon as she asks me a question, My Angel dodges the entire scene and flees to her guest room next to Leonie's suite.

As she hurries away, I watch her retreating back. Once Haley finishes, I call My Angel's mobile and send text messages eager to speak with her. No. Fucking. Answer.

I finish my sad story and glance over at Baz.

He doesn't show any judgement on his face that mine resembles. At only two years apart, I'm his absolute doppelgänger: same six feet, four inches in height; gray eyes; black hair; clean shaven or 5 o'clock shadow covers a firm jaw. People often confuse us or think we're twins.

It used to drive me crazy as a teenager. I strove for my own identity, hating being in Baz's shadow. It resulted in my rebel ways for years. Now we're good, and I see Baz as a confidante and not as a competitor. Still similar driven and dominant playboys—well, not anymore.

Baz gave up his one fuck and done ways after he met Lola. I gave up the sub contracts after I met My Angel. Call us reformists…

"I get how frustrated you must be, given how Lola iced me out of her life so abruptly. Did you do or say anything that may have upset Starr? Even if you don't think it bothered her?" Baz asks as he frowns.

A moment passes while I consider the last few times My Angel and I were together. Nothing untoward comes to mind. Hell, I was planning our next trip!

"No, bro, nothing. Not a damn thing," I respond as I stroke my five o'clock shadow thoughtfully.

Baz nods, then pulls out his mobile. After a finger presses on the screen, he lifts it to his ear.

"Hey, babe. Are you near Starr? Okay. Question, what's she saying about Malcolm?" His gaze remains on my questioning face while Lola speaks. Then he ends the call with an *I love you, too*.

Lucky fuck.

"Well, Starr has mentioned nothing to Lola. And she doubts Starr said anything to Leonie or she would have told Lola," Baz starts, then runs his fingers through his hair. "Either Starr doesn't want to interfere with Roger and Leonie's moment, or Starr isn't ready to disclose anything to them yet."

I nod in agreement.

"So, just leave it for now. Give her a couple of days once she's not as busy with Leonie"—he claps me on the back, and angles us toward the door of the waiting room—"Go to your President's Suite at STEELE Place Vendôme, shower, and eat a good meal. Then come back to the hospital refreshed. You need to clear your head, bro."

I take his advice and head out after I check in on the new parents. My heart swells with love when I see them holding Rodolphe and Gaspard. Could that be My Angel and me one day?

"THE NEXT GENERATION of Steeles is born! May they carry on our clan name and STEELE and Beaulieu forever!"

Declares our father as he holds his day-old grandsons proudly.

"*Oui, Mon Trésor* extends her family's line with males,

one for Beaulieu and one for STEELE!" Guy—Leonie's father—adds proudly as he plucks Gaspard from Morgan's arm.

The rest of the conversation fades into the background as I lean against the wall, watching My Angel across the room. Fuck if I don't feel like a lost puppy hoping to be reunited with its loving owner.

When at last she raises her gaze to mine, my heart thuds in my chest. At last!

Then it crashes to the ground, cracked.

She averts her eyes and chats with Anita—the wife of Norman Green, the former world heavyweight champion, STEELE's partner in his eponymous chain of luxury fitness facilities, and Roger's personal trainer.

My feet no longer propel me towards My Angel. Instead, I slouch back against the wall with a frown marring my face. Okay, this shit will not fly for much longer. Enough.

I am far from one who bows in defeat when I want something. No matter the challenge, I stand firm and get what I want. And I want my brown-eyed Angel back in my arms and writhing beneath the sting of my palm and the pounding of my ten-inch cock.

* * *

"Oh!" My Angel exclaims as she bumps into me when she closes the door behind her to Leonie's suite at the hospital with a click.

Her head tilts back to see me glowering at her. It's been

two days since Leonie gave birth and one since our hallway encounter. Yesterday I resolved to put an end to this limbo.

Without a word, I take My Angel by the elbow and usher her next door to her guest room. I cock my eyebrow at her wordlessly, demanding she unlock it for us to enter. This intervention requires privacy.

She does.

Once inside, I grab her heart-shaped face between my sizable hands and crush her mouth with mine in a possessive, toe-curling kiss. I don't let My Angel catch her breath before I hoist her up and slam her back against the door.

Automatically, her long, toned legs wrap around my waist and lock at the ankles. Her hands dive into my hair, tugging at my scalp.

The pressure of her warm pussy against the front of my shirt coupled with the pain from her frantic tugs makes my cock jump to life. It's been too long since I buried it balls deep in her tight, wet core.

With a growl, I rip at her wrap dress, pulling the hem up to her waist. The sound of my zipper, then the feel of my Prince Albert piercing's balls jewelry against her pussy lips drive me to the brink. Only to be jerked back from the edge of carnal bliss.

My Angel pushes me away.

Her palms against my broad chest offer no help to dislodge her from my firm hold. She squirms in my arms and tries to get down.

I lap at her tongue with mine as I continue to breach her pussy.

"RED!!!"

My Angel's scream against my mouth jolts me—her safeword.

Fuck. Me.

At once I let her go and step back. My gray eyes darkened to obsidian with lust, now peer at her dazed and questioningly.

Despite her body's betrayal—flushed face, pebbled nipples, swollen clit, wet pussy—she wants me to stop. My Angel closes her eyes and takes a deep cleansing breath. Then she smooths her dress before she brings her gaze back to mine.

Meanwhile, my heart continues to race.

I scrub my hand over my heated face and run my fingers through my mussed hair. Now I tug in frustration. I too take a deep breath and shake my head to clear it. The wild look leaves my eyes as I stare back at My Angel.

She breaks the silence.

"Malcolm... I... You told me we could explore one another. That it will have no negative impact on our business. You swore to uphold your promise to me for our business to proceed, no matter the result of our 'interaction.' I hope you are a man of your word," she says and pauses for my confirmation.

My mouth opens and closes, then opens again as I remember my words to her so many months ago. I try to formulate an answer. One that will get us beyond this line of questioning.

She holds up her hand and asks, "Yes or no?"

I cock my head to the side and raise my eyebrow as I study her face intently.

My Angel holds her ground, lifting her chin to stare back at me. Her sorrel brown eyes defiant, no longer filled with passion or submission. Or us.

My face shutters, and I grow taller, aloof. So be it. Malcolm *The Enforcer* Steele begs no one.

"Yes," I respond blandly.

"Good. I no longer wish to pursue the D/s relationship with you. However, I intend to continue as planned with Starr Light Fitness & Wellness' partnership with STEELE International. Agreed?" She asks.

Without hesitation, I respond coolly, "Agreed. Anton will continue as your contact. Goodbye, Starr."

"Goodbye, Malcolm."

That answers my question: Starr Knight is no longer My Angel.

resent

"Oh, God, Malcolm, baby! You feel so fucking good! I missed you so much, too!" She cries out.

A month later, and icy fingers still grip my broken heart in a vice.

That hussy Vicky Reynolds!

I should have known better than to trust Malcolm and his former or current or whatever sub. She's a Hollywood royalty actress who tends to name-drop her great-grandfather the founder of a movie studio, her father a major producer, and her mother a screen siren.

After over two years of her being my client, to me she was like a little sister. Albeit a petite, blonde-haired, blue-eyed sister from another mother. Four years younger than my thirty-two, her acting career and travels make her worldly. But she appeared to look up to me. Often asked my advice. It could have been the yogi tenets I shared in my dharma talks.

That is, until I started my D/s relationship with Malcolm. Vicky used to tell me about her escapades with her Dom, but never mentioned his name.

Her erotic tales made me want the same experience. I would fantasize about being submissive to a sexy, powerful Dominant. After I bumped into Malcolm at Lola's wedding, it was his visage that appeared on my faceless dream Dom.

My pussy clenches at the vision and at the memories of his calloused palm spanking my tender ass and his massive cock tunneling into my virgin bottom hole. And he made me want even more. Submission. Pleasure. Pain. Love?

Damn that man for making me want him!

Vicky picked up on my relationship with my new Dom at SLFW's demo fitness retreat at STEELE St. Barth's. Unfortunately, she caught My Dom with me in an intimate embrace on the path to the villa I was staying in.

I did not know the Dom who dumped her was none other than Malcolm Steele.

Vicky showed up to Malcolm's high-profile members-only luxury BDSM and dance club LEVELS Beverly Hills opening night gala drunk off of her ass. She accused me of stealing her Dom in front of the guests.

Afterwards, she made my life miserable with the media, gossip blogs, and paparazzi hounding me. It reached the point where Malcolm provided a security detail for me and upped the systems at my Benedict Canyon Drive mansion and at SLFW.

If that wasn't enough, Vicky went so far as to tamper with my business. That was the last straw!

I canceled her membership and banned her from the center. Some members sided with her and left while others stayed loyal to me. It's one thing to talk shit about me, but not to fuck with my company and the good it provides for our clients. No ma'am!

Thankfully, Malcolm took full responsibility and protected me from the worse of the scandal.

We made it past that unpleasant blip in our relationship. But this? Him inviting me over to talk, and he's fucking Vicky like a stallion? No way, no how will Malcolm and I ever rekindle our relationship. The End!

"Hey! You're not even listening to me, Starr!"

Adrienne Anthony's accusatory voice cuts into my reverie. My CMO and General Manager of SLFW Beverly Hills and best friend of nine years scowls at me.

We met at Stanford Graduate School of Business. Everyone referred to us as Night & Day since we contrasted in our appearances and attitudes. From our long, curly hair with Adrienne's light brown and mine dark brown to her green feline eyes and my sorrel brown angelic eyes to her buttery pecan-colored skin and mine the color of warm chestnuts. I have dimples to her sharp cheekbones. But we're both five feet, six inches with curvy fit bodies from our years of yoga, Pilates, and strength training as certified teachers and students.

Again alike with our hippie vibes, independent nature,

and outgoing bubbly personalities. We're loyal and open to a fault. Resourceful and trustworthy round out our traits.

Where Adrienne has a tattoo of a peacock wrapped around her foot up her ankle to symbolize success, I have shooting stars on the back of my neck for wishes.

We hit it off immediately at Stanford and work well together with SLFW.

Our first location outside of Beverly Hills has its grand opening celebration in two weeks, seven days after the soft opening with VIPs and health and wellness editors and bloggers. Starr Light Fitness & Wellness Resorts at STEELE St. Barth's will open its doors for the world. And I cannot wait!

St. Barth's will serve as the center's first global location. Malcolm's team recommends more centers at STEELE properties in Cabo San Lucas, Monte Carlo, and Koh Samui in Thailand, initially with others as demand requires.

The Jackson Hole at STEELE Resorts is Lucien Jackson's latest concept of members-only, high-end beach clubs for the jet set where SLFW will host retreats. Our fitness and wellness programs will offer more amenities for Jackson Hole and increase activities for guests and provide accommodations for retreat participants.

LEVELS—with locations in New York, Paris, London, and now Beverly Hills—is another one of many business partnerships that STEELE has with Jackson Corporation. World-renown for their award-winning eateries, choice cigars, and distinguished liquors and wines, their products pair well within STEELE's casinos, hotels, resorts, and residential and retail properties.

The Steele family's cousins—if not by blood—the Jackson clan has several business ventures with them. Shelley Steele is best friends with Lucie, the Jackson matriarch. They spent most of their adult lives together forming a closer bond than they have with their blood siblings and relatives. Not sharing DNA doesn't keep their families from being a close-knit group.

And SLFW benefits from their partnership, too.

At least, the business partnership survived the arrogant Malcolm Steele…

"Oh! Pardon! I'm listening now," I respond to Adrienne as the thoughts of my ex recede like the waves from the shoreline before Adrienne and me.

We're up on the rooftop terrace of SLFW Resorts St. Barth's sitting on chaise lounges facing the Caribbean Sea. The breeze off of the turquoise water wraps around me as I straighten my legs from lotus position and inhale deeply. Salty air fills my lungs, and the warm sun soaks into my toasted skin. It's early morning, so no one is out. So peaceful.

As much as I'd rather practice my latest class asana flow on the warm powdery sand, work calls. I turn my attention to my bestie.

Adrienne smiles knowingly. She doesn't take pity on my tryst with the playboy billionaire. She's too caught up with Anton Alexeyev—Malcolm's Vice President of Development and college friend. The giant six-foot-six-inch, blond-haired, glacial-eyed Russian has Adrienne in his sights. Her erotic tales with the Alpha Dom rival mine!

"Glad to hear you're with me…" Adrienne quips with a smirk, her green eyes sparkle with mirth.

We discuss the upcoming soft opening: two-day retreat activities, guests, media, staff, and the STEELE team's responsibilities. Having worked together for so many years, Adrienne and I finish our agenda quickly.

We head down to the beach for phase two of our meeting. I take her through my new flow class followed by a meditation focused on nature and the body. Afterwards, Adrienne practices her Beach Barre class with a couple of the SLFW teachers who now live on site and me. I don't blame some of the girls for requesting a relocation from Beverly Hills to St. Barth's. I'm tempted to stay after being here for a week!

Later we have lunch on the patio in front of the center. The delicious menu crafted by Anita. Besides her fitness certifications, she completed culinary school at Le Cordon Bleu and started a meal plan delivery service. Norman added her customized plans to the paid offerings of the elite facilities and complimentary healthy snacks to the youth. She also took over the food services in both chains of his gyms.

When I was in Paris five months ago, she told me more about the meal plan side of her business and her goal to expand it to other wellness companies. I agreed SLFW would partner with her and couldn't be happier.

The flaky local fish and steamed vegetables over cauliflower rice melts on my tongue. The flavors burst across my taste buds in a profusion of tantalizing spices. Even the fruit punch dazzles my palate. Delicious.

I look forward to Anita's arrival so I can rave in person! Without a doubt, the guests will love her food selections, too.

As we finish our meal, one teacher shifts the conversation to the fun she had last night at the resort's beachfront dance club. Everyone laughs as she recounts the sexy as sin men who flirted with her and another teacher shamelessly.

My mind drifts once again to my sexy as sin Dom turned boyfriend. I recall the nights we danced to the sensuous island music as we melded our bodies together. Then the dancing we continued between the sheets. My empty pussy throbs with need.

Damn that man!

MALCOLM

"This chalet hasn't sold yet. It's the largest with five stories, twelve bedrooms, sixteen bathrooms, four fireplaces, an oversized ski room, and the usual entertainment rooms including a sixteen-person cinema room, game room, gym, and wine-tasting cellar. The indoor-outdoor heated pool pavilion with spa is an added bonus. Staff quarters are above the six-vehicle garage."

I nod my head as the project manager rattles off the details of the luxury chalet. As always, the spectacular view of Verbier and the Swiss Alps through the floor-to-ceiling windows captures my attention.

Roger and I have business in the chichi ski town.

After a month of being with Leonie, Rodolphe, and Gaspard, they only left *Le Beaulieu Manoir*—Leonie's ancestral home—to attend their friends Joel and Hettie's wedding. He couldn't put off the final walk-through of

STEELE Residential Properties Division's latest Swiss project.

I oversaw the STEELE Verbier Hotel & Resort's grand opening during last year's ski season. It's been a success from day one. Roger planned his division's completion of the by-application-only compound of ten state-of-the-art chalets and private clubhouse to take occupancy for this year's season.

Verbs, as the in-the-know jet-set call it, is a town in the Swiss Alps. A part of the Valais canton in the southwest of Switzerland, France borders Verbier to the west with Italy to the south. It's the most exclusive ski destination in the world and one of my favorite for heli-skiing off-piste.

It's the winter version of Monaco, with the difference being people who go to Monaco want to watch or be watched. Whereas Verbier has an understated style where wealth is glamorous, stylish and tasteful. People are here for the reasons one goes to a ski resort—the superb skiing. Not to mention the phenomenal bars and restaurants; the après-ski is perfect for party lovers. Verbier is a glamorous winter playground.

The luxury chalets occupy the area south of the Médran lift. They're slightly away from town along Rue de Médran, where the extra space means they are rarely overlooked and have a private, exclusive vibe. The residential compound is opposite to the STEELE Verbier that's closer to the heart of the village square. The concept is for the STEELE Verbier Chalets to access the resort for its five-star amenities. The most important include the luxury thermal bath spa and the three Jackson Corporation restaurants headed by our cousin Lucien the *Sexy Chef* as he's known by his millions of followers.

I'm surprised this chalet is still on the market. The decor is modern Alpine chic with traditional materials of timber and stone complemented by the high-quality fixtures and fittings and custom furniture. Combined with the view, it's an incredible property.

"Well, damn. Maybe I'll buy it."

Roger says as he glances over at me and raises his eyebrow questioningly.

"Why not? We all ski and could use a place here to hang out," I reply with a shrug.

We're all close. And close enough to hang out together regularly. We even spend lots of time with our parents going on vacations, the holidays, birthdays. What can I say? The Steeles enjoy each other's company.

Roger's thought leads to a brilliant idea.

"I'll buy the chalet and gift it to Leonie for Christmas. She loves to ski, and winter is her favorite season," he says with a broad, goofy smile.

"We can have our wedding at *Le Beaulieu Manoir* as planned two days before Christmas Eve. The next day we come to Verbier to celebrate the holiday and New Year's Eve with our families, then our honeymoon alone. Leonie and I didn't want to travel too much with The Twins since they will be with us. Perfect!" He adds now grinning like the Cheshire Cat.

"I'll buy it," Roger says with finality as he glances from me to the project manager.

I cock my head to consider his pronouncement. Then I nod.

"Sounds good to me, bro," I respond. "Leonie will love it. Man, what a way to celebrate, new babies, new wife, new beginning. I'm happy for you, brother."

He smiles at me. We're only a year apart, so I've never lorded over him with an age difference. Harris and Haley get ribbed the most for being the youngest, especially Haley for being the only girl. Her declaration that we're not her father never gets old.

"Thanks. Sebastian, me... Now it's your turn..." Roger says, waggling his eyebrows.

He's on a roll with his love matches—Luc and Blair, now he's focused on Starr and me.

I thought no one was aware of my feelings for the brown-eyed beauty. But I made it clear at Baz and Lola's wedding Starr was on my radar, as evidenced by my mother's comments and Roger's smirk. Neither Starr nor I have said much recently. But Roger must think that ends now.

"How's Starr by the way?" He asks.

Uh no...

I dodge the answer and pull out my mobile.

"Listen, I have a conference call with my team in five minutes I have to take, then some work at the resort. I'll meet you for dinner later," I say over my shoulder as I hightail it out of the chalet.

A nod to the project manager, who hides his laugh with a cough at my fast exit, and I'm out the door.

. . .

"Hello, you look like you could use a friend, Mr. Steele."

A glance to my right reveals a statuesque platinum-haired stunner. Her obsidian eyes—a sharp contrast to the paleness of her waist-length silky tresses and porcelain skin—level on mine. She all but purrs as she brushes her hand along my muscular thigh, then leans in to press her surgically enhanced tits against my side.

"How would you like to join me by the fireside with your drink?" She whispers in my ear, her Swedish accent thickening.

I shudder, not from interest but from irritation at her bold behavior when her palm grazes my groin.

"My, my, you're a big boy, aren't you?" She breathes lustily.

In a flash, my hand grasps her wrist and removes the wandering digits from my flaccid cock. A scowl covers my face. I shake my head, then angle my body away from her.

The thought of canoodling with another woman makes my stomach roil. Fuck.

"You—"

"Hey, bro! My bad for keeping you waiting."

I turn back around to find Roger standing behind the handsy woman.

She tosses the curtain of hair over her shoulder to peer at him. Her eyes widen to see another Steele brother within reach. She had her sights set on one ultimate prize and found two.

Just like many others, she's more than willing to have a one-night tryst with one of the STEELE Quaternity, as the media has labeled my brothers and me. They've dubbed us the most sought-after of the world's eligible multibillion-aires. Our near-limitless wealth, power, and good looks attract women like bees to honey. They clamor for a taste, even one night.

Behind her dark lust-filled eyes, her mind goes into overdrive thinking of how to snag Roger and me. The tip of her little pink tongue pokes out to glide along her glossed full lips. A sultry smile spreads across them as she sizes us up, glancing at us from head to toe.

"Well, aren't I the lucky one tonight?" She purrs as she reaches for Roger's arm.

He steps aside deftly and raises his hands to ward off her grasp.

"Neither of us are available," Roger adds with a firm shake of his head. "Pardon, my brother and I have dinner plans. Good night."

I take my cue and hop off of the barstool. Without a second glance, I walk past the woman and follow Roger to the maître d's station at STEELE Verbier's STEAKhouse restaurant. It's run by Lucien through one of their many Jackson Corporation partnerships. A reservation at the three Michelin star restaurant is the most sought-after in this part of Switzerland. The host leads us into the dining room to a prime table with unobstructed views of the slopes lit for night skiing.

He places menus in front of us that offer the expected fare typical of steakhouse cuisine of choice cuts of beef, chicken, lobster, and the fish of the day with favorable sauces and sides. Lucien complements the tantalizing dishes with an award-winning wine list and delicious desserts.

As to be expected, the client care is impeccable. So, I don't flinch when the server quietly appears at my side and places a napkin-covered basket with an assortment of warm, fresh-baked breads on the table. I glance up to see a twenty-something woman who is model-perfect and polished with coffee-colored hair pulled in a neat, low ponytail, minimal makeup, and bright hazel eyes. Her all-black uniform of a long-sleeved shirt, knee-length skirt, butcher apron, and sensible heels is spotless—the de rigueur fashion for restaurant employees.

"Welcome to STEAKhouse, sirs. My name is Denise, and I'll be your server this evening. May I take your drink orders? We have some lovely specials tonight. May I share them with you?"

Roger and I give her our drink and meal selections, then catch up on STEELE business. His Residential opening still on track and exceeds revenue expectations. With the hotel and resort still booked years in advance, the one-year anniversary party RSVP list includes the über-wealthy, royals, and celebrities. Baz sent emails to each of us commending our divisions' performances in Verbier.

As we finish our entrées, Roger pulls out his mobile. He grins and hands it to me.

It's a text message from Leonie. The sounds of babies ah-gooing along with their mother singing a lullaby to them in French floats from the speakers. The adorable scene plays on the screen. I can't help but to chuckle.

Too cute!

I hand the mobile back to Roger. When he doesn't let go, I glance up at him.

He pins me with his intense, gray-eyed stare and quirks his eyebrow at me.

Oh boy, here we go. I should have known I couldn't keep the situation with Starr known to my parents and Baz only…

"Could be you, you know," Roger says pointedly as he pockets his mobile and stands.

The server automatically places the bill on the Steele family account, so no need to waste time signing the check.

Roger strides from the dining room to the floor-to-ceiling stone, double-sided fireplace in the lounge. We settle on leather club chairs before the roaring flames. The scent of the pine kindling fills my nostrils. Another server approaches to take our after-dinner drink orders.

I sip my Rémy Martin digestif as I watch Roger over the Baccarat crystal snifter. Might as well let him ask. It's been a month since Starr ended us. Perhaps he can enlighten me as to the cause of her abrupt change of heart.

"So?" He asks with no room for dodging an answer.

I incline my head and nod. Then tell him the latest. Just like Baz, Roger listens intently without interruption, his gaze unwavering.

He agrees it's best I don't attend the grand opening celebration for Starr Light Fitness & Wellness Resorts at STEELE St. Barth's out of respect for Starr's wishes. Leonie told him the possibility of me making a scene or of me making her feel uncomfortable if I showed concerned Starr.

Now the grapevine news continues…

But I appreciate my family's involvement since their chatter provides a clue to Starr's mindset. Sure, I told her goodbye. However, that doesn't stop me from wanting her, needing her. Or wanting a video of her singing to our babies.

"Starr!! This is spectacular!"

"Yes! I'm so proud of you!"

"Absolutely amazing!"

I smile at Haley, Billie, and Lola. Along with Leonie, Blair, Anita, Adrienne, and her younger sister Claudia, my girls flew in to SLFW Resorts at STEELE St. Barth's early. I want them to experience the center before the guests and media arrive tomorrow for the soft opening, then stay for the party.

"*Félicitations!*" Leonie chimes in as she hugs me. "Your dream came true, *chérie!*"

"And in a big way! A brand-new center designed to your specifications on a beautiful resort property," Anita adds, then grins. "Not to mention your sexy boyfriend!"

The smile slides off my face. From such a high to a terrible low…

Anita's brown eyes widen as they dart from me to the

other girls. Lola, Leonie, and Haley quirk their mouths and lower their gazes. Billie and Blair stare back, unaware of Anita's unintentional flub.

"Sorry, honey! I didn't realize!" She recovers quickly. "No matter, you did it and I'm beyond happy for you!"

We hug, and I return her smile.

"No worries. Remember, we must embrace the good and the bad. They have equal purpose in our lives," I respond despite the crack in my heart reopening like a chasm.

Adrienne told me Anton confirmed Malcolm won't attend the soft or the grand openings.

I pretended not to be bothered, but it hurt. All along I envisioned us together celebrating my triumph. With a sigh, I turn my attention back to those who love and support me, thankful for their presence in my live.

"Well, let's get started with our morning yoga session, ladies!" I say as I clap my hands and gesture for them to sit on their mats.

They scuttle to their seats, and we spend the next hour and a half absorbed in our pranayama, asana, and meditation practices.

Fortunately, my disappointment in Malcolm floats away on the warm sea breeze.

"TELL ME, how do you really feel?"

Billie says in her Southern Belle accent. Her Granny Smith apple green eyes search my face as we sit on the patio of my beachfront villa sipping mojitos later in the evening.

She and Blair are Lola's administrative assistants. With Billie based in Las Vegas, we've grown close over the last couple of years. We meet up in Vegas or Beverly Hills at least once a month. Hitting the baccarat tables at STEELE Las Vegas as frequently as the massage tables at SLFW.

With her wavy, medium-blonde balayage hair and pecan-colored skin, everyone says she's Tyra's doppelgänger. Billie is curvy like the megamodel, but a petite version at five feet, four inches.

"I miss him. I won't deny it. Hell, I can't deny it. The thought of Malcolm makes me want what we had," I respond sadly.

Billie takes a sip of her cocktail and stares out at the setting sun hovering on the horizon of the Caribbean Sea.

The streaks of fiery red, orange, and gold dapple the surface. A few seagulls soar above the waves, seeking their dinner. Their cries fill the salt-scented air.

"Well, what happened? You seemed happy—both of you," Billie says as she shifts on her chaise lounge to face me again.

I hadn't told Lola or Leonie about overhearing Malcolm speaking to Roger the last time Malcolm and I were at STEELE St. Barth's over two months ago.

"Who says I love her?" he asked with an arrogant chuckle. "We're just in the here and now, bro. Not all of us are ready to run down the aisle to the love of our life!"

I gasped at his callous words, and my stomach dropped as I stood in the doorway behind him. The noise made him shift in his chaise lounge on the deck. A fleeting expression of shock ghosted across my face, but it was too fast for Malcolm to decipher it.

From his expression, he appeared just as shocked as me.

I pulled on the strength of my inner Independent Woman warrior. Then I smiled. She gave me just enough oomph to move my lips, but not enough for the smile to reach my eyes. Fortunately, they're covered with giant glamour girl shades, so he couldn't tell.

Malcolm smiled back and held his hand out to me.

I took it and pretended all was fine for the next three days.

And definitely didn't tell them about discovering Malcolm fucking Vicky on the rooftop terrace of his Sunset Boulevard penthouse...

After I recount that sad tale, Billie nods thoughtfully.

"I can understand why you haven't told Leonie and Lola. We're girls and all, but Malcolm is the brother of their men. But don't discount the loyalty Leonie and Lola have to you, too," Billie says.

"Loyalty to you for what?"

Billie and I startle at the unexpected question coming from the path beside the villa.

Lola appears with Leonie and the rest of the girls.

"Well?" Leonie adds to Lola's question.

Billie rises and pours the mojito in the pitcher into the other glasses on the table before us. Once everyone has a glass, she lifts hers and inclines her head towards me.

"Here's to girl power and the support we give to each other," Billie says, then continues in a great impersonation of Bette Davis' voice. "Now, fasten your seat belts, it's gonna be a bumpy ride."

I take my cue and tell my girls everything.

* * *

"CONGRATULATIONS, Starr, sweetheart. You accomplished your dream. I'm happy for you."

I smile up at my ex-boyfriend Quinn, who's taller than me by six inches. His chocolate brown eyes sparkle in his just as chocolatey face.

My parents introduced us years ago since he's an attorney at their law firm. They thought we'd have a lot in common.

I finally gave in to his dinner requests, then to spending time with him. Finally, we started seeing each other. The sex began shortly thereafter. Not at all what I expected or wanted.

After six months, I decided I needed more, and Quinn couldn't give it to me. I broke up with him.

But before I flew down for the soft opening, he reached out to me, wanting to talk. I agreed to meet him for dinner. We spent the evening being honest about our prior relationship and where we stood now.

Quinn admitted he was wrong and had gotten engaged to someone who resembles me because he wanted more with me. He ended the engagement and courted me instead.

I told him I was not in the headspace to date or to rekindle our relationship. Not one to bounce from one pillar to the next, I prefer time between relationships. Time to get back to me.

"Thank you, Quinn," I respond.

Then smooth my hands over my vintage Versace outfit. The saffron yellow corset top with a sweetheart neckline and lacing in the front accentuates my perky D-cups. The matching ankle-length skirt with a full leg slit held closed with more lacing on my left hip drapes across my lower body. Strappy yellow sandals elongate my toned legs. Red lipstick is the extent of makeup and my long curls spill down my back.

My body is my best advertisement for SLFW. I flaunt it for the grand opening celebration—and any chance I get!

Quinn's eyes burn into my skin as his gaze follows the path of my hands.

I ignore his lustful heat and move away to mingle with the other guests and the media.

My parents beam as we pose for the cameras. Quinn slips into the frame, and his hand locks onto my left hip possessively. The pressure from his fingertips on my bare skin makes me flinch. He takes my reaction as an invitation and pulls me closer to his side.

Not wanting to ruin the photos, I stay in place.

"Starr, we need you over here. Kindly come with me now."

I thank God and every deity in every religion's pantheon for Adrienne.

Deftly, I extricate myself from Quinn's clutches and follow her. As I pass Anton, he quirks his eyebrow at me. I widen my eyes and shrug questioningly but keep moving. His icy glacial stare pierces my back.

Great, I can only imagine the report he'll make to his boy...

Then I pass Borya Alexeyev and Lucien.

Oh, it just gets better.

Lucien inclines his head and raises his flute of Krug Clos d'Ambonnay Champagne—my favorite and despite it all, Malcolm arranged cases for the celebration.

Borya scowls at me—the brooding Russian cousin of Anton and a close friend of Malcolm.

I suppress an eye roll and keep strutting.

"You have every brute here imaginable!" Adrienne exclaims as we weave through the throngs of guests. "He who shall not be named may not have deigned us with his presence, but he made certain his cronies attended. Or should I say spies?!"

Her bright green feline eyes flash and narrow.

Adrienne looks fabulous in a coral Swarovski crystal embellished mini slip dress with sky-high strappy sandals. Her long, curly brown hair pulled up into her version of a messy bun—perfectly coiffed. Simple, clear lip gloss coats her full lips.

I have to wonder if she's not dressing to impress another certain Russian more than advertising SLFW's benefits...

"I know right!" I respond after I greet a VIP new member of the Resorts' center.

Malcolm assured me residents of St. Barth's would apply for membership. With over fifty on file from day one of the list opening, I have to give him his credit. He knows his market.

No matter how much I try to keep him out of my mind tonight, I. Just. Cannot.

Damn that man!

"Hey there, Ms. International!"

I turn to find Norman and Anita approaching.

My friends came all out to support me, *The Champ* included. Guests went gaga and angled to get selfies with him. He posed and signed autographs with a smile graciously.

"Ha! You know it!" I giggle.

"I agree. Well done, Starr!"

Sebastian and Lola emerge from the crowd with Leonie and Roger.

Billie, Blair, and Claudia join us.

I glance around our circle and smile ruefully. It's a happy, but bittersweet moment. But I am grateful for my success and my supportive friends and family.

"You. Are. Mine. Naughty. Girl!"

Comes his snarl as he roughly yanks me from the arms of my would-be playmate for the evening.

I nearly stumble in my feather mules as the caveman, gray-eyed stranger pulls me close, my back to his firm chest. I tense as his massive cock thickens and lengthens against my round bottom. His possessive behavior triggers my core. My juices immediately gush from my pussy and drip down my clenched thighs.

I peer up and over my shoulder at this dominant man. His upper lip curls, his nostrils flare, his eyes the color of molten platinum shoot poisonous darts at the Dom who was preparing me for a scene.

My unknown cockblocker wants to take me as his very own.

As I decide whether I want him more than the Dom who first drew my attention, he puts his hands up, palms out in surrender.

My mouth gapes at his retreating back.

Suddenly, I'm hoisted onto the stranger's shoulder in a fireman's carry as though I weigh next to nothing. He swiftly strides to one of the darker areas of the BDSM dungeon. I kick my legs and pummel his back—my small fists ineffectively hit a wall of steel and earn me four swift spanks on my exposed rear. A lightning bolt shoots through my pussy, liquifying more of my juices to pool on the shoulder of his bespoke suit jacket.

A gasp pops from my mouth as he sits on a red velvet sofa in the alcove and drapes me over his hard, muscular thighs. My belly presses against his engorged cock that twitches when our bodies collide.

He makes quick work of lifting my silk negligee and snatching the matching thong down to bind my knees. My bare ass and throbbing pussy exposed to his view. He runs his hands over my lush curves gently—quite a contrast to his previous brutish behavior. I shiver under his delicate touch; his calloused hands caress my soft skin.

"Holy mackerel!" I yell as the first slap of his rough palm against my ass shocks me from the gentle lull.

I reach my hands behind me in an attempt to block his painful blows.

The caveman grabs my wrists in one sizable hand and presses them against my lower back. His other hand never misses a beat and continues to punish me—left, right, left, crease of my ass and thigh, right, left.

I squirm on his lap pitifully as the pain blooms across sore ass.

"You are mine. No one else will ever touch you again, Naughty Girl," he growls.

He punctuates each word with a hard spank, drawing heat and pumping blood to the surface of my bare, jiggling ass.

An unexpected shift in his movements brings two of his thick fingers to my seam—I'm soaking wet for him.

"Is this all for me?" He asks seductively.

His voice deepens with lust as he slides his fingers in and out of my pussy, fucking me, the wet sounds loud in my ears.

As if I were a puppet on a string, I widen my legs to allow him better access to my slippery pussy, but refuse to respond.

My lack of a verbal answer results in another volley of spanks—left, right, left, crease of my ass and thigh, right, left.

"Yes, Sir!" I scream as I wriggle on his lap, attempting to get out of his reach and to close my legs.

"Open!" He demands.

Instantly, my thighs part. My traitorous body takes over from my logical brain.

"So, sweet, Naughty Girl," he rumbles.

The sound of the caveman lapping his fingers with the

flat of his tongue to clean off my erotic essence makes me gush even more than before.

A wicked chuckle slips from his full lips as he smirks at my carnal reaction.

He bends to press his lips against the delicate shell of my ear to whisper, "You like being mine and receiving the sting of my palm on your luscious ass, do you not, Naughty Girl? How would you like to have my colossal cock in your little, virgin ass?"

I cry out and shudder, aching to have his thick cock in all three of my holes. I can't deny I want this caveman to take me in every single one roughly, bent over and fucked by him like a feral animal...

"Ohhh... Malcolm!"

The sound of my hoarse voice screaming aloud rips me from my dream. I bolt upright in the bed sweating, breathing heavily, wildly looking around for the LEVELS members, the Cellar, and My Dom... Malcolm.

I flop back down against the pillows, noticing the sheets tangle around my body in disarray. Not the arms of my former Dom-cum-boyfriend holding me in his warm embrace as I dreamed. The realization sinks in my mind past the veil of my sexy fantasy that I'm not in Beverly Hills at all. Rather, I'm in the villa at STEELE St. Barth's after the party.

With a groan, I roll over and leave the stifling confines of the empty bed. I rip the damp, silk tank top and sleep shorts from my hot, drenched body that's still reeling from a sleep-induced orgasm. Then head to the en suite bathroom for a cold shower.

The first tendrils of the sun's morning rays breach the dark blue sky.

I might as well join the morning yoga class on the beach and release the last of the sexual tension from my humming body.

Damn that man!

MALCOLM

"Cut it out, Harris! Pass the cranberry sauce to me already!"

Haley growls, frustrated with her twin's antics as he teases her relentlessly. Her gray eyes flash like a stroke of lightning as she glares at him.

"Harris Steele! That is enough, young man. Stop taunting your sister and give her the platter at once," our father commands in full-on Alpha Dom mode.

Immediately Harris complies—albeit grudgingly, with a smirk on his face—and hands Haley's favorite Thanksgiving side dish to her.

"Jerk," she mutters under her breath as she snatches it from him.

He in turn mimics her response wordlessly lest our father hear his new gibe. I hide my laugh with a cough and shake my head at Harris. He smirks until our father pins him with a steely stare.

Then I can't help myself, and I laugh out loud.

Those two will never stop. It's their usual behavior at any of our family gatherings. When we were younger, Haley would sometimes leave the dining room in tears. Our parents would chastise Harris and send him to his room.

Now it's our first Thanksgiving as a family with Leonie, Rodolphe, Gaspard, Guy, and Josy. Even Luc joins us. My gaze travels around the dining room table of my parents' new penthouse on the twenty-eighth floor at The STEELE Tower Paris designed by Leonie. Everyone smiles and appears peaceful. The atmosphere is one of gratefulness and happiness.

Our family has a lot to be thankful for: the pretrial judge declared Roger innocent and STEELE International clear of all charges; The Twins were born; my division's revenue outpacing last year. All is right in the Steele World.

Well.. almost.

I lost my mind when Anton gave me a recap of the SLFW Resorts' grand opening celebration.

All was routine and went as expected until he recounted seeing Starr kissing that fucker Peters—her supposed ex-boyfriend. The last we saw him, he was engaged to some Starr lookalike. I should have known he wasn't over her then.

It was bad enough the photos of Peters holding her possessively in the event photos made my blood boil. I damn near crushed my mobile when the Google alerts linked to a gazillion social media and blog sites showing the laughing, lovey-dovey couple.

Nothing prepared me for Starr to move on to another

man so soon after she and I ended our relationship. Starr really didn't seem the type to jump around so easily.

Now I know better.

I wish I could just say fuck it and move on, too. But in the six weeks we've been apart I haven't been able to scene with anyone despite going to LEVELS New York. Each night—and morning for that matter—my palm meets my aching cock, and I spill my jizz down the shower drain.

What a sad schmo I've become.

Fuck. Me.

"Leonie, you did such an incredible job with the redesign of our penthouse!" My mother declares as she raises her glass of Chateau Lafite Rothschild. *"Merci ma fille aussi!"*

"Well done, Leonie!"

"It's marvelous!"

"Cheers!"

Congratulatory comments draw me back to the room. My thoughts of Starr disperse as I refocus on my family.

"It was an honor. Thank you for entrusting me with your home," Leonie responds humbly.

Luc shifts in his seat to face her and asks, "When do you expect to return to your new career, *chérie*? We know how important interior design is to you."

Leonie glances at Roger, then turns to Luc.

"Roger and I haven't spoken about it yet. But I was thinking once Rodolphe and Gaspard reach six months, I could return to STEELE's Interior Design Team part-time as a project designer."

She glances at Roger from beneath her eyelashes and smiles.

He returns her smile and kisses her hand.

"Whatever you want, my love. We have Nanny Grace to help us. Plus, you can even design a nursery for The Twins next to your office if you want to keep them close," he says.

"Oh, *merci, Mon Cœur!*" She squeals as she pulls his mouth to hers and plants a kiss on his lips.

We rib them for their PDA. Me included even though I wish I cuddled Starr in my arms for our family gathering…

"Well, that means you have to make time for your Lola's Coterie campaigns, too! And we need to work on more designs for the pre- and post-natal collections. They've been a colossal hit!"

"*Oui, oui! Absolument!* I cannot wait. I have some new sketches for you, *Chérie,*" Leonie says giggling as Roger continues to plant kisses on her cheek.

"*Très bon*! That's splendid news," Luc says. "Excellent idea, Roger. Leonie, you should consider a specialization in interior design for children. What I've seen of three of the… What is it? Nine? Nurseries for The Twins, they're incredibly well done. You could design nurseries, play-rooms, bedrooms—"

"Ooh, and playhouses that match the families' mansions!" Haley adds. "I've read they're extremely popular with chichi parents."

Luc's thoughts are never far from revenue-generating ideas. Haley, the nerd, more than likely read about the mini mansions during one of her many Internet searches.

"That's an area STEELE International doesn't cover.

The focus has always been on the main properties and amenities. Perhaps you'd like to lead your own division?" Sebastian asks.

With a nod to our brother he adds, "If Roger is game, we can set it in motion as a subset of his division."

"That would add another offering to our clients, and we would include it in future projects. Another revenue stream," Morgan adds, ever the CEO even while retired.

Leonie looks at Roger, her amber eyes glow with excitement.

He scowls, then chuckles.

"How can I deny my love anything? Not to mention the CEO and Steele Patriarch… Thanks, Luc, for an excellent idea!" Roger proclaims as he raises his glass of Chateau Lafite Rothschild. "Here's to Leonie's new division!"

"Hear, hear!"

"*Félicitations!*"

"Cheers!"

Leonie claps her hands and turns to Roger with a grin to kiss him again.

Roger grins like the Cheshire Cat.

Lucky fucker.

"How did you like Thanksgiving dinner, Josy?" Shelley asks as we sip Rémy Martin digestifs in the library.

Josy gestures to my mother with her Baccarat snifter, "It was delicious, *merci!* Guy and I spent Thanksgiving with Lola at her Parisian penthouse on many occasions. She would cook a delectable multi-course meal. Luc would bring scrumptious pastries, and I would bring my double-chocolate soufflés for dessert."

She turns to Leonie and quirks her elegantly arched eyebrow at her daughter.

"Leonie, however, brought the wine since she doesn't cook despite my best efforts to teach her our Tunisian family's recipes."

Lola scoffs, "That's a wasted effort, *Maman* Josy! I've told you so for years!"

Leonie's golden caramel cheeks flush red, and she shakes her head.

"Don't tease her, *Mon Amour*. She takes after her Beaulieu side with her love for beautiful things," Guy responds as he winks at Leonie.

Daddy's Little Girl blows him a kiss in thanks.

"Well speaking of food, Nanny Grace just sent a text to me. The Twins are ringing their dinner bell! So pardon me," Leonie says.

Roger rises with her, but she pushes him back to his seat gently.

"Stay, *Chéri*, Nanny will help me," Leonie says as she smiles lovingly at me while she runs her fingers through his hair, massaging his scalp.

I clap my hands, and everyone glances at me in surprise.

"Do bring my nephews back. I haven't spent enough time with them," I say. "I don't want them to forget their favorite uncle!"

Sebastian sputters on his sip of cognac.

"Hell no! I'm their favorite uncle. So bring them to me!" He exclaims.

Harris and Luc join in, all proclaiming their place in The Twins' lives.

Leonie laughs, and her eyes twinkle.

"Simmer down, boys! You're all their favorite!"

Roger chuckles as she leaves the library.

"Well, don't get me started on their favorite aunt!" Lola adds.

"Yeah… Me!" Haley cuts in, lifting her snifter in salute.

Everyone laughs good-naturedly.

"Since Leonie is out of earshot, I'll tell you some stories about her as a child," Josy says gleefully.

We listen and laugh some more until Leonie returns with The Twins.

Roger goes to Nanny Grace and takes Gaspard from her arms with a word of thanks. Then he kisses his rosy cheeks as he coos happily.

"That's it. Hand him over, bro," I hustle over and pluck Gaspard from his arms just as Sebastian scoops Rodolphe from Leonie.

Roger rolls his eyes at our antics and shakes his head.

"Hey, you could have your own, you know…" he ribs us.

Baz smirks and inclines his head towards Lola.

"Yeah, no need to tell me. Have that conversation with your sister-in-law," he retorts.

Lola gives Roger the stink eye, and he opts to not comment. Instead, he cocks his head at me.

"So what's your excuse, lover boy? How're things with—"

"You mean the sexy AF yoga teacher? Because if you're not interested, I'll step in without hesitation!" Harris says.

The hairs on the back of my neck bristle. A growl erupts from my chest. The Alpha Dom in me rears his possessive head as I glare at our youngest brother.

Harris snickers and pulls out his mobile, typing on the screen.

"Oh, hi Starr… Yes, Happy Thanksgiving to you, too… I wanted to wish you a wonderful holiday and ask how the new surveillance system is going… Mmm… Right… Okay, great! I'm looking forward to the retreat, too. Thanks for inviting me… See you soon."

Silence descends on the library, making the sound of my ragged breathing loud.

10… 9… 8…

"You. Little. SHIT!" I explode. Steam pours from my ears as I flare my nostrils.

Roger reaches for Gaspard. But I pull away and turn my glare on him.

"I know what I'm doing with a baby! Lest you forget, I used to wipe the snot from your nose," I snap before I pin Harris with another heated stare.

"You'll pay for that when you least expect it, little brother. And lest you forget, I'm. Not. Haley," I snarl viciously.

Harris' smirk falters since he knows I'm *The Enforcer* amongst us.

"Ha! Good! Get 'em for me too, Malcolm!" Haley shouts, punching the air in victory.

I wink at her and respond with a dark chuckle, "Will do, Baby Girl, will do."

"One day you'll learn, little bro," Sebastian laughs. Then

leans over to Gaspard and adds, "Just ignore your *Oncle* Malcolm's foul mouth…"

Oh, damn…

Now I glance at Leonie, chagrined.

"Sorry, sis. It won't happen again," I promise.

Leonie's laughter morphs into snorts as tears fill her eyes. She shakes her head and waves her hands in front of her flushed face.

"No worries, *mon frère*! They don't understand words yet, just emotions," she tells me as she pats my shoulder. "But, Harris, boy oh boy, I feel bad for you!"

LATER WE GO UP to Roger and Leonie's redesigned triplex penthouse for a tour.

Leonie did another excellent job with combining my parents' former penthouse below my duplex to create one large home for their growing family. It's on the top three floors, thirty through thirty-two.

Located in the Front de Seine district of Beaugrenelle in the *quinzième*, the property, like The STEELE Tower New York, is mixed-use with commercial and residential space plus the largest mall in Paris. The views of the Seine and of the Eiffel Tower are incredible, especially now at night when the spectacular light display flits across the monumental iron structure.

"Nicely done, Leonie," Luc says when we return to the main living room on the first floor. "*La Tour Eiffel* resembles a sparkling Christmas tree!"

"My favorite room is your Pilates and yoga studio," Lola

gushes. "I need one! Then I can get a good workout at home."

Sebastian snorts and whispers in her ear.

Lola blushes scarlet red, but her hazel eyes spark with desire. Playfully, she swipes at Baz. He chuckles, wrapping his arms around her waist and pulling her back to his front. He places his hands possessively on her lower belly as he nuzzles her neck.

Leonie slips her hand into Roger's and smiles up at him knowingly.

I guess it won't be long before Baz and Lola have a baby of their own.

And my sad story continues…

"This is the most high-end karaoke place I've ever been to before! It feels more like a night-club for dancing than for getting on a stage drunk reading from the teleprompter! I'm glad I listened to you and came out after all."

My gaze goes around the well-appointed interior of the multilevel club in West Hollywood. The sleek decor of black leather, chrome, and gray velvet with glass touches breathes luxury. They covered one wall in floor-to-ceiling mirrors with rows of top-shelf liquor shining like jewels in their crystal bottles. Sofas and club chairs on two levels like an arena face the stage. A female DJ with diamond-covered Beats by Dr. Dre headphones stands behind her Plexiglas booth spinning the latest tunes and the all-time favorites for karaoke lovers.

Then there are the fabulous glitterati attending the club's grand opening night. The current box-office block-buster action hero and his sexy guy friends; *Los Angeles*

Confidential magazine's cover girl for November with her tech mogul husband; the heiress to a private jet company and her entourage. All decked out in their finest attire.

And so am I.

A red, long-sleeved, sheer mock turtleneck with glossy ruby red leather motorcycle pants custom made to hug my curves taper to cover the backs of my cinnamon-hued stilettos. My curls blown straight, brush the top of my ass and sway with each step. Subtle shades of smoky red highlight my eyes while the rest of my makeup remains in nude tones.

Yeah, I want to look fierce since we're at the newest addition to Malcolm's portfolio: STEELE Karaoke Club West Hollywood.

Adrienne confirmed my former lover won't be in attendance since he's still in Paris with his family for Thanksgiving, according to Anton. So along with Claudia, we came for a much-needed night of fun—karaoke, my favorite!

"I'll never steer you wrong, girl!" Adrienne says as she dances to the song being performed. "This club is amazing!"

I nod and raise my tall glass of mojito in salute. Then pick up the song scheduler to cue my choice. It's time for me to enter the contest. First prize, a week's stay at STEELE Cabo San Lucas. Who'd pass up the opportunity to visit stunning Palmilla Beach?

"Ready to go up? You're the last of us, bring it home, Starr!" Claudia says as I take a sip of my mojito and stand.

"You know it!" I respond, slapping high five with her.

I leave our VIP cluster and strut to the stage. My heart pumps with excitement the closer I get to the stage. Then it drops when I join the queue of performers.

Malcolm Steele!

He's here after all and with a group of people including two women clinging to him as he laughs at something one of them said in his ear. His handsome face lights up, and he turns to the woman on his left to whisper something in her ear.

Really?!

Well, I've got something for you, you arrogant…

When my time comes, I ask the coordinator to change my song selection. Let's see how he laughs now.

Game on!

I take to the stage like I'm Annie Lennox herself. The sound of a motorcycle revving as it blares from the surround-sound speakers catches the audience's attention. All heads turn to the stage, to me standing like a diva gripping the mic like my lover.

I belt out the words to "Would I Lie to You" and stalk the stage with such emotion, it's not long into the song people clap and cheer. I refuse to direct my soulful rendition in *his* direction. Instead, I play to the action hero and his friends seated at the edge of the stage.

When I beckon to the movie star, he jumps up and helps me down from the stage. I sashay around serenading him as he plays along. The audience goes wild with stomps and wolf whistles when my performance ends and the actor kneels before me, bowing down.

The emcee names my group the winners, and everyone cheers even louder.

I kiss the sexy actor on the cheek, and he swings me in the air before setting me back onstage to collect my trophy.

Adrienne and Claudia join me, and we thank the audience. I chance a look at Malcolm only to find he's gone.

Couldn't stand the heat? Good riddance, Mr. Steele!

"I'm going to the ladies' room to freshen up," I tell my girls as we exit the stage.

It's not until I stand before the mirror I let the hurt sink in.

How could Malcolm just move on so easily? And with two women?!

Hell, I knew he was a playboy. But I didn't expect him to forget me so soon. It's been almost two months. I'm the one who should have moved on weeks ago! Quinn's still in hot pursuit. Maybe I should give him a booty call. BOB just isn't doing it. A battery-operated boyfriend doesn't compare to a full-blooded dick…

I shake my head and reapply my lipstick, then leave the ladies' room.

"Oh!" I exclaim as I bump into a wall of muscle when I step through the door.

My head tilts back. A red-faced Malcolm scowls down at me. I frown back and jut out my chin in defiance.

Fuck you, Mr. Steele!

Without a word, he grabs my elbow and forces me along the hallway.

I pull back, but he's having none of it. When I punch his

side, he lifts me over his shoulder and stalks further down the corridor.

He slaps his palm on the wall; I hear a lock disengage. Once inside the room, he kicks the door closed, re-locks it, and puts me on my feet.

I clutch the front of his black cashmere sweater to steady myself as the blood rushes from my head. Then jerk back at the sensation of his heaving chest under my hands.

"What the hell, Malcolm?!" I yell as I pivot to open the door.

He slams his palms on either side of my head and presses his firm body against my back, boxing me in. His heavy breathing sends chills down my spine—and makes my nipples tighten and my pussy clench with need.

I push back against him to get space. But he refuses to budge.

"Get the fuck off of me, Malcolm!" I screech, slapping my palms on the door in frustration.

He continues to breathe and not answer me. The massive bulge in his trousers lets me know what's on his mind.

Oh. Hell. No!

"Get... the... fuck... off... of... me... I said, Malcolm!!!" I repeat yelling again.

Someone has to hear me, I guess.

His sizable hands cover my smaller ones, and his fingers intertwine with mine, locking us together. He leans his forehead against the back of my head, and he inhales deeply.

My body continues to respond to his nearness and

need. I can't help it. He's trained me to crave him, to cum on command, to submit to his dominance. To love him.

Damn this man!

We stay melded together. Malcolm bent at the knees to angle his groin to cradle my ass. My body caught between his and the office door. The urge to flee dissipates, the fight in me gone.

I press my forehead against the door and inhale deeply.

"Why, My Angel?" Malcolm whispers in my hair.

The fact he doesn't consider his callous words to Roger about love and marriage not enough for me to end our relationship makes my body tense once again. How could he be so hard-hearted? To me?

I resolve not to let him hurt me any further. With a sigh, I straighten and unwind my fingers from his. He's proven twice now I'm not enough woman for him. He desires others more.

"Talk to me, My Angel," Malcolm says softly in a voice full of raw emotion.

"Malcolm, you know very well I'm not *your angel*. Listen, I don't want to argue with you. Especially since Leonie and Roger's wedding is next month, and we're partnered in the bridal party. I will not upset my friend during a special time of her life," I respond and push back again. "Please, just let me go."

When he doesn't move and seeks my fingers, a small cry falls from my lips. I can't hold back the tears much longer.

"Red," I whisper my safeword hoarsely, lowering my head in defeat.

Malcolm squeezes my fingers, but steps back, respecting my limit.

I unlock the door and open it, then pause facing the hallway.

"Some people cherish love and marriage, even if you do not, Malcolm."

STARR

"**H**ey, hey, hey! The gang's all here and ready to celebrate the blushing bride-to-be!" I say, then blow my party whistle upon entering the living room to Leonie's wing of *Le Beaulieu Manoir*.

Billie and I with her boyfriend Patrick Rockett flew to Paris for Roger and Leonie's wedding on his private jet. Her Scottish billionaire beau and the CEO of Rockett Construction Company—the competitor to STEELE International, Inc.—went to their suite at STEELE Place Vendôme while we continued to *Le Manoir*. When they first started dating, Lola had to calm Sebastian down when she reminded him Billie signed an ironclad nondisclosure agreement and she swore her allegiance to Lola.

Leonie, her mother Josy, Shelley, Lola, Blair, Anita, and Hettie gather in the East Wing. Leonie, Roger, and The Twins stay here while their STEELE Tower Paris triplex penthouse reconstruction completes. They took over her former bedroom suite.

The rest of the wing comprises several bedrooms and bathrooms, kitchenette with eating area, library, art studio, media room, and living room. In essence, it's a house within a house and was all hers before Leonie bought her duplex in the *seizième*. It's where she stays when she visits her parents.

"Let's get this party started right! Let's get this party started quickly! Time to set it off!" Billie chimes in as she dances into the living room.

"Hey, *chéries*!" Leonie squeals as she jumps up from the navy blue velvet sofa and rushes to embrace us. "I'm so glad everyone made it!"

"Is it too early to break open the Taittinger Comtes de Champagne Blanc de Blancs? Since Leonie is marrying her very own Double-O agent in a couple of days!" Lola asks, giggling as she pretends to pop a bottle open.

"It's five o'clock somewhere in the world!" Blair cosigns, tapping her gold Cartier Panthère watch.

Leonie is a huge James Bond fan. In *Casino Royale*, 007 requests the decadent libation and makes history. Now, it's her preferred champers.

Everyone laughs at their antics.

"Now, now… Time to review the wedding activities schedule," Josy says.

"Yes, work before play, ladies," Shelley adds.

Leonie and Lola giggle at the drill sergeants. We remember how in control Shelley was for Lola and Sebastian's nuptials. Somehow no one expected Josy being just as commanding!

We settle down instantly.

An hour later, we finish just in time for The Twins' feeding. Leonie excuses herself when Nanny Grace rings her mobile. Josy and Shelley go to help Leonie.

While she's gone, we catch up on our lives since we last saw one another a month ago at SLFW Resorts. After Billie fills us in on her latest escapades with the bonnie Scotsman at LEVELS Beverly Hills, she turns to Blair.

"So, Miss Secretive, what's new on your front? I'm still surprised Monsieur Montaigne let you loose to attend Starr's celebration!" Billie quips.

Blair blushes, turning her porcelain skin crimson. As always, she dodges the question and swings her chestnut brown colored hair over her face.

I keep my mouth shut, not wanting to draw any unwanted attention to myself. Instead, I rise and walk to the window. The majestic property features manicured park-like grounds, stables, tennis court, swimming pool and cabana, and a palatial French Rococo mansion. A part of the 16th arrondissement, it's in the wealthiest neighborhood.

The picturesque view extends past *Le Manoir's* twenty acres of land to Bois de Boulogne. I can visualize a young Leonie riding her horse on the trails. Now her sons will grow up in its splendor.

Wistfully, I turn back to the room. My gaze meets Shelley's as she re-enters the living room. She smiles and heads towards me.

"It's such a magnificent mansion. I can't keep my eyes off of the landscaping either," she says as she loops her arm through mine.

After a moment of gazing at the grounds, Shelley speaks again.

"Everything wrapped prettily isn't always what it seems. Sometimes we have to search deeper—past the facade—to get to its depths. If we give up and don't dig deep enough, we miss out on the gem inside."

She squeezes my arm and smiles when I glance at her. Obviously she's referring to Malcolm. But I don't know what to say. So I nod respectfully.

"OMG! Look at my handsome nephews!"

Shelley and I turn at Haley's words to find Leonie and Josy carrying the three-month-old twins into the living room.

We gather around the babies, oohing and aahing at the adorable duo. They've grown so much and resemble their father even more than before.

As we take turns holding Rodolphe and Gaspard, my mind drifts back to the dreams I had of mini Malcolms swaddled in blankets held in my arms; smiling up at me as I breastfeed them; coos as I talk to them. All the while, his magnetic presence hovers on my periphery. Watching his sons, me.

By the time we leave for the rehearsal and the dinner, my ovaries ache.

"Hello, Starr."

My heart flips.

Malcolm stands behind me, dressed in a bespoke three-piece charcoal striped suit. The ruby red silk tie and pocket square pop against the bright white dress shirt. His tousled hair—longer than usual—brushes the collar. The two-day stubble surrounds his lush lips that curl up at the corners in a hint of a smile. His dove gray eyes sparkle in the fairy lights of the Chapel of *Le Beaulieu Manoir*. But his eyes lack their usual luster.

We're lining up to practice for the ceremony. With everyone milling about, I didn't notice his arrival. But as I inhale deeply to calm my nerves, I smell his John Varvatos - Dark Rebel Rider cologne. The orange, balsam, leather, and amber fill my nostrils, promising long nights of rough fucking.

I'm wet instantly.

Damn this man!

"Hello, Malcolm," I respond, hoping he doesn't notice my arousal.

"You look beautiful—"

"How have you bee—"

We laugh awkwardly as we speak over each other. Then again, when we repeat the same slipup.

"You first," he says, bowing his ebony head graciously with his typical smirk.

I nod and start to speak. But this time it's the wedding planner who interrupts our reunion.

Malcolm gestures with his hand for me to proceed ahead of him to the front of the pairs. Roger stands at the altar with Sebastian as his best man. So Malcolm and I take the lead for the processional, followed by Haley and Lucien, Blair and Luc, and Billie and Harris.

"You look beautiful, Starr."

Malcolm's words whispered in my ear along with his warm breath tickling its delicate shell make me blush and preen.

My hands smooth across the stretch-knit of my one-shoulder midi dress—ruby in keeping with Leonie's Christmas theme. The shoulder ruffle leads to a figure-skimming fit. Heeled sandals bring the top of my head with my hair in an elegant chignon close to his lips.

"Thank you, Malcolm," I murmur as I take his proffered arm.

What I really want is for him to lower the gold zipper on the back of my dress, slam me against the wall—Chapel or not—and fuck me senseless…

The rehearsal goes well and doesn't last long. We travel in Mercedes-Benz Sprinters to the rooftop ballroom at STEELE Montaigne. Funny enough, the city named the street for Luc's family.

In the *huitième* arrondissement the five-star hotel has extraordinary views of the Champs-Élysées, Arc de Triomphe, and the Place de la Concorde, not to mention the Seine. At night, with the lights of Paris shining brightly, prove a spectacular venue for the rehearsal dinner.

When we arrive, dozens of guests—the rest of the Jacksons clan, STEELE associates, high society, friends—mingle during the cocktail hour. Leonie's Winter Wonderland Wedding theme continues at the ballroom with shades of cranberry, gold, champagne, and ivory. If this is any sign of the actual ceremony, we're in for a sumptuous fairytale!

With the amount of people, I don't spend any more time with Malcolm. The way he tended to me during the rehearsal reminded me of our time together, especially during aftercare or spooned together sated from our lovemaking.

The exuberant sound of his laughter carries over the band's background music and the murmurs of guests' conversations.

I peek over my shoulder and spy him sitting with his boys—Anton, Borya, Lucien—and others. They're talking animatedly, gesticulating, and egging each other on. Malcolm tosses his head back and roars with laughter.

A chuckle falls from my lips as I watch from across the room.

As if sensing my presence, Malcolm glances around until his eyes meet mine. His narrow as he finds the source. Pinned by his possessive wolf-like gaze, I bite my bottom lip and lower my eyes submissively.

Hell, I might as well roll over and show him my belly.

Before I can go through with the silly thought, Anita hands me a flute of Champagne. Coming back to my senses, I turn away from temptation and gulp down the bubbly.

"Well, I guess you needed that, huh?" Anita teases as she lifts her hand to snag full flute from a passing server's tray. "Here, have another!"

I giggle, feeling the effects of the Champagne and nod.

"Yes, well, I need something to get me through the next two days!" I respond, saluting her with my crystal glass.

This time it's our laughter that floats through the air.

I ignore the sensation of Malcolm's eyes on me for the

rest of the evening. His magnetism is strong, but I'm stronger.

My Independent Woman roars in agreement.

* * *

"YOU WERE PUTTING them back last night at our Girls' Night In, Little Miss Moderation…"

I attempt a smile at Lola, then winch. The next French Martini I see, I'm going to run from it!

While the guys went to Roger's bachelor party, we played karaoke and games at *Le Manoir*. Leonie stuck with water since she's breastfeeding. She'll pump today and indulge for her wedding.

We had an amazing time chilling out. But the cocktails packed a punch.

Fortunately, Roger transformed the living room of the East Wing into a mini spa so Leonie and her girls could get pampered before the wedding. He arranged for her favorite day spa in Paris to set up multiple stations and rooms for our treatments.

She and her mother have facials done in an area separated by an antique, hand-painted Chinese partition. While Lola, Shelley, Haley, Blair, Billie, Anita, Hettie, and I have five-star massages, scrubs, and waxings. We'll all end up together in the manicure and pedicure chairs.

We started the day with a vigorous yoga flow led by Anita, followed by meditation with me. So this is a much-needed respite. So relaxing and rejuvenating!

"Remind me all day and night," I moan.

Once we're done, we troop into the living room to find Leonie laughing.

"What's so funny, love bunny?"

Billie's silly question evokes more snorts from Leonie. She sits up from the facial table and fans herself. Cucumbers roll off her eyes and plop onto her lap.

"Ha! She's hysterical! Leonie is losing it, folks!" Lola says, bouncing on her feet and clapping her hands.

Everyone laughs, even the aestheticians, albeit discreetly.

Shelley walks over and plucks the cucumbers from Leonie's lap and says, "Oh, let her be. It wasn't so long ago you were in the same position, Mrs. Sebastian Steele."

Then with a wink, she adds, "Although I can understand why… My sons are fine catches!"

She glances at me, and her smile broadens.

I, however, bite my lower lip and suddenly find interest in the nail polish selection.

Shelley snickers.

"I remember how nervous I was before I walked down the aisle to Joel," Hettie starts. "It terrified me he'd get cold feet and duck out of the church!"

We laugh.

"Up and at 'em! We've got a schedule to maintain," Leonie's mother says as she slips off her table and joins the others at the mani/pedi chairs.

Lola and Leonie glance at each other and bust out laughing.

As our nails finish drying, one servant enters the living

room-cum-spa with a beautifully wrapped box in her hands.

Leonie thanks her before she lifts the top. Inside is a flat blue velvet box. She presses the sapphire cabochon closure, and the lid lifts to reveal an exquisite suite of diamonds set in clusters of pear-shaped stones in various sizes: a pair of earrings; a bib necklace; a bracelet. They glitter as the light bounces off their flawless surfaces.

"Whoa! Someone pass my shades to me, stat!" Exclaims Blair as she shields her eyes from the brilliance of the diamonds.

Haley claps and adds, "My brother knows how to treat a lady!"

"Shelley, *chérie*, you are right. Your sons are fine catches!" Leonie's mother says.

We head to the solarium in the East Wing that faces the Bois de Boulogne for the bridesmaids' luncheon. To go along with the spa theme, the menu comprises green salads, grilled herb-crusted salmon, roast chicken, and citrus-infused water. We prefer to eat light before putting on our gowns.

Leonie giggles to herself.

"There she goes, again," Lola says gleefully as she twirls her finger in a circle by her temple. "Looney Tunes alert!"

I can't blame Leonie. She and Lola married the men of their dreams. One day, I hope to do the same.

MALCOLM

"*Some people cherish love and marriage, even if you do not.*"

Starr's words continue to haunt me even a month later and while I'm at Roger's bachelor party—or Bro Bonding, as our cousin Laurent calls it.

After our encounter at STEELE Karaoke West Hollywood, I realize I hurt Starr. No matter how hard I try, I can't figure out what I did to drive her away. The reference to love and marriage makes me wonder if she wants a ring. Since I've given her collars only, she's given up on us.

I resolved to find out before the wedding, but Starr ignored my calls and messages. I stopped trying since we'd see each other for the festivities.

And boy, did we...

Starr was smoking hot in her red dress last night. The material cluing to her luscious curves and reminded me of what I've missed. The gold zipper was like a beacon begging me to lower it and slide my hands inside to cup her round ass and bare pussy. My lips ached to plant a trail of open-mouthed kisses along the shooting stars tattooed on her exposed neck then shoulder before I turned her and suckled her plump brown nipples. Hard.

Hard. Exactly what happened when I laid eyes on Starr. My cock awoke from its slumber—a beast hungry for the succulent morsel of its mate.

And I wasn't the only one aroused by our reunion.

Starr shuffled on her feet, obviously rubbing the apex of her thighs to manipulate her swollen clit. Her chest heaved when she inhaled, and my lust-filled eyes followed the lift of her full tits happily.

I wanted to bury my face between the pillowy mounds. Then lave and lick her beaded nipples until she climaxed a dozen times. Her soft coos in my ears, and her sweat-slicked skin warm against my tongue.

Fuck. Me.

I shift in my club chair, just fantasizing about the moment.

Starr thought she could avoid me the rest of the night after I spied her watching me with desire written all over her gorgeous heart-shaped face.

I allowed her to flit around the ballroom of the rehearsal dinner, sipping Champagne and engaging in conversation with other men. She sensed my possessive stare and chose to ignore it. Fine. For now.

However, I dodged single—and some married—female guests who thought they could wrangle a ride in the sack with the rebel of the Steele family. No thanks. I have my hands full with roping in Starr again. Besides, she'd flip if I so much as glanced in their direction, and she definitely would never speak to me for life.

The promise I made to respect her limits and not pursue her before or during the wedding will remain intact. Once Roger and Leonie finish their eternal vows, game. Fucking. On.

For now, I'll focus on my brother and his happiness.

We're at Jackson Smoke&Scotch Lounge Paris—what's quickly become our favorite spot to unwind with the boys as we partake of their top-shelf Scotch offerings. I rarely smoke their fine Cuban cigars, but tonight is a special occasion and all of us join in.

I take a long draw on it and settle back in my leather club chair. The tasting notes of the spicy, earthy, and woody flavors linger on my palate. They blend well with the smoky, dark berries flavor of the Jackson Reserve Scotch. Its trademark bite drags along the back of my tasting.

Much like my delectable and tantalizing Starr. As Pam Grier says in *Foxy Brown,* "the darker the berry, the sweeter the fruit, honey." And Starr is all that, and then some, even if she no longer wants us together.

Joel raises his Baccarat crystal snifter in a toast.

"Well my friend, this time tomorrow you'll be a happily married man and join the likes of Sebastian, Norman, and me in the bliss of wedlock. Here's to you and your beautiful bride-to-be!"

"Damn, man! Get a grip on yourself with that goofy ass smile on your face!"

Busted, Roger laughs along with Joel and Norman, Luc,

our brothers, our cousins Lachlan, Lucien, and Laurent guffaw.

"Who would have thought from one meeting over two years ago would bring us to two Steele men capturing the hearts of my mentees and friends?"—Luc shakes his head and his navy blue eyes sparkle with mischief—"Roger, *oui*. But Sebastian… mmm mmm. A surprise!"

Harris, Lachlan, Roger, and I chuckle remembering how jealous Baz was of the Silver Fox's relationship with Lola.

Luc may be in his early fifties. But as Leonie and Lola pegged his nickname, he can go toe-to-toe with any of us for a woman's affection. Hell, he may even win! An Alpha Dom at six feet, four inches with salt and pepper hair, a clean-shaven face that highlights the cleft in his chin. He could pass for a movie star. Not to mention being a billion-aire duke, the last of his noble line.

We laugh some more when Baz bristles.

Only after he put his ring on Lola did he loosen up a smidgen on Luc. Obviously, it's still a touchy topic…

"Ha! Just fucking with you, Steele," he chuckles. "I trust you and your brother will do well by Lola and Leonie. That is, if you know what is best for you."

He pauses to pin both of them with a don't-fuck-with-them stare, then raises his glass for a toast.

"*À la tienne, mes amis!*" He proclaims with a smirk.

The rest of the night we rib each other and reminisce about our time growing up. Damn, who would have thought we'd end up with two Steele brothers down so

close in time? And if I have my way, another falls in line…
Soon.

I ARRIVE BACK at my suite in STEELE Place Vendôme, a slight sway to my step. Fuck, I drank more than I thought. The need to distract myself from images of Starr drove me to take the shot challenge Laurent put forth.

That fucker can drink like a fish!

As I walk into the room and my eyes light on the empty bed, I know what needs to happen next… Let my fantasies free.

I toe off my Gucci loafers and strip out of my cashmere sweater and trousers, tossing the garments to the ground with my boxer briefs. I pad to the bathroom.

The light bounces off of the white marble as I flick the switch. While I shield my eyes from the opulence, I make my way to the oversized glass-enclosed shower.

As I duck under the spray from multiple shower heads, I let my eyes close and tilt my head back. The warm water sluices down my rock-hard body as I brace my palms on the marble wall. The ache in my cock—and surprisingly in my heart—increases. I drop my head and groan aloud.

Fuck, I miss My Angel.

My thoughts drift to her—my celestial beauty—so bright and out of reach.

I groan as my cock lengthens, and the girth thickens. The Prince Albert piercing makes my tip super sensitive. The platinum piercing glints in the light.

The wings of my tattoo ripple as my back flexes. The mantle lays heavy.

Only when I'm buried balls deep in My Angel's tight, wet heat do I feel free completely. She welcomes me into her willing body and becomes one with me. No burden is too heavy when I'm wrapped in her warm embrace.

I groan again when I think about how much time we've wasted. Days… Weeks… Months. Damn.

Flashbacks play across my mind's eye.

Her bodacious curves in the coral-colored long-sleeved dress at Baz and Lola's wedding.

Starr in a tiny bikini on the beach when we met officially in St. Barth's.

My collar of intricate platinum lacework covered in tiny sparkly diamonds on her long neck.

Her sorrel brown eyes shining as she giggles at my lame joke.

That red fuck-me dress…

My hand slips from the steam slick wall and slides down between my eight-pack abs, the well-defined ridges taut beneath my calloused fingertips. The texture of the trail of hair leading from below my navel to my groin contrasts with my bare skin.

I suck in a ragged breath as my fantasy begins…

My Angel sub naked on her knees before me with her mouth open wide, eager to receive my engorged ten inches. Her eyes— darkened with lust—stare back up at me as she pokes her little pink tongue out.

My hand grips the base of my dick and taps the reddened tip against the flat of her tongue. A pearl of pre-cum drops onto it.

She moans and sways as she closes her soft mouth around my dick. Her eyelids droop as she takes my swollen length down her throat. Her gag reflex spasms sending a zing to my seed-heavy balls.

I squeeze my eyes tight, not wanting to lose the vision before I'm ready to blow my load.

After a moment, I regain control and my fantasy continues…

"Just like that, take it deep, Little One," I praise her, pulling on my Dom. "I want to see tears meet the drool on your chin before I give you my seed to swallow."

My hand dives into her wet curls. I grip the back of her head as I snap my hips forward until the tip of her nose meets my happy trail.

She sputters and gags. Her widened eyes fly back up to gaze into mine as she panics.

"Breathe through your nose. Understand, Little One?" I command.

She nods, then winces from my grip on her scalp.

When her breathing evens out, I pull back until my tip leaves her mouth with a pop. A string of saliva runs from her lips to my cock. Tears flow down her reddened cheeks. She stares at me as she licks her swollen lips.

Fucking beautiful.

"Some more please, Sir."

I nearly bust my nuts.

Instead, I drop my forehead to the slick wall and brace myself on my forearms for what promises to be a leg wobbling experience.

My Angel sub does not disappoint.

One hand massages my sac and the other grips and tugs my turgid dick. The rhythm she sets alternates between gentle and painful, keeping a delicate balance that has me close in moments.

"Fuuuck... Angel... Shit, that feels so good," I growl as my palms slap the wall. She has me slipping between Dom and boyfriend.

A pinch to my tip sends me rocking onto the balls of my feet, driving my hips forward to pump against her hand. My Angel sub senses how close I am to release, so she speeds up her pace.

"ANGEL" I roar as my dick jumps in her hand and ropes of creamy cum splash onto the wall.

My hips move on their own since my brain exploded with my cock. She snakes her fingers that were massaging my balls around my hip and slips one into my ass. Her fingertip strokes my prostrate, and my cock hardens again.

"FUCK!!!" I roar, surprised by the erotic invasion. Then I ride out another mind-blowing, spine-tingling orgasm.

My body slumps, and I join My Angel sub on the wet marble floor as the shower water rains down on us. I pull her onto my lap and bury my face in her neck, still breathing heavy. The feeling of her fingers running through my hair soothes my racing heart.

"I love you, My Angel," I murmur, no longer in my fantasy.

The love is real, and I will deny it no longer.

"Roger, I'm so proud of you. Shrewd business executive, worthy father, soon to be a loving husband. You did it, bro! Congratulations!"

"Yeah, well, as long as Leonie doesn't leave him standing at the altar looking like a love-lost puppy!"

"Shut the fuck up, Harris!"

He laughs and grabs his big brother in a bear hug that lifts him a few inches from the floor.

"You know I love you, man!" Harris chuckles. "I just can't help myself!"

"Obviously! But I love you, too!" Roger replies, mussing Harris' hair.

"Aw damn, dude! Cut it out already!" He groans as he rushes to the mirror to fix his ebony waves.

Along with Roger and Harris, Baz, Lucien, Luc, and I gather in a tent beside the Chapel awaiting our time to enter for the nuptials.

We rode in one of the Sprinters from STEELE Place

Vendôme earlier, already dressed in our bespoke tuxedos. Suited and booted in white-tie attire for Roger's big day.

He attempts to maintain his cool Alpha male demeanor. But we see straight through it. He's nervous as fuck!

"You are already on my list, Little Harris. Keep messing around, and you will be on Roger *The Responsible*'s ugly side," I warn our kid brother with a smirk.

"Exactly!" Roger adds, pointing his index and middle finger at his eyes, then at Harris. "I see you, bro…"

Baz chuckles and flips his fingers through Harris' hair as he turns from the mirror. He huffs and fixes his artfully tousled locks again.

"Roger, you make Leonie thrilled, *mon ami!*" Luc says.

"Gentlemen, it is time for you to take your places in the Chapel."

We face the tent entrance at the sound of the wedding planner's voice.

"All right, Roger. Time to rock and roll!" Lucien says as he claps Roger on his shoulder.

I grin as a smile filled with love spreads across Roger's face. He takes a deep breath, adjusts his diamond and platinum cuff links—a gift from his bride-to-be—and strides to his future.

ENCHANTRESS.

Words fly from my head. But that's the only one to describe the sight of My Angel.

The bridal party stands in the anteroom of the Chapel, alight with tiny lights and covered in flowers as the background. She looks like a celestial being. My fantasy come to the Earth.

Her strapless dress has layers of silk chiffon with a neckline of a confectioner's sugar swirl of the silk. An intricate appliqué of gold, champagne, and touches of cranberry attaches at her waist and crosses her body from one hip up to cover the opposite breast.

I want to unwrap my early Christmas present. Right. Now.

"Hello, Starr," I say instead as I approach her.

"Hello, Malcolm," she responds a bit tense.

To rib her, I repeat my words from before.

"You look beautiful, Starr," I whisper in her ear. Then smirk when she trembles slightly.

"Thank you," My Angel murmurs.

I hold out my arm, and she slips her hand under and around my elbow. Locking her forearm to my side, I turn to face the wrought-iron gates at the entrance to the Chapel's primary space.

Thousands of fairy lights twine with the dark greens leaves and red berries of holly around the gates, the columns, and up the walls to the ceiling bathing the Chapel in a soft, golden glow. An abundance of wreaths and flowers ranging in hue from deep cranberry and burgundy to champagne and ivory fills the Chapel. The sweet, hot spiciness of cinnamon mixed with the floral scents waft through the air. The space is at once elegant and festive.

Leonie and her father Guy arrive behind us. The bridal party turns to face them, and everyone smiles as we shower the beautiful bride with our praises. Then the music changes for the start of the procession. The Trans-Siberian Orchestra perform their "Christmas Canon." The strains of the violins swirl around the Chapel.

The wedding planner cues us to proceed.

I glance down at My Angel, and she tilts her head back to gaze at me. Tears shine in her sorrel brown eyes. I ache to kiss her eyelids but smile at her instead. With a nod, we march down the aisle.

While we walk, I wonder what it would be like if this were our wedding day. I know My Angel will make a stunning bride. But is she ready for more?

We settle in place and await Leonie and Guy. Roger's hands twitch as though he wants to race up the aisle to claim his bride before she reaches him.

"Slow down, bro. She's yours forever."

Sebastian stills him. But nothing can hold back the beaming smile on Roger's face when Leonie comes into view.

She resembles a princess bride floating towards her prince on an ethereal carpet of fragrant white rose, camellia, and gardenia petals. Through Leonie's veil, we can see her brilliant smile rivals the diamonds in her ears and on chest. Their eyes lock, and the grin that spreads from one ear to the other threatens to split Roger's face.

After the couple exchanges their vows, the officiant pronounces them husband and wife.

Roger kisses Mrs. Roger Steele until she's breathless.

The bridal party whoops while the guests stand and clap.

Lola places Leonie's bouquet in her hand and straightens

her long veil and the hem of her gown as the pair turn to the guests. Roger grasps Leonie's hand, and they scoop The Twins from their grandparents. As a family, they stroll down the aisle to the cheers of family and friends.

Baz and Lola leave the altar next.

I stride to My Angel and extend my arm. She peeks at me from beneath her wet eyelashes, damp with tears. This time I brush my thumb beneath her eyes and bring my fingers to my lips. She ducks her head and loops her arm through mine.

We follow the newlyweds down the aisle and to the closed door of the separate room off of the Chapel's ante-room. My Angel disengages herself from my arm and dabs her eyes with a handkerchief.

Lola knocks at the door, and Roger calls out to come in.

"Yeah, yeah, yeah… Time for pictures in this Winter Wonderland Chapel, Love Birds!" Lola teases as her hazel eyes sparkle with mischief. "The guests head back to the *Manoir's Grand Hall*. The wedding planner said to hang out in here until they're all gone."

My Angel laughs, "Lola, you are no good!"

I stand close to My Angel with my front inches from her back. My focus remains on her the entire time we're in the room.

Hell, I can't take another moment without My Angel. I don't know what it's about weddings. But it's hard to evade love when it swirls around you. The very atmosphere charged with the electricity of two people deeply in love.

I chuckle at myself, waxing poetic.

My Angel faces me, and for a moment we're lost in our own world.

Leonie cracks up about something, drawing everyone's attention to her and Roger.

The wedding planner enters and ushers us into the primary space. Hairstylists and makeup artists touch up the girls' before we pose for the cameras.

The Twins steal the show. The photographers and videographers came prepared with colorful fuzzy balls suspended from sticks to keep Rodolphe and Gaspard looking toward the cameras. They reach for them and track the balls as an assistant moves them through the air. Pros just like their *Maman*—the world-renown megamodel.

A photographer and a videographer captured the guys in candid and posed shots. The girls did the same. So we spend little time on the group photos.

When we exit the Chapel, everyone laughs at the golden coach led by four horses with a driver and two footmen waiting to take us back to the mansion. Their liveries just as formal as our white-tie attire, harkens to days of the centuries past.

The beauty of the snow-covered lawns and twinkling trees remind me of being inside of a snow globe for a wintry fairy-tale. The stars glitter in the ink-black sky and the air is crisp. Sound muffled by the falling snow. It's fantastical.

While Roger and Leonie climb into their carriage, the bridal party boards the Sprinters for *Le Beaulieu Manoir's*

Grand Hall. The girls take one of the luxury mini coaches. My Angel thinks she can evade me. Not happening.

When we arrive at the *Grand Hall,* the bridal party gathers at the closed double doors and partner up again for our introduction to the guests inside.

I skim my hand along My Angel's flank to rest at her lower back. A shudder runs through her.

Gotcha!

Baz and Lola enter the massive room, dancing to the music. The rest of us strut in laughing and clapping. I hold My Angel's hand in the air and wave them around. She squeezes my hand back as she shimmies.

My cock jumps.

We take our seats at two tables below the dais where the high table waits for Roger and Leonie. Set on the other side of the dais, our and Leonie's parents sit at tables with their closest friends. Our Uncle Connor and Aunt Lucie Jackson—parents of Lachlan, Lydie, Lucien, and Laurent— join them as the women have been best friends since before either married their billionaires.

Everyone turns their attention to the double doors when the music pauses.

"Ladies and gentlemen, presenting Mr. and Mrs. Roger Steele and their sons Master Rodolphe Beaulieu Steele and Master Gaspard Beaulieu Steele!"

The room breaks out in applause for the couple and The Twins. They make their way to our parents' tables and hand their sons to them before they have their first dance. When the song ends and they dance with our parents, the rest of us join in.

"Starr, will you dance with me?" I ask as I rise and extend my hand to her.

She nods and takes my hand.

I pull her close and whisper in her ear, "Words, Angel. I will have your words."

It's a risk, but I'm going full throttle.

I'm rewarded with another shudder and her sweet words, "Yes, Sir."

My world rights itself. I want to fist pump and holler but hold back. I am an in-control Alpha Dom, after all.

The feel of My Angel in my arms is so right. Her body melds to mine as I hold her close. The alluring scent of her perfume's sandalwood, jasmine, and vanilla notes makes me want to bury my face in her neck and suck on her tender flesh. The urge to mark My Angel grows stronger.

My cock rouses and presses against her flat belly.

A small gasp falls from between her lips when she feels my desire for her. Instead of pulling away, she lays her head against my chest.

Fucking perfect!

Céline Dion finishes the song, and we return to our seats. I have to shake my leg surreptitiously to adjust my burgeoning erection.

My Angel giggles, then stops when I peer down with a raised eyebrow at her. She coughs and averts her gaze.

Between courses of our meal, I circulate amongst the guests and dance with Haley, who seems forlorn whenever Lachlan comes near.

Baz already told that fucker to back up off of our baby

sister. We don't give a damn if he claims nothing is going on between them. Haley acts like a sad puppy around him.

From the time we were kids growing up together, Baz and Lachlan were best friends. Haley would trail after them from the time she could walk. Then she stopped as a teenager. Now she's flustered with him.

I've already warned Baz if I have to step in, it'll be a problem. Hell, I love Lachlan like a brother, but he better not fuck with my baby sister. He's an Alpha Dom like me and a big-time Global All Access member at LEVELS, so I know his proclivities…

Purposefully I don't interact with My Angel. I want her on the edge, wondering when I'll follow through on my dick poking her. I can tell my strategy works whenever I catch her watching me with a burning hunger in her eyes.

After Leonie gives a touching speech to her new husband, Sebastian takes the mic followed by each of the siblings. Then we listen to our family and friends regale Roger and Leonie with fond memories and best wishes.

They cut the cake and toss Leonie's bouquet and garter.

Funny enough, My Angel catches the flowers. She giggles and waves the bouquet over her head. The girls tease her, and she avoids my gaze again.

When Roger prepares to toss the garter, I position myself in the center of the bachelors' group behind his turned back.

"All right now! Who will be the lucky guy to catch the garter and match up with the lovely Starr Knight?!" He challenges those gathered.

I brace myself.

"Watch out, sucker! This is all mine!"

Harris makes a grab for the garter; he'll never learn.

With my three inches on him, I snatch it mid-air.

"Take that. Take that. Take that!" I say à la Puffy and stalk towards my prize, swinging the garter on my index finger.

We lock eyes.

I pull My Angel into my embrace, dip her into a deep arc, and capture her mouth in a mind-blowing kiss. I bring her back on her feet, and she peers at me dazedly while I grin wider than Roger.

"Time to go, My Angel," I murmur against her luscious lips.

"Yes, Sir," she whispers, then nips my lower lip.

I growl.

My cock thickens down my inner thigh.

We leave the dance floor with her tucked against my side and her head on my shoulder.

Everyone whoops and hollers—Harris the loudest with wolf whistles.

Gotcha, My Angel! Love takes all.

STARR

The buildings and monuments of the City of Light blur by as Malcolm navigates the Parisian streets in his sleek, black on red Aston Martin DB7 Vantage expertly. Funny how he parked it on *Le Manoir*'s driveway. Pretty convenient…

Where we're going, I'm not sure. To his hotel suite at STEELE Place Vendôme or to his private suite at LEVELS Paris? Either destination would suit me just fine.

I squeeze my thighs together as my arousal increases in anticipation of his carnal touch—fingers, lips, tongue. My pussy clenches at the thought. Best to stare out of the tinted window to prevent a puddle of my juices from forming on his plush leather seat.

How much further?

An unbidden sigh escapes my lips.

Malcolm's heavy hand placed on my thigh makes me jump and gape at him.

Dammit! I feel like a jittery virginal bride.

"Relax, My Angel. We'll be there soon," he says as his gaze shifts from the street to me briefly.

The rumble of Malcolm's deep baritone voice heightens my desire for him. I return to watch the city fly by, still uncertain of our destination.

When the obelisk of the Place de la Concorde appears before us—lit up in the night sky like a beacon—I know we're headed for the hotel. In a matter of minutes, we'll be at his suite.

Thank God and every deity in every religion's pantheon! I almost shimmy in my seat.

We pull up to the hotel's grand entrance, and a doorman helps me from the low sports car. A hair-raising growl draws my attention from smiling in gratitude at the man.

Malcolm curls his lip in a snarl as he glares at the doorman, pointedly moving his eyes from the man to my leg, exposed by the slit in my gown.

Apparently Malcolm doesn't appreciate the doorman staring at what he believes is his. The Possessive Caveman returns.

He flicks his wrist to wave the man off and takes my arm.

"Pardonnez-moi, Monsieur Steele," he stutters, now realizing Malcolm's identity. *"Je veux dire aucun manque de respect, monsieur."*

Malcolm gives a cursory nod to the doorman's apology of no disrespect. French being one language in which he's fluent. But he doesn't slow down as he bustles me through the hotel's glass and wrought-iron doors held open by another doorman. He too nods to Malcolm as a sign of respect to a Steele.

I smile as I move as briskly as possible in my heels and gown.

More staff greet Malcolm before we reach etched-glass, double doors where yet another doorman allows us entry to a separate foyer. Beyond sit three reception and two concierge desks, four sitting areas, and a bank of three private elevators. Malcolm ushers me into one and places a keycard on a plaque for access to the most exclusive suites.

He stares at the floor numbers as though counting the minutes, equally eager to arrive at his rooms. The warmth of his palm on my lower back grounds me.

The entire time, I can't keep my eyes off of Malcolm. He looks fine in his elegant white tie. So very debonair. He shaved the growth from his chiseled jaw and trimmed his hair. Whether rugged or polished, Malcolm Steele is sex AF.

No sooner do the doors open than Malcolm guides me through them and down the hall. Our steps muffled by the silk carpet quicken the closer we get to the double doors at the end of the corridor. Soft music plays over hidden speakers as the rustle of my gown hints at my speed.

"After you, My Angel," Malcolm purrs as he holds the right door open.

I sashay past him, putting an extra sway in my hips. All the more to entice my... Dom, boyfriend, post-wedding-love-haze hookup?

Not clear on the status of our situation, I shrug inwardly. *Just go with the flow, Starr,* I admonish myself.

Interesting how my inner warrior remains silent. Either she wants to reunite with Malcolm or is just horny; I'm grateful for her compliance.

"Would you care for a glass of Champagne? I noticed you enjoyed it at the rehearsal dinner," Malcolm says as he appears at my side.

For a moment I'm transfixed by the magnificent view of the Tuileries Gardens, Place du Carrousel, and the Louvre beyond. Lights placed strategically to exhibit the former royal residence to its finest. The other day Anita and I had pastries and tea at Angelina Paris—the legendary 1903 tearoom near the gardens.

"Oh, yes, thank you"—I start as I turn with an arched eyebrow to face him—"I didn't realize you were watching me so closely, Mr. Steele. What else did you spy?"

Malcolm chuckles wickedly and clasps my chin between his thumb and index finger, holding my head in place. He stares into my eyes intently.

"Oh, so much more, My Angel. Such as you flirting with a few of the male guests and letting them dance with you, giggling when they whispered in your ear. Not very nice. I believe your transgressions are rather punishable. Do you not agree?"

Huh! He did not go there with accusing me of flirting when he was fucking Vicky Reynolds! I had planned to leave it in the past and see what the future held. But no, Sir!

"*Flirting*, you say? Well, then what is *your* punishment for *fucking*?" I narrow my eyes to glare at him as I jerk my chin from his grasp, then explode. "And is it double for your tryst being with Vicky Reynolds after you tricked me in to going to your rooftop to WITNESS YOU FUCKING HER?!?!"

Malcolm pales and staggers back. His gray eyes bulge, and his mouth drops open. Then he squints his eyes and cocks his head, never taking his eyes from mine. He stalks back to tower over me.

"What are you talking about, Starr?" He asks in a deadly tone.

I blink and step back to put some space between his hulking frame and my smaller one.

He has none of it and moves within inches of me again. The heat radiates off of his body in waves.

"Starr?" He questions; his deep baritone sending a shudder down my spine.

"You heard me, Malcolm!" I retort, recovering from his threatening posture quickly. "Do not attempt to scare me, either, *Enforcer*! You're the one who's wrong here. Not... me!!!"

I deliver the last words with pokes to his solid chest, not that they budge him in any way. But they make me feel stronger. I refuse to cower before him.

"I heard you, but I do not know what you speak about. Give me details, when, where?" Malcolm demands.

Now it's my turn to stagger back, eyes wide, mouth agape.

He doesn't know what I'm talking about? How the hell is that possible?!

I yank my mobile from my clutch and unlock it. My fingers tap with fury on the screen—fury at him, or Vicky, or me, I'm uncertain. Then I shove the mobile in his face.

"Here! See your text for yourself, Malcolm!" I screech.

He takes the mobile from me and reads the text message, once, twice.

It's imprinted on my brain: *Hi Starr. I'm on my way to LA and want to see you. Come by my place at 8 tonight. I'll be on the rooftop.*

Malcolm with an eerie calm hands the mobile back to me.

"I presume you used the code I gave to you to enter my penthouse?" He asks quietly.

When I nod, he continues.

"What did you see when you arrived at the rooftop?" He questions as he stares into the depths of my soul with turbulent gray eyes.

I recount the horrible night…

I walk through to the stairs that lead to the rooftop deck. With a smile on my face, I climb my stairway to heaven. When I open the doors, I almost call out to him. Instead, I stare, a bit confused.

Ahead of me is a naked woman straddling a naked man on a chaise lounge. His back is to me. But she faces my direction. The sounds of her moans and his grunts, their skin slapping skin fill my ears.

My vision tunnels on them. Everything else fades out of view.

I step closer, my mind attempting to process what my eyes see before me and my ears pick up distinctly.

When we're only yards apart, the woman tosses her long blonde mane of wavy hair over her shoulder and pins me with her blue eyes. Her mouth a moment before contorted in a cry of ecstasy now morphs into a wicked smirk.

She leans back and her large breasts bounce from the man's brutal upward thrusts into her pussy. Then she leans forward—never taking her eyes from mine—and cups the man's face. Her red manicured fingernails poke through his ebony waves above the back of the chaise lounge.

"Oh, God, Malcolm, baby! You feel so fucking good! I missed you so much, too!" She cries out.

Blindly, I back away and rush through the door and stumble down the stairs to the elevator, then to my car to careen out of the parking garage...

A deafening roar fills the rooms surrounding us.

I jump as Malcolm detonates. WTF?!?!?!

He storms around the salon ranting and raving, pulling at his hair, and ripping the white tie from his neck.

I stand stock still, shocked by his unusual behavior.

Suddenly he stops, whips his mobile from his trousers pocket, and jabs at the screen.

"Nightingale! Do... it... NOW!!!" Malcolm barks when his call connects.

He keeps his back to me as he places his mobile on the coffee table and slides his hands into his trouser pockets. Then he faces me.

The placid expression on Malcolm's face hides the whirlwind from moments before. His still-wild eyes bore into me as he scans my face. He holds his hand out to me.

My eyes dart over his face to gauge his mindset. In my heart, I know Malcolm would never harm me or anyone. Well, those who don't deserve it, that is...

I keep my eyes on his wild ones while I walk to him and place my hand in his.

A calm settles over Malcolm. His features soften, and his body relaxes, releasing the fury. He squeezes my hand and lifts it to his lips to kiss it gently. Then he leads me to the sofa. He cradles me on his lap and buries his face in my neck. His warm breath tickles my skin.

"I was in Verbier with Roger. I do not know who pretended to be me. But I guarantee you I will find out. The matter is being taken care of as we speak," Malcolm says as he cups my face. "I wondered why you shut us down—"

With a shake of my head, I place my fingertips on his lips. He needs to know all of it. We need to clear the past to make way for our future. A future I know I want with this man.

"I overheard your conversation with Roger in St. Barth's, Malcolm," I start, then continue when he frowns. "When you were on the deck of the villa, you told him you didn't love me, and we were just a thing for now, not ready for marriage."

He moves his lips to speak, but I cut him off again.

"I love you, Malcolm Steele, even if you don't love me. It's impossible to deny my feelings for you any longer. I miss you... us and hope you feel the same. Perhaps not love, yet... But much more than a fuck," I finish as I shrug, resigned to love a man I hope will love me someday.

In a flurry of movement, Malcolm has me over his knees, my head hanging, and my gown bunched around my waist. He slides my G-string down to bind my legs.

THWACK. THWACK. THWACK. THWACK. THWACK.

I buck beneath his punishing blows as he spanks my ass, one cheek after the other, followed by the tops of my thighs and sit bones.

The swift smattering of spanks has me gasping and squirming on his lap, his massive erection pokes my hip. When I squirm almost free, he wraps his arm around my waist and puts his leg over my thighs to rain a sequence of left, right, sit bones, right, left smacks.

I squeal and beg for his forgiveness—and for his dick inside of my sopping wet pussy. My safeword never comes to mind.

Obviously not caring to succumb to my pleas, Malcolm continues until I hang limp, and wetness from my juices coats his trousers. The sight of it draws a groan from deep in his chest.

Malcolm lifts me to straddle his thighs—the cool air swirls around my reddened ass and swollen pussy. He cups my face and kisses me until I feel nothing but erotic elation coursing through every cell of my being.

His chest heaves as much as mine while our tongues tangle. He demands dominance, and I willingly give it to him with a mewl for more.

Malcolm complies readily.

I nearly cum from the sound of his zipper lowering and the rustle of his shirt and boxer briefs moving to free his ginormous cock. A moan slips from my mouth when the cool platinum balls from his Prince Albert piercing brush against my heated pussy lips. His engorged tip seeks the entrance to my core.

My knees widen to spread my thighs, giving him better access.

His dick breaches my folds. One thrust of his hips, and I'm impaled on his incredible girth. The platinum balls graze my G-spot, then press against my womb.

"Aaaahhhh, baby…"

"Fuck yes… So tight, My Angel… Still mine!"

Once my core adjusts to his size, Malcolm grips my hips, fingers digging into my flesh. He lifts me to his tip, then flexes his thighs to snap up and bring me down at the same time.

Shooting stars dance before my closed eyelids as I grip his shoulders to brace myself. So fucking good…

Malcolm sets a controlled tempo of slow and deep stokes. His eyes never leave mine after he commands me to open them and to not look away. His hooded gaze burns with passion.

I'm mesmerized.

He continues his thrusts but refuses my cries for release. His commands of *not yet* set my thighs aquiver and my breath to come in pants.

Malcolm bands his arms around my waist and hoists me into the air with ease to settle me onto my back. His knees brace on the sofa cushions as he leans up to remove his jacket and open the vest and shirt. His mussed hair falls into his eyes as he places his hands on either side of my head to loom over me.

Did I say sexy AF, or what?

His hips go berserk as he pistons in and out of my greedy little pussy, my thighs tight around his hips.

Squelching joins his grunts and my moans. He rides me like a thoroughbred stallion, taking his mare in heat.

My fingernails dig into his biceps as I hold on for dear life.

"Cum… for… me… NOW!" Malcolm demands.

The pent-up orgasm rips through me from the top of my head up from the tips of my toes. My back arcs off of the sofa as I throw my head back, my mouth open wide in a silent scream. The muscles of my pussy spasm. My juices gush as Malcolm tweaks my engorged clit.

Another orgasm followed by another has my mind floating in erotic bliss. The sensation of Malcolm's dick expanding then jerking as his hot seed spurts in copious amounts to paint my pussy walls and to fill my womb sends another orgasm through me.

A carnal roar rips from his mouth as he yells through his climax to the ceiling.

The air is rich with the scent of our arousal and the mingling of our perfume and cologne with our natural musk. I inhale deeply and close my eyes to savor this moment.

Sill hard within me, Malcolm lowers his head to my heaving chest. We remain locked in our embrace until our breathing returns to normal.

I brush my fingers through his hair, wanting skin-on-skin contact beyond the intimacy of our groins.

Malcolm lifts his sated gaze to mine.

"Only you, My Angel. No one since, and no one after. I am yours and you are mine," he declares as he holds my chin in his fingers. "I will allow no one to hurt you. Only I will give you pain and know that pleasure will always follow."

I nod, then correct myself and respond with words.

Malcolm caresses my lips with the pad of his thumb.

"I love you, My Angel."

With a contented sigh, I nuzzle against his neck. I guess that answers my question about what he is to me—Malcolm Steele is mine, all mine.

And I am *his* Angel.

MALCOLM

*A*s the sun rises and Paris awakes, I lie in bed and stare at My Angel who sleeps so peacefully. Her lips curl up at the corners when I brush my knuckles along her soft cheek. A soft sigh escapes her mouth at my feather-light kiss.

"You're mine again, Starr Knight—My Angel," I murmur. My eyes never leave her gorgeous face. "I love you."

A smile spreads across my face, pleased to admit the words aloud with ease. At last.

"Good morning at last, Mr. and Mrs. Roger Steele! So nice of you to join us..."

The cabin explodes with a ruckus of wolf whistles, stomps, and laughter as Roger and Leonie board one of STEELE's Gulfstream G700 private jets. They had us waiting on the tarmac at Le Bourget Airport for twenty minutes. Leonie may be notoriously late, but I have my suspicions for the newlyweds' tardiness.

We're bound for Verbier to celebrate Christmas through New Year's Day as a family—the Steeles, Beaulieus, and My Angel. Then Roger and Leonie will remain for their honeymoon with The Twins as he planned.

The ultra-plush G700 easily accommodates both our families and staff. The spacious interior boasts the tallest, widest, and longest cabin of all private jets. Its size suits the Steele men and Leonie's father, whose large frames range from six feet, one inches to six feet, four inches.

"Leonie, I'm surprised you were on time to your wedding!"

Lola cracks up at her clever remark.

"Leave the newlyweds alone," Morgan says as he chuckles. "We added a buffer to the flight plan. So, we have plenty of time to spare."

Roger and Leonie thank him and head for Rodolphe and Gaspard. Haley and My Angel hold them playing with colorful rings on their laps. They're seated on the sofa across from where I sit at the table near the center of the large jet.

Roger murmurs in Leonie's ear as he nods towards Starr. Leonie's amber eyes shine as she grins, her gaze darts between My Angel and me.

I ignore their whispers.

"*Bonjour, mes beaux fils*," Leonie coos, as she lifts Rodolphe from My Angel. "And to you too, *mon amie*. Nice to see you spending Christmas with us."

Leonie's eyebrows waggle as she purses her lips.

My Angel attempts to hold in a laugh unsuccessfully. Her kissable dimples deepen as a flush reddens her smooth chestnut complexion.

"Well, the more the merrier. Right, Malcolm?" Roger adds as he scoops Gaspard in his arms.

I roll my eyes and stretch my long legs in front of me with a huff. Fucker.

Roger and Leonie take the fifth living area behind us. They settle The Twins in their car seats, one next to each of them at the dining table.

Everyone has space to enjoy the luxury of a custom-built seventy-five-million-dollar aircraft.

My Angel reaches across the aisle to squeeze my arm and winks.

I bring her hand to my mouth to kiss it. My eyes drift to the diamond-pavé letter S in its platinum mesh center gleams in the sunlight from the oval windows. My collar rests securely on her neck once again. Where it belongs and will forever stay.

We stare at one another and smile as only couples who are in tune can communicate without even speaking. Smiles that say, nothing can bother our love.

Haley smirks.

"Yeah, I gave Haley and Lola my AMEX Centurion Card to buy everything Leonie will need for our winter honeymoon—ski gear, après-ski, clubbing. Plus an entire wardrobe to leave here. Based on the walk-in dressing room, they splurged… Shelley and Josy bought everything for The Twins. So that will preoccupy them for a while," Roger says, shaking his head.

Women and clothes. Good grief.

Although I must admit I take great selfish pleasure in buying lingerie for My Angel, particularly from Lola's Coterie. My sister-in-law's luxury lingerie, loungewear, and evening wear company makes the most delightful little pieces. Wait until My Angel sees her closet in our room.

As soon as we arrive and walk into the great room with its magnificent Christmas tree, Leonie's mother declares we'll spend every Christmas and New Year's here. "One big happy family," Shelley claps in agreement.

Roger gives us the grand tour of their new residence Leonie named *Chalet de la Joie* since the home will bring everyone such joy to spend family holidays here.

The girls head to the primary bedroom and nursery.

The rest of our family migrate to different areas of the chalet. Our parents choose babysitting duties, or as they say, "important bonding time with their grandsons." So their nanny retired to her suite of rooms above the garage.

My brothers and I stand in the garage to check out the new snow toys he ordered. We take the snowmobiles out before we meet back up for an early dinner with a meal prepared by one chef from STEELE Verbier.

When we return, I shoot a text message to My Angel to ask her whereabouts in the massive house. Moments later, I stride into our room with my hair disheveled from the cap and my olive-toned cheeks reddened by the icy mountain air. My eyes dance when I see her stretched out in a red silk and lace teddy with matching G-string on the furry rug in front of a roaring fire.

In no time, I strip and prowl over to her. Stalking my prey.

My Angel squeals when I burrow my face between her thighs to nip at their apex. The stubble on my cheeks rasps her sensitive skin.

I slide the string aside and plunge my tongue and two middle fingers inside her wet pussy. The walls flutter as she squirms from the stretching of her inner muscles so quickly. Unceasing licks and suckling on her clit along with my fingers stroking her G-spot send My Angel spiraling over the edge.

Once.

Twice.

Three times.

A trial of open-mouthed kisses leads me to her succulent brown nipples. I take my time to pay homage to her full tits until she climaxes again. I grip her hips and flip her onto her knees—ass high, head low—and sink my turgid length balls deep into her still-quivering pussy.

Then ride My Angel until she screams and begs for no more. I thank the architect for soundproofing the bedroom suites.

* * *

"LAST ONE DOWN!" I yell as I—like Roger before me—race past Leonie towards the finish.

It's Christmas Eve morning and we're out en masse for

an early morning run. My Angel—who I just zipped past—the entire Steele clan, and Beaulieus make our way from the top of the mountain piste to the base lodge. It's a popular time to come out, so other skiers bob and weave around us.

I laugh at My Angel and Leonie muttering and tuck to bullet my way down the piste. My movements unrestricted by my white and green Bogner ski suit. I bob my head covered by a green helmet and mirrored googles over my eyes.

"That was incredible!" My Angel exclaims when she reaches the base lodge.

One by one, everyone arrives. Our ski butlers help us remove our equipment and hand us our heated après-ski hats, sunglasses, and footwear.

My Angel loops arms with her friend, and they follow our group inside for a hearty breakfast on the deck kept warm by heat lamps. As we walk through the great room of the lodge, we wave at friends who happen to be on holiday in Verbier, too. It's a popular destination for the low-key of the chichi crowd.

"So what's the plan for the rest of the day?" Harris asks as he piles his plate high with eggs, bacon, sausages, and toast from the table laden with delicious food and steaming beverages.

We turn to Roger *The Responsible*—always prepared. He claps his hands like a group excursions guide. Leonie giggles at a private joke.

"Yes, my darling wife, we will have loads of fun! We'll go for another run, then return to the chalet. Shower and change to stroll through the village with The Twins. Take in the sights and do gift buying for those who are always last minute…"

Roger raises an eyebrow at Harris, who shrugs.

"That may be true. However, I always have the best presents. This year, you'll get coal in your stocking if you keep it up, big bro," he retorts as he takes another giant bite of his food.

Everyone laughs and digs in.

"IT'S JUST SO beautiful here! Usually, we go to Aspen."

My Angel says as we meander through Verbier Village for its bustling Christmas market.

The cloves and spices of mulled wine mix with baked goods like bredele, semi-sweet cakes, pretzels, and macarons to scent the crisp air. Carolers dressed in costumes stroll through the aisles singing cheerfully and ringing bells. Vendors fill their stalls with handcrafted music boxes and toys, knit sweaters, scarves, and gloves, and candles and ornaments.

"The festive atmosphere fills me with such joy!" She continues with a sparkling smile.

I lean over and kiss her lush lips, then pull the bottom one with my teeth.

"I'm glad you like it, My Angel. Verbier has the best off-piste trails, so more expert skiers choose the town. The après-ski partying is just as attractive as the slopes. We'll take advantage of both."

She grins up at me as she squeezes my arm.

"Let's find the others, then get back to the chalet. I have plans for you and that syrup you bought…" I tell her with a smirk.

We catch up with Roger, Leonie, The Twins, Sebastian —similarly laden with shopping bags—and Lola who's squatting in front of the stroller. My Angel replaces her as she chats with Rodolphe and Gaspard.

Roger and Sebastian laugh out loud. I smirk.

AFTER RETURNING FROM THE MARKET, we add our new gifts to the already vast number beneath and around the tree's base. The colorful boxes of all shapes and sizes fill the space. Harris winks at us and adds more.

We're gathered in the great room with a blazing fire in the sizable stone hearth. Mariah Carey's "All I Want for Christmas Is You" plays in the background from my favorite Christmas playlist. The classic songs of Nat King Cole, Johnny Mathis, Céline Dion, Gladys Knight and the Pips, Frank Sinatra, and of course the Trans-Siberian Orchestra.

The chef prepared steaming mugs of delicious hot chocolate and mulled wine for us to enjoy with the tasty morsels we bought.

In keeping with the French tradition, we unwrap two presents each on Christmas Eve and the rest tomorrow before we partake of le *Réveillon de Noël* for the Christmas meal. The dishes include Beluga caviar, foie gras, oysters, lobster, scallops, fresh truffles, roast goose, venison, and cheeses. We end with the paramount French Christmas dessert *la bûche de Noël*—the Yule log. All the while, a selection of wines and champagne please our palates.

To incorporate a Steele clan tradition, we move to the cinema room to watch *It's a Wonderful Life.* I settle My Angel between my thighs on the suede chaise lounge with popcorn to enjoy the film.

"What do you want from Santa this year, Little One?" I growl in her ear.

She shivers and whispers, "Only you, Sir."

I chuckle wickedly.

Yeah, it's a brilliant start to the holidays. Like Josy, I look forward to making Verbier our traditional gathering spot, especially with My Angel on my lap.

* * *

STARR

Lola, Leonie, Haley, and I finished a few runs and kick back on chaises at the base lodge deck sipping hot cocoa.

Malcolm and his brothers skied off-piste on Chassoure, as the locals call it, or Tortin to everyone else. It's one of the most challenging runs in Verbier and well-known in the ski world. The terrain and the level of difficulty concerned me, so I bowed out of going with him. But for his safety, he assured me they would take precautions with a trail guide, and each of them set with high-tech tracking devices and satellite phones.

In fact, all of us wear the gadgets and carry the mobiles whenever we're on the mountain slopes.

Still, I told Malcolm we just reunited, and I don't want to lose him again!

He promised me they'd be perfectly safe and would meet us back at the chalet later. After a mind-blowing kiss, he spanked my ass and strode from our room. Always My Dom…

But damn if juices didn't saturate my pussy and my nipples pebble. Yeah, I can't wait for my virile caveman to return.

Leonie's loud singing draws me from my musings.

We're on a Girls' Day Out of good friends, laughter, and plain ole silliness!

"What's going on?" I ask as I lean forward from her chaise.

Lola hesitates for only a moment. A giant smile breaks out on her face, and the gold flecks in her hazel eyes glitter more than the bright sun. She launches into the details of her conversation about having a baby with Sebastian. Afterwards, she stares at Haley and me pointedly.

"So, who's next? Hmmm? Lachlan… Malcolm… Do not consider for one second we haven't noticed signs and sexual tension between you guys!" Lola says, waggling her perfectly shaped eyebrows. "Don't even try to deny it."

"Yeah! Sparks were zipping amongst you at my wedding from the rehearsal dinner through the reception," Leonie adds, tossing her mahogany mane, daring us to dispute the obvious.

Shy Haley flushes crimson while I glance away, flustered.

Lola and Leonie rag on us some more, but all in good

fun. We make a bet on who will come back next Christmas with whom. Included in the lineup are Luc and Blair and Billie and Patrick. Both couples showed their affection for one another openly during the nuptials.

"Well, Starr's already in this year and Malcolm is not one to bring women around at all," Lola says. "In over two years, I've never seen him with anyone seriously. But you had him disconcerted the morning after my wedding."

Leonie agrees.

"I know. But I'm not sure if I'm ready to get involved with anyone, and I've been putting him off for quite some time now," I admit. With a sigh, I tell them about our difficulties and how we seem to be better for now. I'm staying positive and letting fate take us where we're meant to be.

They offer words of advice and encouragement.

"And you, miss?" Leonie asks.

"Right… What's your story, morning glory?" Lola chimes in as we turn to Haley.

Normally she would push her glasses up her nose, but she's taken to wearing contact lenses recently. She says it's better for her peripheral vision. So instead, she pushes her mirrored Ray-Ban Aviators to rest better on the bridge.

Not one of Haley's big brothers would appreciate Lachlan getting involved with their baby sister. Particularly Sebastian since he and Lachlan are best friends and Baz knows he's an Alpha Dom. Malcolm told me the idea of his little sister being a sub to Lachlan makes him want to finish him, cousin or not.

Even though they refer to the Jackson siblings as their cousins, there's no blood relationship—only their mothers being BFFs for decades. So technically, the boys should stay out of it—if an it exists truly.

The girls and I think Haley and Lachlan make a cute couple—shy, curvy Haley and movie-star-looks, dominating Lachlan.

"What's so funny, Leonie?" Haley asks self-consciously.

Leonie waves her hand and responds, "Thinking about your overbearing brothers. Better you than me!"

Haley shakes her head and purses her lips. She fills us in on her latest escapades with Cary Grant lookalike Lachlan.

"Speak of the devils... Look who shows up now. I thought they were meeting us at the chalet," Lola says, nodding towards the entrance.

As Haley finishes, and we were ready to dive deep with an analysis and strategic plan, the boys walk out onto the deck.

Every woman's head turns to gawk at them—young and old alike.

They're like a pack of Alpha males whose high testosterone levels call to every women's womb with an aching need to be pounded and filled by them. The STEELE Quaternity live and in full effect.

I'm overcome by the urge to jump up and yell, "Malcolm Steele is mine!" So I guess I'm more ready than I thought.

All of us but Haley salivate at the sight of them. She groans and throws her head back against her chaise in annoyance at the interruption of her relationship advice session.

"Give me a fucking break already," she mutters.

Malcolm tilts my head back and takes my mouth in a possessive kiss.

Yup, he's got me good! My Dom-cum-boyfriend sexy AF Malcolm Steele.

* * *

MALCOLM

"Dude, you need to open a LEVELS Verbier. Ski in, ski out style! A little action on the slopes and in the playrooms."

Harris says as we take shots of Oval Vodka.

We hit all the hot spots leading up to New Year's Eve since we'll celebrate it at the chalet. The other night we went to Farm Club Verbier, the dance and nightclub famous since the early 70s. It's maintained its popularity for decades, symbolized by its glamorous vibe and great reputation. It's like the Studio 54 of Verbier—if the walls could talk.

My Angel and I made the bathroom walls talk—or rather scream—when I pounded into her, braced against the vanity. Her sequin mini dress rode up her toned thighs as they gripped my hips. She threw her head back, calling my name on repeat. Ah, such sweet music to my ears.

Tonight it's Public Verbier, the swanky spot and counterpart to Public London.

"You know, that's not a bad idea," Sebastian adds, slamming his glass down with a smile next to the Swarovski crystal bottle of vodka. "Of all the clubs we've partied at, none can compare to LEVELS. Bring the heat to the Alps!"

"Yeah, spoken like a true Alpha Dom," Roger chuckles.

Baz's laughter rings out. He's been in an exceptional mood.

"I can see that being a profitable possibility. Surprising how a tech geek can think beyond code," I rib Harris good-naturedly.

Yet, he's still an Alpha male, who like the rest of his brothers seeks release within the LEVELS clubs.

I continue thoughtfully, "We can take over one property near the hotel and close by the other clubs for accessibility. I'll run it by Lucien tomorrow, thanks."

We fist bump, and everyone downs another round of shots.

Our server appears with an assortment of finger foods including Russian pancakes with Beluga caviar, marinated mushrooms, and cheddar olives. The leggy blonde bends over the table to reach for my plate, nearly spilling her ample tits out her top.

Nope, not gonna happen. I ignore her and carry on my conversation with Baz.

She lingers to throw a meaningful glance Harris' way. Then leaves satisfied he made plans with her.

"Obviously you're doing all right without the play-rooms," Roger says, smirking.

Harris sits back and plants his feet wide on the floor, spreading his arms along the back of the booth.

With a smug expression he responds, "You could say so. I'll have some not so little action tonight."

I lift my shot glass in a toast, "Here's to ski in and ski out, my brothers!"

"Hear, hear!"

"Abso-fucking-lutely!"

"You can say that again, bro!"

We raise our glasses and toss back the vodka shots.

Leonie slides up behind Roger and whispers in his ear. With her off of the dance floor makes me glance around for My Angel. They must finish shaking their asses.

"Come bump and grind with me, Sir."

I grin as my cock twitches at My Little One's seductive purr in my ear.

Time to take our club sexcapades to the dance floor or bathroom...

* * *

STARR

"What did you and Sebastian get up to today?"

Lola, Leonie, Haley, and I stretch out in the chalet's spa sauna before our deep-tissue massages start. Ninety-minute of pure decadence.

As a treat, Malcolm arranged for a Girls' Spa Day with masseuses and aestheticians from the hotel's facility to pamper us prior to our New Year's Eve dinner and party. He said we were good girls and deserved special goodies.

Haley and Leonie rolled their eyes at the "good girls" part. But Lola and I grinned from ear-to-ear. My Dom-cum-boyfriend is so sweet!

I'm grateful for the treats. Between Malcolm's marathon lovemaking—"to compensate for lost time"—and

112

the rigors of skiing, tobogganing, and ice skating, my muscles need a rubdown.

"Oh, a little bit of this and a little bit of that," she hedges.

I shake my head, causing long, curly tendrils to escape my messy topknot. As I tuck them back in to the Scünci, I laugh.

"What kind of evasive answer is that?" I ask. "What exactly does that entail?"

Lola giggles and waggles her eyebrows.

"Well, if you'd prefer all the details… Sebastian bound my arms and legs to the four bedposts with red silk cords—"

"Uh, no, thank you!"

"TMI!"

"Girl! Not all of those details! Please!"

Lola's giggles turn into snorts as she doubles over, cracking up. Her hazel eyes twinkle with mischief when she lifts her gaze. The petite firecracker strikes with her sex tales again.

"Okay, okay! I mean, you did ask for it!" She starts. "After a morning of multiple orgasms, we went ice skating. Boy, when I tell you my legs were wobbly—"

Haley throws a towel at Lola's head and she ducks, laughing hysterically.

"Lola!! I do not care to hear of my brother's sex life!" Haley shouts. "And that goes for the two of you, too. Not interested in the least."

Leonie and I exchange looks, then throw towels at her. Lola grabs the one Haley threw and tosses it back at her.

We end up laughing and exchanging our tales for the day, minus the sex scenes.

A gentle knock on the sauna's door draws our attention. A masseuse reminds us it's time, so we troop out to rinse off.

Aside from the sauna and showers, the spa accommodates a steam room, plunge pools for hot and cold therapies, a tranquility lounge, and four of each manicure stations, pedicure chairs, and treatment rooms. We settle in the rooms for our sessions.

The rejuvenating massages put us in even higher spirits when we reemerge. They added a body polish treatment, so our skin glows and feels like satin. The warm oil soothed my achy body and added to the softness.

The aestheticians help us into the pedicure chairs first. We gab some more while they set to our feet and hands. The start of a new year excites everyone. We're ready to leave all the drama behind and to begin anew!

"So, who's the bonnie Scotsman with Haley?"

I ask Leonie and nod towards the other side of the wine cellar.

She glances at me before she turns to the cuddled-up couple.

"Well, don't you look fabulous, darling!" Leonie tells me.

I feel super sexy in a slinky metallic lamé brown and gold wrap-effect mini dress. My long, toned legs end in brown sky-high sandals with gold serpentine metal straps wrapped around my ankles. The long curls of my chocolate-colored hair frame my heart-shaped face, the dimples pop as I giggle.

"You remind me of Christie Doll, Barbie's friend!" Leonie laughs.

"Why thank you! We're hot babes, huh?" I respond.

"Very hot indeed."

Leonie and I startle at the unexpected gruff voice of Malcolm. He chuckles and strokes the five o'clock stubble on his chin. His eyes rove up and down my body as I shift from one foot to the other.

He ignites a passion deep inside of me with one word or a glance.

Leonie laughs and pats his shoulder as she makes a fast exit. Our erotic energy pulsating between us, too hot for her to handle.

We're enjoying pre-dinner cocktails with our families and friends, including some we meet up with on holiday. The bartender and sommelier for STEELE Verbier crafted a selection of drinks and wines for our dinner and party.

"Is your shiny new gift still in place, Little One?" My Dom asks with a raised eyebrow.

"Yes, Sir," I answer as I flex my ass muscles around the platinum butt plug with its sapphire—for its faithfulness and sincerity—embedded base.

"Excellent, Little One. You will receive another gift if you are a good girl," he murmurs in my ear as he pats my butt cheek.

A shudder passes through me and threatens to undo the plug. I gasp and squeeze tight.

My Dom smirks, "Good girl. Do not allow your gift to slip out. I want your ass ready for my ten inches at the *stroke* of midnight."

THE DJ from Farm Club spins a range of music perfect for everyone.

We party it up in the disco next to the wine cellar. The set up works well with people moving seamlessly from the bar to the dance floor or the banquettes along the walls. A gigantic screen shows scenes of countries around the world celebrating the start of the New Year with Sydney, Australia first.

Malcolm twirls me, then pulls me close. He buries his nose in my hair as I drape my arms over his shoulder. We move as one, allowing the past to fade away with each move we make.

A piercing whistle blasts, and we turn to see Sebastian on a raised platform with one arm around Lola and the other beckoning to Leonie and Roger. Then Sebastian raises his champagne flute.

"Before midnight strikes, I want to congratulate my brother on his new bride and darling Twins, my new sister and nephews. We love you all. Steeles for life!"

Everyone claps and stomps with more wolf whistles.

Roger picks Leonie up and swings her around before dipping her and kissing her silly.

The DJ calls for more champagne with five minutes to go.

Earlier, Harris angled the exterior cameras toward

Verbier Village and relayed the footage to the screen. Now, he switches the feed, and the live view appears for the countdown clock and fireworks display.

As the lights dim for the countdown, My Dom guides me from the disco and to one of the many rooms on this level of the supersized chalet.

"Ready to make our own New Year's fireworks, Little One?" He rumbles, his eyes hooded with carnal need.

I spin to face away from him, wiggle my ass, and toss my hair to glance over my shoulder then purr, "Yes, Sir… Happy New Year…"

"Baby, you're my best Dom boyfriend!"

My other gift for being a good girl is a surprise trip to Laucala Island, the private retreat in Fiji.

We flew from Verbier to New York City for a walk down Fifth Avenue to see the Christmas lights and the Rockefeller Center tree. Gazing down from Malcolm's penthouse terrace on the fifty-third floor of The STEELE Tower to the giant crystal snowflake star above Fifty-seventh Street and Fifth Avenue was a highlight.

After two days of ice skating at Rock Center, store window gazing, and making love, Malcolm had us back on his private jet.

I thought headed to Beverly Hills when we landed at LAX. But no, it was a fuel stopover. He refused to tell me our destination even when I threatened to deny him access to my body.

Well, my sore ass and pussy say otherwise. My Dom's

spanks and strokes won me over to his way of thinking in no time...

"You mean your *only* Best Dom Boyfriend," Malcolm growls, eyeing me briefly.

I lean over to kiss his cheek as he drives the golf cart along the frangipani-lined path to our cliffside villa. Then inhale the luscious floral scent as I shift in my seat to take in the island's extraordinary view.

The sparkling, cyan-colored South Pacific Ocean reaches the horizon. The hues range from the darkest to the lightest blues and greens so varied in depth captivate me. Nearby verdant islands with rings of coral rise from the ocean.

Gulls and terns hover over the waves while shadows of fish schools appear below the crystal-clear surface. The birds swoop in and out of the water to catch their meals.

Malcolm removed the canvas roof before we hopped into the golf cart. I tilt my head back to gaze at the cloudless, blue sky. The sun beams down on us. My bare shoulders and arms appreciate its warmth. Such a welcome 180-degree change from the cold of Switzerland and New York!

"Glad to be back, My Angel?" Malcolm asks.

I grin from ear to ear.

"Absolutely! It's divine! Have you ever been here?" I ask. When he shakes his head, I continue. "Oh! You'll love it. I can't wait to show you the rain forest and the white sandy beaches!"

I prattle on until we stop in front of the villa.

When I was here for my retreat two years ago, I stayed

at a beachfront villa. It was spectacular. But this villa and its views are breathtaking!

A butler, chef, and maid greet us as we step from the golf cart. The butler gives us a tour while the maid unpacks our belongings. The chef explains he stocked the refrigerator and prepared a light meal for our arrival. Back at the entrance, they smile and leave us. The staff is present at our call only, so we can enjoy complete privacy.

"What shall we do first, Sir?" I purr glancing up at My Dom through my eyelashes.

"That swing facing the ocean appears the best place to begin our holiday," he responds. His hooded gaze travels from my pink-painted toes up my bare legs, past my strapless romper to linger on my lips. "Strip."

Without hesitation, I rip my clothes and sandals off. My hands grasp my elbows behind my back, and my feet widen. With my head bowed, my long curls skim the bottoms of my heaving breasts. Eager to play on the swing, my breath quickens.

My Dom tsks as he sweeps my hair behind my back and braids it.

"Never cover your tantalizing tits from my sight, Little One," he chides me. "Understand?"

An unexpected whack to my ass makes me jump and gasp. My mind distracted by the scent of his cologne and the sensation of his thick fingers in my hair delayed my answer.

"Y-y-yes, Sir!" I yelp rising to my toes from the impact of his palm on my butt cheek.

My Dom chuckles wickedly, "Come."

I follow him back through the villa to the rear terrace overlooking the Pacific Ocean. Its natural splendor extends for miles. I sigh, content to be miles from the bustle of our lives.

My Dom takes my hand and helps me to sit on the cushion of the rope swing. It hangs from a palm tree surrounded by more frangipani shrubs. The white flowers symbolize Fiji and remind me of my previous tropical vacation each time I smell them.

To position me to his specifications, My Dom places my hands on either side of the swing at shoulder height with my fingers wrapped around the ropes. Next he pushes me back gently as he tells me to put my butt on the edge.

I take a deep breath when he steps back and undresses.

Each garment comes off with slow, precise movements. Saliva fills my mouth at the sight of his sculpted chest and the feathered line of dark hair from below his belly button to his trimmed pubic hair. I have to swallow as his massive dick springs free from his shorts and boxer briefs. The platinum balls glint in the sunlight.

A shiver runs through me at the memory of them rubbing my inner walls just right each and every time. My pussy creams.

My Dom notices and chuckles again. His eight-pack abs ripple.

Damn!

He stands before me and grips the base of his cock. Slow, long strokes followed by a tug draw a pearl of pre-cum from his swollen tip. He uses the pad of his thumb to smooth the delicacy around his piercing.

How I'd rather it were my tongue.

To show My Dom, I poke the tip between my lips and curve it up to brush against the top one. A moan escapes.

My Dom's eyes narrow as a growl rumbles from his chest—now rising and falling in sync with mine.

"Want a lick, Naughty Girl?" He asks in tone sultrier than the humid air surrounding us.

"Yes, please, Sir," I reply with an eager nod and full-on lip lick.

He stalks closer and places his hands on either side of my hips to steady the swing. I entwine my legs with his muscular ones and bend at the waist.

My mouth engulfs his dick from tip to mid-shaft. Yum…

He groans at the dual sensation of my hot, wet mouth and my small fist around the rest of his girth. My other hand kneads his heavy balls.

"You will suck me, Naughty Girl. Every. Single. Inch," My Dom grinds out. "Suck. Me. Well."

I hum in pleasure.

My tongue performs acrobatics on his shaft. Swoops, circles, laves, twirls. All to bring him erotic ecstasy.

His cock swells and pulsates.

"Enough," My Dom commands as he grips my braid, and his dick pops from my mouth. "Give me your pussy, Little One. I want your slick heat wrapped around my cock. Now."

I pout because giving him head gives me power. I love to see My Dom with jelly knees when he spills his seed down my throat.

But I comply because nothing compares to the feel of his dick filling my weeping pussy to capacity. I lean back again, then unwrap my legs from his and spread them wide. The heady scent of my arousal mingles with the frangipani.

"Fuck, you're beautiful, My Angel," Malcolm says slipping into boyfriend mode.

He dips his head to place his nose against my dripping folds and inhales with a groan. When he stands, he grips the swing and aligns his erection with my gaping hole. The swing jerks forward to impale me on his dick.

"FUCK!!!" We cry in unison.

Once my inner walls adjust to his length and girth, Malcolm pushes the swing backwards. I arc through the air, then close my eyes as the pendulum reverses.

He rolls his hips against me, filling me with his cock to the root.

"So good, My Angel," Malcolm says in my ear gruffly.

We continue our adult playtime until I'm panting from multiple toe-curling orgasms and a sheen of sweat glistens on our skin.

"Give me one more, Little One," My Dom returns to make demands of my body.

A demand I give in to happily.

A final arc brings me home, and an all-encompassing orgasm overtakes me. My pussy spasms around My Dom's massive ten inches and showers it with my juices. They run down the crack of my ass to pool beneath me on the already-soaked cushion.

"MALCOLM!!!" I wail as my body convulses.

Now it's his turn.

He lifts my limp body from the swing. Automatically, I drape my arms over his shoulders and wrap my legs around his hips. His fingers dig into the fleshiest parts of my ass, and he pistons his hips.

Malcolm's feral caveman grunts and growls punctuate each deep thrust.

Another climax rocks my world, and I scream his name.

He responds with my name—a howl to the sky—as his dick expands, then jerks his seed inside of my wrecked pussy. Malcolm lowers to his knees. He continues slow strokes in and out of me as he suckles my nipples until our minds return from our carnal trance.

"Welcome to paradise, My Angel," Malcolm murmurs as he lays his head against my breast.

WE STRETCH out in the sunken tub on our villa's veranda to soak our sore muscles—nothing beats aftercare with My Dom lover. Five days of hiking through the rain forest, scuba diving, and the pleasurable rigors of marathon love-making fade away. And each one makes me love this man even more.

Malcolm is so attentive and loving. The words *I love you, My Angel* flow from his mouth with ease. From the moment we reconnected in Verbier, he's made it his mission to make up for the time we spent apart.

I relish in every second of it. Just like now.

It feels fantastic to lean back against Malcolm's solid

chest and allow the fragrant essential oils—amplified by the warmth of the water—lull us into a peaceful state. The sounds of the ocean waves lapping against the rocky cliff mesmerizes us.

"Ready to return to reality tomorrow?" He asks.

I sigh and shake my head.

The soapy sponge he smooths up from my lower belly to the hollow between my breasts as he bathes me makes me wish we never have to leave.

Malcolm chuckles and nuzzles my neck, pulling me tighter in his embrace.

"I'd rather stay too. But duty calls for both of us," he says wistfully.

Water sloshes onto the stones as I turn to straddle his powerful thighs. I cup his face with my palms and press my forehead and nose against his. We share each other's breath for a peaceful moment.

"Fine. But promise me we'll come back," I tell him.

He grips my hips and lifts before lowering me onto his throbbing cock. When his groin meets my ass, he sighs.

"I promise, My Angel."

"All rise... This court is now in session. The Honorable Judge Dixon presiding."

From my peripheral vision, I see Vicky stand with her legal team. She smooths the skirt of her conservative navy blue suit, then adjusts the headband holding back her blonde hair.

When My Angel, her parents, Sebastian, Harris, Haley, and I arrived with my legal team, Vicky glanced over her shoulder at us. Fire filled her cornflower blue eyes as she glared at my hand interlocked with Starr's then at me.

Now Vicky pulls on her acting skills for the performance of an innocent young woman.

Fuck that. I have to suppress the snarl in my chest. Keep it together, Steele. This shit will be over soon enough.

At the call to order, the hum of voices and sounds of shuffled papers quiet. Everyone stands for Judge Susan Dixon's entrance.

Part two of Nightingale begins. Game on.

The hearing starts with an opening statement presented by Judge Dixon as a summary of the trespassing claim and the parties involved.

I'm suing the hell out of Victoria Anne Reynolds. For the last time, this bird is going to learn to not fuck with My Angel and me. She damn near ruined my chance for happiness.

Obviously it wasn't me she was fucking on my penthouse rooftop terrace. The security footage revealed the mystery man as Dante Rossi, the new concierge for my apartment building—a STEELE International residential property. Who happens to resemble me in hair color and body build.

Vicky seduced him for access to my penthouse for her grand scheme of hurting My Angel and ending us. Vicky led Rossi to believe she was interested in him. Starstruck, he fell for it. After a couple of weeks, she persuaded him to show her the nighttime view of Sunset Strip from my terrace.

Gullible, he used the passcode security keeps for emergencies to enter my penthouse's private elevator. Once on the rooftop, Vicky instigated sex on the chaise lounge angled with his back to the access door. She put on an Oscar-worthy performance when My Angel stepped onto the terrace as depicted in the security camera's lens.

The expression of raw pain on her face nearly undid me. My Angel looked as though someone ripped her beating heart from her chest and squeezed it before her eyes. The anguish was so intense she stumbled down the stairs and to the elevator. She sped through the garage and out to the street. Her sobs still echo in my ears. Damn that bird!

I clench my fists on my thighs as the judge finishes.

Engelbert Douglass—my lead attorney—presents my case. He plays the security footage from the time Vicky entered the garage to the time My Angel drove away. Afterwards, he calls Rossi to the witness stand where he spills his guts. Poor sucker.

The lead attorney for Vicky cross-exams Rossi. He doesn't waiver in his previous testimony. But he agrees he was wrong in giving Vicky access to my property. The attorney doesn't have much to smirch Rossi. As a STEELE employee—now former—he went through an extensive background check and proved spotless. The attorney ends his questioning.

Next Douglass calls My Angel to the stand to testify.

I want to grab her in my embrace to shield her from Vicky's bullshit. Pride wells in my chest when My Angel strides to the stand confidently. I also can't help but appreciate the sway of her hips in her dress and how her heels lift her lush ass just so…

Once she's settled in the chair, she flicks her gaze to Vicky, then to Douglass.

"Ms. Knight, kindly share for Judge Dixon what led you to Mr. Steele's penthouse rooftop terrace on the night in question," Douglass says.

My Angel maintains her composure as she recounts from the text message through Vicky's words during the sex to her return to the garage. Her nostrils flare when she glances back at Vicky as she finishes her testimony.

Douglass provides the judge and the opposing counsel with copies of her cell phone records. Then yields the floor to Vicky's attorney.

He attempts to discredit My Angel. But being the daughter of brilliant legal eagles, she avoids any pitfall he puts before her. I can sense their pride in her as they sit behind my table. When it's apparent her testimony is irrefutable, the attorney ends his cross-examination, albeit begrudgingly.

When he returns to his seat beside Vicky, she whispers to him fervently. He shakes his head, and she gesticulates as she raises her voice. He tries to calm her, but she's not hearing it.

"Get your client under control, counselor," Judge Dixon warns with her eyebrow arched in reproach. "I am prepared to issue my summary judgement."

"Apologies, your Hon—"

"Wait one minute! Malcolm Steele is a liar! He's trying to ruin my fucking life! My film deals ended... Clothing contracts canceled... He beat me... He... He tied me up—"

Bam! Bam! Bam!

"Silence your client, counselor! Now!" Commands Judge Dixon as she slams her gavel with a frown.

"Order in the court! Order in the court!" The bailiff demands.

The room explodes with Vicky's wild rantings of BDSM, torture, lies, bullshit. Her madness pisses the judge off, and she calls for counsel in her chambers.

Two other members of Vicky's legal team escort her

still screaming from the courtroom. Once they leave, the room is silent.

I shift in my seat to face My Angel and the others. Her sorrel brown eyes dance as she grins. Baz smirks and nods his head. I sigh, relieved she's not mad at me.

"Well, Ms. Reynolds was entertaining…" Harris snorts. "I wouldn't pay to see her though."

Haley giggles at her twin's dry wit.

"I know Judge Dixon. She's fair and will not allow that woman's unsubstantiated claims to interfere with her judgement. They're irrelevant to this hearing," Peace says while Sun nods in agreement.

"Not at all," she says.

My eyes never leave My Angel, and she reaches over the railing for my hand. I smile and clasp her dainty hand between my larger ones.

"You did well, My Angel. How are you?" I ask.

Her grin broadens.

"Fine! I just can't wait to smudge everyone when we leave that woman's toxic presence!" My Angel quips.

Everyone laughs, and the tense moment passes.

Douglass returns to the table. Vicky's team agreed to a monetary settlement with me and extended the original three-year civil harassment orders to five years. To ensure she doesn't have time to fuck with us, Judge Dixon added options for five additional years to protect My Angel and me. The seven figures will go to STEELE Foundation.

Our mother Shelley runs our family's foundation that builds and manages attractive, affordable housing for urban, lower-income families. The name is a play on the house foundation, being strong and supportive like steel. Appropriate since Vicky broke into my home she'll pay for others' homes.

When a subdued Vicky and her legal team return, Judge Dixon re-enters the courtroom.

She announces her summary judgement as Douglass informed us and ends the hearing with one more strike of her gavel.

I can sense Vicky's glacial glare from across the aisle. A glance at her face makes a cold band of iron squeeze my heart. Such blatant hate surprises me. A shiver races down my spine.

A hand pressed into mine draws me from the chilly abyss of Vicky's blue orbs. I look down into My Angel's warm gaze and shake off the morose gloom that permeates my soul.

"Let's go, baby," she smiles as she tugs my hand.

I ignore Vicky's ire and leave the courtroom, fingers locked with My Angel's again.

Peace and Sun and my legal team head for their respective offices. The rest of us go to my penthouse.

"Thank fuck that's over with quickly. We've had enough with the courtroom drama between you and Roger. Give it rest for a while, will you?" Sebastian sighs as he sips his Jackson Reserve Scotch.

"Hear, hear!" Harris agrees, raising his Baccarat crystal snifter. "Moving on, fellas!"

I nod and take a sip from my glass, then hug My Angel closer to my side on the sofa. She rests her head on my shoulder, and I kiss her curly top.

"Not that I want to hear about your sex life—never! But her accusations concern me. Especially given the situation with Roger and that other hussy. We don't need another he-said-she-said situation to arise later," Haley says.

"I have videos of our sexual encounters and her signed contract for her consent, including the taping," I respond. "That's standard for any sub relationship I've had. No chance for misinterpretation."

My Angel stiffens in my arms and leans back to look at me.

"You record us, too?" She asks with wide eyes. "I don't recall—"

I place my finger on her lips and shake my head.

"You're the only one I have never recorded. Well, except for—"

My Angel claps her hands over my mouth, shaking her head vigorously. She looks at my siblings, horrified I'll disclose our private activities.

Baz chuckles while Haley sings with her fingers in her ears.

"Bro... Messy Malcolm!" Harris guffaws.

It's been a month since the hearing—Nightingale Part II— and no disturbances from Vicky.

Nightingale Part I...

Ruin her acting career: video surfaced of her disparaging remarks on her co-stars, crews, industry heavy hitters led to every top agent, producer, director refusing to hire her.

Destroy her paid endorsements: documentation of her lies and manipulative behavior goes against the clean-reputation clause of her contracts.

End her sexual partnerships: her medical record of STI treatments circulated on the Internet.

They don't call me *The Enforcer* for nothing. I handle bullshit my way. Just like I did for Roger that gold digger Delia Fucking Shaw.

I returned to New York City a week after the hearing. Working from STEELE Los Angeles makes it easy for the bicoastal relationship with My Angel. Although I'm encouraging her to open Starr Light Fitness & Wellness New York.

She's hesitant to take on more than one at a time since Cabo San Lucas is under construction and St. Barth's just opened its doors—doing extremely well, in fact. With Monte Carlo on the list next, she wonders if New York should come before it.

I say, hell yeah!

The expansion to Jackson Hole at STEELE Resorts for her international retreats also proves popular. Not only her regular clients attend, but wellness buffs from around the world bringing new guests to our resorts. Those who happen to be at the properties for their holidays tend to join the classes since they receive the schedule at check-in.

The new revenue stream impresses STEELE CEO Sebastian. He's given the green light for any future SLFW projects. My Entertainment Properties Division continues to surpass expectations.

My Angel laughs that the media coverage from the Vicky situation boosted SLFW and her social media followers and e-newsletter subscribers.

I follow her channels to watch the yoga videos she posts. Damn if she's not the most flexible little thing!

A knock at my office door causes me to shift in my chair to adjust my burgeoning erection. Then I call for the person to enter.

Anton strides in for our weekly meeting with a shit-eating grin on his face.

"Adrienne is still in town, I take it?" My question makes him smirk even harder.

"*Da, moy drug,*" he responds. "Unfortunately, my little *khlopushka* leaves tomorrow."

I clap my friend on the back before I sit at the conference table.

"And your woman? All good?" Anton asks as he pulls out his chair.

Now it's my turn for a shit-eating grin.

"Ha! That good, huh? Well, I'm happy for you, my friend! Don't let her get away like you did before..." He chuckles as he shakes his head. "We took care of that *cyka*. Now enjoy a real woman!"

Nah, not this time, I chuckle to myself with a shake of my head. My Angel is going nowhere. I've got her on lock!

"Good morning… I guess. Why are the lights off? Some new welcoming of clients I'm not aware of?"

I joke to one greeter as I stride through the entrance to Starr Light Fitness & Wellness Beverly Hills.

Clients mill about the darkened interior, sitting at tables near the café, browsing in the boutique, and on line for check in at the front desk. It's time for the first group classes and private sessions to start in fifteen minutes.

Everything appears normal, but no lights.

Adrienne stands beside the front desk. As I approach her, she glances up from a tablet with her mobile to her ear, a frown on her face.

Okay, now I'm concerned.

What the heck happened? I wonder, glancing around the lobby.

Now I notice no sound of the blenders for smoothies or

the piped-in music. It's not just dark, the center is silent. WTF???

A client walks over to me with a quizzical expression.

Not wanting to seem worried, I smile at her.

"Good morning, Gail. How's your husband doing?" I ask pleasantly.

We take great care to familiarize ourselves with SLFW's clients—their names and the life happenings they share willingly. They appreciate the human connection and don't feel as though they're only dollar signs to me or to my staff. SLFW clients pay a sizable amount of money each year on the annual membership dues, semi-privates, duets, privates, and retreats. Not to mention the ancillary services including the spa, boutique, café, kids' club, and the valet. SLFW values our clients.

"Good morning, Starr. He's doing much better, thanks for asking! Your suggestion of turmeric tea—"

"When can we go inside the Pilates studio? I want to get my preferred tower!"

Inwardly, I sigh. Not every member is laid back. Some Type A personalities—ultra competitive, demanding, impatient—exist, even in SLFW's mellow environment. They come for the amazing bodies our yoga, Pilates, Barre, and strength training sessions develop. The infamous Yoga Butt...

I excuse myself from Gail and turn to Ms. Tower with a smile.

"Good morning, Shelby. I've only arrived. Let me check the status," I respond, then nod as I continue to Adrienne.

Just as I reach her, the lights turn on, and everyone

claps. Immediately, the front desk staff check in the clients and the café blenders whir.

"Hey, girl. A mix-up with the electricity company. They thought I canceled our service. Everything's back in order. Crazy, huh?" She says as we walk towards our offices.

We nod and smile at clients along the way. They return our greetings as they go to the studios. I giggle when I notice Shelby rush past everyone. Good grief. Take it easy, girl!

"Ah, Shelby…" Adrienne laughs outright.

"*Buenos días!*" Says Márcia Souza, my administrative assistant and a yoga substitute teacher. "Thank goodness the power is back on! A flashlight would not work…"

The Brazilian petite spitfire follows Adrienne and me into my office and shuts the door.

"I know, right! Simple error on the electric company's part. It's fixed now," Adrienne says as she sits across from my desk.

Márcia joins her in the other chair while I take my seat and plug my MacBook Pro into its docking station on my desk.

"Tell me what's going on today," I say as my monitor screen flicks on.

We settle into our morning routine: the day's agenda; administrative tasks; client and staff concerns; upcoming events; the expansion status. More teachers clamor for a transfer to St. Barth's and Cabo San Lucas. Even Monte Carlo has a wait list, and its construction not scheduled for months!

We set the international retreat schedule for two every

other month. I'll lead one while one of our top teachers leads the other. They rotate based on the fitness focus of yoga or Pilates; Barre and strength training occurs with both types. Based on the location, we'll include additional activities for wine tasting, cooking, hiking, painting, or whatever the place is known for. Clients book the retreats as soon as we promote them.

I'm beyond pleased with the success of our STEELE International partnership. Their team from Malcolm to Anton to the directors and their staff have been phenomenal. Malcolm says we impressed Sebastian, and he's given the okay for more SLFW Resorts. Whoohoo!

"So when do you leave for the retreat in Monte Carlo?" Adrienne asks as she we sync our calendars.

I swipe through to next month on my app, then give her the date for two weeks from now.

I'm looking forward to it since I'll have time to see Leonie and The Twins while I'm in Europe. I miss the little munchkins. It's their six-month birthday party. Unbelievable how time flies so quickly. Leonie and Roger return from their two-month honeymoon, so we'll gather at the family's newly renovated triplex in Paris.

Adrienne, Márcia, and I finish our meeting. I go to my studio for my first private session. My day won't end until four this afternoon with my last group class. Then I'll have a massage at the spa before an early dinner with my publicist and a fitness magazine editor.

As I enter one of the group yoga class studios, my heart swells with gratitude. From the continued success of my company to my friends to the love of my life, the Universe shines its blessings on me.

The smile that spreads across my face is genuine as I sit in lotus position before my students. I place my palms together at heart center and bow my head.

"Let us start our practice with the Anusara chant, Niralambaya Upanishad…

Om Namah Shivaya Gurave

    Satchidananda Murtaye

    Nishpranchaya Shantaye

    Niralambaya Tejase

My heart opens to the power and source of grace that takes form as truth, knowledge, bliss. Always present, boundless peace. Shining source, limitless and free."

* * *

"*Joyeux Anniversaire!*"

"Happy Birthday!"

Josy, Guy, the Steeles, Luc, and I celebrate The Twins' six-month birthday the day after Leonie and Roger returned from Verbier.

Yesterday, Malcolm flew in from New York City with his parents and his siblings to update Roger on another legal claim involving that woman, Delia Shaw. Ninety minutes ago, I flew up from The Jackson Hole at STEELE Monte Carlo after SLFW's retreat. Malcolm met me at the airport, and we fooled around like a pair of hormone-crazed teens in the back of his Black Badge Rolls-Royce Cullinan.

After a quick shower, we joined the family in Leonie and Roger's new triplex penthouse. We're gathered around the dining room table with Rodolphe and Gaspard sitting in their high chairs. They're bedazzled by the flickering candles on the identical cakes before them.

As everyone sings, The Twins bounce and wave their arms in amusement. Each has one little tooth that gleams in the light. I laugh when I recall Leonie's stories about all their drooling and tears. Now The Twins have their first tooth each!

I still can't believe it's been half a year already.

Roger and Leonie bend over to blow out the candles. When they lean in to kiss The Twins' chubby cheeks, Gaspard says, "Dada, dada!"

Leonie's eyes fly to Roger, who looks stunned.

"Dada, dada."

Everyone looks over to Rodolphe, and he waves his arms, repeating the words.

Roger has tears in his eyes as he lifts first Gaspard, then Rodolphe into his arms. He kisses their cheeks and holds them close.

Leonie wraps her arms around the three of them. Roger buries his face in her hair. It's an unexpected, momentous occasion that overwhelms the first-time parents.

The room is silent save The Twins and their baby sounds.

"Well, Dada, don't get all sappy on us!" Harris chuckles and smacks his lips. "I'm ready for some cake, bro!"

Everyone laughs at the jokester.

While Roger continues to hold The Twins and chats with Sebastian, Lola helps Leonie cut the Gateau St. Honoré cakes. She shares it's made by Josy from the recipe tips their Verbier chef shared. The Twins' birthday gave Josy the perfect excuse to try her recent version.

I glance up to see Josy nervously watching Lola and Leonie cut into the flaky confections. Her mother looks relieved after Harris takes a bite and raves about the delicious factor being off the charts.

I take a bite of my piece and swoon at the delicious flavor. It's incredible!

Then I turn to Lola with a question that's been burning in the back of my mind since we had dinner last month at Spago Beverly Hills with Billie and Blair. A mystery man—Simon Blanchett—had his eyes on Lola from the moment we sat at our table until he left from speaking to her. She waved us off with assurances nothing was amiss when we asked her about the sexy Frenchman.

But I want the deets.

"So, how was your business dinner with Simon Blanchett?" I ask when we're away from the others.

Lola blushes and darts her hazel eyes in Sebastian's direction.

As I thought, something's there. I won't pry, but we've grown close enough to share our lives. I arch my eyebrow and cock my head to the side questioningly.

Lola clears her throat and brings her gaze back to me. Her eyes fill with guilt, then sadness.

"He was a lover for a brief time years ago. I ended

things when he wanted more than I was ready to give. It took him a while to give up. Then I met Baz," she says, then sips her Champagne. "Simon owns Blanchett Retail Enterprises, SAS, the largest online luxury retailer in the world. At dinner he asked me—rather Lola's Coterie—to partner with his company."

I smile and congratulate her. But she shakes her head sadly.

"Baz is jealous, you know, Captain Caveman. No different from Malcolm... Baz and I are supposed to be working on a baby. But I want to hold off until—"

"Time to open the presents!" Haley exclaims.

Lola shakes her head, and I nod. Now's not the time.

We spend the next half an hour opening presents. With The Twins' development in mind, the gifts include stacking toys with different-sized rings and multi-colored cubes; cars, trains, and balls that roll, light up, and make music to encourage crawling; roly-poly toys; sturdy toys that encourage pulling up to standing; to keep them entertained, colorful board books.

Harris and Haley—the Dynamic Duo—give them some gadgets claiming one is never too young for technology.

Luc bought them their first stock portfolios. The men were more impressed and had a lengthy discussion about the growth potential.

Afterwards, we go to the cinema room with aperitifs.

Haley surprises Roger and Leonie with a compilation movie of our first family Christmas and New Year's. No one even realized she was taking footage while we were together. Some scenes from us skiing, the angle straight on as though we were still on the piste; making s'mores at the outside firepit; The Twins first snowfall; the New Year's Eve fireworks in the village.

She has it set to some of Leonie's favorite Christmas songs, including "Christmas Canon" and Andrea Bocelli and Céline Dion's "The Prayer."

She gives Haley an enormous hug as tears well in her amber eyes.

Haley impresses everyone, and we request copies. Always prepared, she hands out artfully packaged copies to each of us.

Then everyone departs since we have a busy workday tomorrow. Lola to her atelier with Leonie; the Steele siblings to their Paris offices; Luc to his Banquet Montaigne; me to guest teach at Norman Green's Elite Training Facility.

Morgan, Shelley, Lola, and Sebastian take the family's private elevator to their respective penthouses on the two floors below Roger and Leonie. Their residences occupy the top floors, twenty-eight through thirty-two.

The Tower is in the Front de Seine district of Beau-grenelle in the *quinzième*. Like its New York City counter-part, it's mixed-use with commercial and residential space plus the largest mall in Paris. The views of the Seine and of the Eiffel Tower are incredible, especially at night when the spectacular light display flits across the monumental iron structure.

Malcolm, Harris, Haley, and I return to our suites at the STEELE Place Vendôme. Guy and Josy leave for their family's ancestral home, *Le Beaulieu Manoir*. Their driver will take Luc to his mansion first as both live in the posh *seizième* arrondissement.

"Good night, Haley and Harris!" I say as we part ways at the elevators once we're back at the hotel.

"Sleep tight!" They chorus, then laugh.

"See you tomorrow at the office," Malcolm tells them as he takes my hand and leads me down the hall at a hurried pace.

"Slow down, bro! I promised I wouldn't steal Starr from you!" Harris chortles.

Malcolm growls and flips him the bird while Haley and I laugh.

Once inside our darkened suite, Malcolm whirls me around to face the wall of windows and slaps my ass to push me along.

"Strip. There. Now," My Dom commands in a husky voice.

I hesitate, concerned someone may see my naked body from the street to the Tuileries Gardens beyond. Warm breath on the shell of my ear and hands gripping my hips startle me.

"You do not trust your Dom, Little One?" Malcolm murmurs in my ear as he grinds his impressive erection between my butt cheeks.

A shudder travels along my spine, and I close my eyes with a whimper, leaning into his muscular embrace.

"I trust you, Sir," I reply breathlessly. "I'm just nervous someone will see me."

He nips my ear lobe and growls.

"No one but I will ever see your naked beauty, Little

One," My Dom corrects me.

I jolt with a yelp from the pain caused to my sensitive flesh.

"The windows—as in all STEELE properties—have treatments. No one can see in, while those inside can see out," he says. "Now, go do as I told you, Naughty Girl."

My ass jiggles from another harder smack. I hasten into position and remove my silk wrap dress and lace Lola's Coterie lingerie. When I lean over to unwrap the strings from sandals, My Dom stops me with an ah, ah, ah. I bite my lip and rise—feet planted wide apart; arms behind back grasped at opposite elbows; head bowed slightly with eyes downcast.

The lights of Paris shine against the ink black sky before me.

My ears strain to hear any movement from My Dom. The silk Aubusson rugs hide his footsteps. Tinkling of ice in a crystal glass makes me aware he's at the bar on the side wall of the salon. Liquid splashes in to the snifter, undoubtedly his favorite Jackson Reserve Scotch. The ice clinks. He must take a sip of the smooth, amber liquid. Another clink, then silence.

Time passes—a minute, five, one hundred???

My only thought: I must maintain position.

Then the opening strains of Edith Piaf's "Hymne A L'Amour" whispers from the surround sound speakers.

The heat of My Dom's naked body reaches into my soul as he stands behind me suddenly. His head dips to brush his lips along the column of my throat.

As I tremble from his touch, I tilt my head to the side to

give him more access. My pulse beats beneath his full mouth rapidly. Fire licks at my skin when his fingers feather down my flat belly to slip inside my soaked pussy and to stroke my swollen clit.

My Dom finger fucks me through two mind-blowing climaxes. On jelly knees, I lean against his sculpted chest. His arm bands around my waist to hold me close. The musky scent of my arousal wafts beneath my nose when he lifts his fingers to my slack mouth.

"Clean them," he demands huskily.

Without hesitation, I swirl the tip of my tongue around his thick digits, then lave them with its flat surface. Our groans mingle from the erotic act. His velvet covered-steel cock thumps against my ass as he bends his knees to align his groin to my crack.

He dips the mushroom head into my pussy, thrusting slow and long, fully coating his dick with my natural lubricant.

"Spread your ass cheeks for me, Little One," My Dom commands while he places his palm between my shoulder blades to bend me forward. "Remember your safewords are green to continue, yellow for a moment, and red to stop all play at once."

I comply and grip my ass, baring my most private hole to him. Then I rest the side of my face against the cool surface of the window. Another shudder runs through me when his tip—balls piercing and all—pushes past my rings of muscle. Instinctively, I clench my ass—he's huge and stretches my tight hole to the max. But I loosen on a mewl when My Dom spanks the tops of my thighs.

"Open for me, Naughty Girl! Who do you belong to?" He grunts as he presses another inch inside.

I stutter, "You, Sir… Ohhh…"

Fully seated within my forbidden hole, I bow to his dominant possession of my body. The submissive in me rolls over to bare her belly under My Dom's sexual thrall.

With no safeword—only throaty moans—falling from my parted lips, he offers no mercy as he pounds my ass fervently. My cries of carnal pleasure spur him to rise onto his toes and lift my hips to take me even more voracious.

"Mine. Mine. Mine." My Dom chants with each toe-curling thrust.

"Please, Sir! Please let me cum!" I beg, clamping the muscles of my hollow pussy.

"No!" He responds with a slap to my butt cheek for emphasis, then increases his brutal pace.

I squeeze my eyes shut and pant through my open mouth. The glass fogs from my heated breaths, and my hands slide along its surface, slick from the sweat on my palms. The lights of Paris blur before my hooded eyes when I open them unseeingly.

"Sir! Please!" I wail as my legs tremble, unable to hold back my orgasm any longer.

"Yes! Now!" My Dom shouts with one last snap of his powerful hips and a pinch to my distended clit.

My mind blanks as the climax of life overrides my systems.

The last cognizant thought: Ms. Piaf is correct; my body quivers under My Dom's attentive hands. I sigh in contentment, his name a whispered breath across my lips.

STARR

"*How* I love my job!"

Haley professes as we stretch out on chaise lounges on the white sand of Palmilla Beach.

We're on a construction site visit of Starr Light Fitness & Wellness Resorts at STEELE Cabo San Lucas.

The beach features a one-mile-long stretch of gorgeous, soft golden desert sands and blue-green swimmable waters. The five-diamond SCSL is the only resort with direct access. It's nestled near the southern tip of Palmilla Beach and commands stunning views over the turquoise water. Guests enjoy complimentary activities including snorkeling, stand-up paddleboarding, and kayaking at SCSL's very own Pelican Beach.

SLFW Resorts sits back from the shoreline behind lush foliage of palm trees and hibiscus bushes. Close to the primary hotel, the center has beachfront footage for our activities without interfering with guests of the hotel. The structure mimics the Spanish-style property with white stucco walls, red tile roof, arches, and blue accents. A rooftop terrace takes advantage of the panoramic view—miles of turquoise water dotted by mounds of earth breaking its surface.

Haley joined me as co-head of STEELE Technology and Cyber Security to oversee the installation of the center's systems.

Malcolm told me the twins are the youngest of the Steele clan and a double surprise for their parents, who had not planned on having more children. Then a twofer to boot. Roger—who's three years older—had been the baby of the family until Harris and Haley popped up. Harris is older by mere minutes.

Although fraternal, they share a similar love of technology, with Haley being a hacker and Harris a coder. Their brothers tease them for being nerds, but they're wizzes at what they do, which led to the approval for them to create their subsidiary. As co-heads, they're responsible for all of STEELE and external clients from around the globe, including Jackson Corporation. They're super smart and their brothers have grown to depend upon them, even if Haley and Harris are the babies now.

Haley is a shy beauty who—like Harris—matches the rest of the Steeles with jet black hair. Hers hangs mid-back in a silky curtain. Their signature gray eyes in her are soulful, set in her heart-shaped face with cheeks that display dimples when she smiles or laughs.

Like she does now.

"Harris wanted your project, but he lost out. My paper

beat his rock. I always tell him brawny doesn't always win!" Haley giggles.

Their antics crack me up. If they weren't so smart, people would think they're crazy to do business based on a random game of chance!

"I'm glad you won, too! Now we can hang out when the workday ends and sip mojitos!" I declare as I clink my glass with hers.

We sip our cocktails as we catch up on our lives. Haley has been pretty mum about some important project she's working on. I can only gather it involves Roger. She said she'll let everyone know soon.

"How do you feel about your collar?" She asks as she fingers her bare neck.

I choke on my drink.

Malcolm would go ballistic if he knew Haley was asking me about BDSM. Especially a collar, which means she must be interested in submission. Her big brother would end any guy who tried to spank her. Hypocritical much?

I don't let the fact Malcolm does to me exactly what he doesn't want someone to do to Haley bother me. He's her protective big brother—albeit his thirty-four to her thirty years. It's not that he's thinks BDSM is bad for her, he just wouldn't want her with a Dom who's inexperienced and could hurt her.

That's why I'm surprised he and his brothers are anti-Lachlan for Haley.

"Why do you ask?" I respond while I consider my response. A bit of deflection may give me time to plan my answer.

Haley sighs and stares towards the horizon.

"I want to be dominated," she responds.

Oh dear.

Well, she's my friend, and I will be honest with her. Besides, Haley needs a woman's perspective and not her fire-breathing brothers acting as naysayers.

"Lola told me how you helped her after she broke up with Baz. She says you offered really excellent advice"—Haley shifts in her chaise lounge to gaze at me—"I'm torn between Lachlan and Callum—you know the Scottish duke I was with in Verbier. They're both dominants. But I…"

She tells me about her desires, heartache, and determination to live her life without her brothers controlling it. We laugh when she says they can't control her, but she'd welcome it from her prospective Doms.

I tell Haley it's the giving up of control to a man who is powerful, cares for me, and focuses on my needs. His dominance doesn't supersede my Independent Woman. Rather, she allows him to take over in the bedroom, not in the boardroom—or any other area of my life. His possessive caveman provides us with great pleasure.

Haley understands when I tell her I wear Malcolm's collar not just as a symbol of our D/s relationship but as a sign of our commitment to one another. The collar may not be a wedding band, but it declares our connection to those in the lifestyle. I'm his and Malcolm is mine.

"See! I knew you'd help me figure things out," Haley exclaims with a grin. "You do not know what it's like having four brothers and two male cousins in my business! Of course I exclude Lachlan from our Jackson cousins."

She raises her freshly topped off mojito to mine.

"Here's to my sisters. First Lola, then Leonie, now you! At least Baz, Roger, and Malcolm are worth something. Harris… Well…" Haley giggles, then tips her cocktail to her smiling lips.

My heart swells from her including me with her sisters-in-law. I love her brother very much. But we were only together for eight months before we broke up. Now it's five months since we reunited. I need to give us some more time before I'm ready for SIL level.

What's the rush?

* * *

"Hey, babe. How's your site visit going? I hate I couldn't come with you."

I smile at Malcolm, whose handsome face fills my iPad screen during our nightly FaceTime call. His dove gray eyes dim with disappointment.

"That's okay, my love. Everything looks great," I respond, then tell him about the status, including the call I received from Adrienne the other night.

The fire department showed up to SLFW Beverly Hills during our peak evening time—sirens blaring and trucks lining the street. The captain told the general manager on duty they received a call about a three-alarm fire.

Despite the GM telling the captain nothing was amiss,

he insisted upon evacuating the premises and doing a thorough search. The hullabaloo upset and scared our clients.

Two hours later, the crew left. No evidence of a fire. At. All.

Adrienne told me other weird things had happened, and I told her I thought the same.

My gut pointed to Vicky as the most likely culprit. But it turns out she's in Europe, as confirmed by Haley.

Malcolm takes it in as he frowns.

I sense he's ruminating about it, so I change the subject and ask him his opinion on other matters.

Fortunately, Malcolm lets the bad vibes of Vicky fade.

His thoughtful recommendations help to iron out some unexpected issues, and he promises to speak with the project manager the next day.

"And how did things go with Haley? She told me the systems cleared their checks," Malcolm says.

My hand flutters to touch my collar unconsciously. I stifle a gasp when I realize my tell.

Malcolm raises his eyebrow and cocks his head to the side.

I lick my lips and clear my throat.

"Perfect!" I answer brightly. "She's brilliant! Did she tell you she beat Harris at Rock, Paper, Scissors to handle my project?"

My voice rises as I chatter on.

"Naughty Girl, what are you hiding?"

My head snaps up at My Dom's commanding tone.

Fuck!

I swallow, then blank my face. No way will I betray Haley's confidence.

I fudge a bit instead.

"Oh, Sir… You're so good at reading me. I told her how much I miss you," I purr while batting my eyelashes.

A smirk grows on My Dom's face.

"Is that so, Little One?" He rumbles as he shifts on his bed to tug at the placket of his silk pajama bottoms.

Distracted him! Yes!!!

I want to whoop, but I keep my cool. Besides, it's not a lie. A couple of weeks have passed since we saw each other in Paris. Video sex and text message games only go but so far as satisfaction…

"Oh absolutely, Sir," I respond honestly.

My Dom smirks wider.

"I'm in Paris again next week. Shall we plan for an in-person playtime at LEVELS Beverly Hills when I return? You have been such a good girl, you deserve an award, Little One," he purrs seductively.

The vibrations ripple over my skin. Now it's my turn to shift on my bed.

The sheer teddy reveals my peaked nipples clearly. Judging by My Dom's dilated pupils, he sees them too. A lick to his full lips confirms my guess.

I bounce a bit under the guise of sitting on my haunches to tease him with the visual of my fleshy mounds jiggling. His passion-filled groan rewards my efforts.

"I'm sorry, Sir. Are you all right?" I tease as I lean into the iPad's camera.

My breasts fill the screen, and he growls outright.

"Are you teasing me, Naughty Girl? Must our reunion start with you trussed up on the St. Andrew's Cross while I flog your juicy brown nipples and tits?" My Dom queries.

My response is a shiver that causes my breasts to bounce even more—this time not purposefully. I still cannot control my reactions to him.

I suck in a heated breath, then sigh as I sit back on my heels, head bowed.

"If that would please you, Sir," I answer, knowing it would please me even more.

He chuckles wickedly, and I steal a direct glance to his face.

My Dom's cheeks infused with blood heated from his lust make his darkened eyes stand out as they roam over my body.

Is it my fault the strap of my teddy slipped below my left breast?

No, but it's My Dom's fault when I cum screaming his name with my fingers plunging in and out of my soaked, greedy, little pussy…

MALCOLM

"Yeah, baby! You got it, Starr! Fly, baby, fly!!"

I yell through the megaphone as I stand on the superyacht's aft deck.

My Angel zips by with her feet strapped in special boots that use a propulsion mechanism from the jet ski guiding her flyboarding experience. It's her second time doing the extreme sport and the first session of our trip. She's become good at it in a short time because of her strong core muscles developed from years of Pilates.

A grin and thumbs-up serve as My Angel's response.

I grin even more than she does as I watch her plump ass in a yellow string bikini bottom when she passes the boat. A life jacket covers her lush tits. I'd have to gouge out the eyes of the crew should a tit pop out of her bandeau bikini top from the jostling of the powerful propulsion. Mine!

We've known each other for two years now. Sure, we split for a couple of months after we started dating, but now we're back together. Seven months. A long ass time for someone like me. A devout playboy with only contracted subs for a few months each before My Angel. Well, aside from Vicky who lasted longer since I didn't see her but for two or three times a month given she lives in California and I'm in New York.

Somehow the distance doesn't make a difference with My Angel. I see her more often—at least every other week. Whether I work out of STEELE LA or my offices at STEELE Las Vegas Resort & Casino, my work gets done and I'm near My Angel. Both of my priorities get my utmost attention. Although I'm still encouraging her to open a center in New York City. Then we can spend even more time together. My woman, my family, and STEELE International in one city. Why not have it all?

That's exactly why I surprised her with a getaway to Bali. I intend to dazzle My Angel with private excursions to the religious sites, the volcanic mountains, and secluded beaches. We'll do more adventures: free diving, wakeboarding, and my favor paragliding over the scenic lands.

The four-hundred-ten-foot superyacht I rented allows us a chance to explore Bali and the surrounding Indonesian islands while we cruise the Indian Ocean. Nights spent in each other's arms as we make love or play. Over the next five days, My Angel will be so awed, she'll only have one word for me, *yes*.

"HOLD ON, bro. Tell me that again."

Baz and I sit at the conference table in his office at The

STEELE Tower after our weekly one-on-one meeting. His face registers shock.

Yeah, me too.

It's our last night in Bali, right before sunset. I scoop My Angel out of the tender and carry her over the water lapping on the shoreline of the secluded beach.

She giggles and kicks her shapely legs as she hugs my neck. The filmy material of the coral-colored maxi dress she wears flutters around us.

Even when my bare feet touch the sun-warmed sand, I continue to carry My Angel. I don't want to let her out of my embrace.

I inhale the seductive scent of gardenias from her coconut oil lotion and bury my face in her curly hair. She's just so soft and sweet, but all woman. My woman. It makes my cock punch the front of my drawstring linen pants.

My Angel squirms in my arms, trying to get down.

I tighten my hold.

"Malcolm! I can walk now. I won't get wet," she insists, unwinding her arms from my neck to brace her palms against my chest.

Her thumbs dip under my linen shirt and brush my pecs as she pushes at me.

"I know you can walk, My Angel. But I want to carry you. Shall I command you stay still, Little One?" I respond with my eyebrow lifted. My Dom transitions from boyfriend seamlessly.

Her mouth drops open, then closes as her eyes widen and narrow. Torn between her submissive tendencies and her I am Woman Hear Me Roar. She doesn't have to choose since we reach the table set on the beach for our dinner.

"Good evening, Ms. Knight, Mr. Steele."

The greetings from the chef and the server distract My Angel.

She swivels her head towards them. Her eyes widen again, and her mouth forms a perfect O. The romantic setting renders her speechless.

A white gauzy canopy with its four posts covered in white hibiscus, frangipani, and orchards floats above the table like a fragrant cloud. The tropical scent of the flowers mingles with the aromas from the tantalizing dishes on the white linen tabletop. Our chairs have more gauzy material drapes over them, with a bow in the back and a floral bouquet at its center. Bamboo torches around the perimeter and white tapers on the table will provide lighting once the sun sets on the horizon.

After dinner, we'll move to the sunbed covered in white sumptuous bedding beneath a gauzy canopy. A bonfire to the side and more bamboo torches situated nearby, ready to be lit. Krug Clos d'Ambonnay Champagne and two crystal flutes chill in a bucket nestled in the sand.

"Oh, Malcolm," My Angel breathes, still staring in awe at the setup.

I take another inhale of her natural fragrance enhanced by the gardenias, then place her on her feet. Cupping her face in my hands, I kiss her softly. The tip of my tongue swipes across the seam of her mouth asking entry. On a sigh, My Angel opens to me. I swoop in and coax her tongue to dance with mine.

She sways.

My hands glide down her neck and flanks to hold her slim waist, bracing her for our soul-stirring kiss. Her gentle moans undo me.

I drop to one knee, then reach into my pants pocket to with-

draw the little navy-blue velvet box. My thumb presses the sapphire cabochon closure to reveal the oval-shaped, twenty-eight carat diamond and platinum engagement ring—a Steele family heirloom. It glitters in the setting sun's orange and fuchsia rays.

I look up at My Angel; the words marry me on my lips.

Her alarmed expression takes me aback.

WTF?

"What's wrong? Are you okay?" I question.

My Angel blinks, then takes a deep breath. When she reopens her sorrel brown eyes, they shine with tears.

Okay. Now a crying fiancée I can handle. A smile spreads across my face as I remove the ring and take her left hand in mine.

"Wait!"

Her startled cry jolts me. Then her hand burns mine as she yanks her finger from my grasp.

WTF???

"I mean... I... I don't want to marry you!" Starr cries out as she backs away from me. Her palms held out in front of her as though warding me off.

Now my mouth drops open. In fact, my jaw hits the sand beneath my knee. I stand to my full six-feet-four-inches with a scowl on my face.

Oh, hell no. Did she just say what I thought she said? Is she running away from me?? What the everlasting fuck!

"Damn, bro. I don't know what to tell you."

Baz shakes his head in pity. Even he can't get his head around the unbelievable situation.

Yeah, My Angel told me no.

I meet the one woman who makes me want to settle down, and she tells me no. No.

No.

"But why? What reason did she give for turning you down?" Baz asks. "I thought the two of you were doing well. Trips together. Family gatherings. The holidays together... You spend more time on the West Coast than you do at any of your other offices worldwide. Damn... How long have you been together?"

Baz babbles on as he tries to make sense of her rejection.

"Well, to be honest, Starr admitted she was 'saying no for now.' Since we broke up so easily and haven't been together for long, she wants to wait. She went on about the Universe and things aligning when they should. You know go-with-the-flow Starr..."

Baz nods, then spins his chair to stare out of the floor-to-ceiling windows thoughtfully.

I leave him with his thinking while I check my mobile for emails and text messages. Then chuckle when I read a message from My Angel.

Hi, my love. You came across my mind, so I want to check in. Are you okay?

"What's got you beaming?" Baz asks.

My fingers fly over my Virtue's screen as I type my response.

Hi, My Angel. Just telling Baz how you broke my heart. But otherwise, all's good...

There's a long pause.

Fuck! I shouldn't have teased her.

"Starr just texted me because I came across her mind. But I think I upset her with my resp—"

My sentence cuts off when my mobile vibrates with an incoming text. I brace myself.

The message opens to a video clip close-up of My Angel using a red lipstick to draw a letter S over her heart in the hollow between her bare voluptuous tits.

My mouth salivates.

The camera moves up to her gorgeous face, and a smile plays on her full lips as she speaks softly.

You have my heart, my love. I can never break yours without breaking mine. I love you, Malcolm Steele.

And just like that, my heart solidifies with her love.

She got away from me once; she turned down my marriage proposal. But I'm a patient man who always gets what he wants.

My collar.

My Red S.

My ring.

With a Cheshire Cat grin on my face, I glance up at Baz.

His platinum gray eyes shine like the band on my ring.

Like Starr, I view it as a sign.

In the end, I will put my ring on My Angel's finger. The brown-eyed beauty will be all MINE.

MALCOLM

"I haven't been to the Hamptons in so long. I forgot how the Atlantic Ocean has different shades of blue around Long Island. Your family's compound sits on the best beach!"

Haley grins at my exclamation as we stroll along their private expanse of golden sand. I close my eyes and inhale deeply. The briny scent of the ocean fills my lungs. The calls of seagulls ring out.

Steele Southampton Village is their beachfront property on ten acres off a private road. Its incredible surroundings include native trees, grassy areas, and closer to the ocean sandy dunes. A security guard in a gatehouse to allow access through the oversized wooden gates set between stone pillars with wrought iron lanterns. A long driveway of pressed oil and natural stone leads to the primary mansion and branches off to driveways for three more mansions—one for each of the elder siblings.

Malcolm's home is a modern contemporary three-story

mansion. The exterior features vertically placed gray weathered shingles, oversized panes of floor-to-ceiling windows, and multiple balconies with white metal railings. A luxurious all-white interior with pops of color from the art and accent pieces has five en suite bedrooms have breathtaking ocean views. The adjacent outdoor entertaining space surrounds a waterside gunite pool with spa, outdoor showers, and outdoor kitchen. A shingle-lined pathway with white metal railings leads from the entertainment patio over the grass-covered dunes to the sandy beach. It's a spectacular home.

Of course being the rebel of the family, Malcolm's mansion is opposite of the others. Their three-story residences with robin egg blue or sea green shutters against gray weathered shingles where blossoms fill the windowsills flower boxes epitomize classic Hamptons-style.

I love Malcolm's home the most! So different and stands out from the crowd, just like us.

Yesterday evening he picked me up from the Southampton Village Heliport in his Black Badge Rolls-Royce Cullinan. We had a delicious dinner with fresh oysters and lobsters with truffle sauce at one of Lucien's restaurants on Main Street before we went to Malcolm's home. Where I ate him covered in whipped cream and strawberries for dessert.

It's been a month, and it relieved me he wasn't angry with me or didn't end our relationship after my negative reaction to his proposal.

Honestly, I love Malcolm, but at this point I'd rather let

us continue as we are without a commitment beyond his collaring me. We need more time as a couple before we marry for life.

Sure, it disappointed him, but he understood my concerns and agreed not to pressure me.

I suppose the daily deliveries of frangipani, orchids, and hibiscus bouquets wrapped in white gauze and silk bows, handwritten declarations of love and our future together, and aphrodisiac delicacies of figs, chocolates, and pomegranates don't count as pressure…

A grin spreads across my face as I giggle at the memories of our last FaceTime tryst. We played strip poker during which he divested me of my new Lola's Coterie cashmere kimono, tank top, and matching boy shorts, not to mention the lace lingerie beneath it.

Malcolm didn't win all the rounds. I got him down to his black silk boxers and one sock. Besides, I wasn't keen on winning. My goal was to tempt him with my body. After treatments at SLFW Beverly Hills' spa, my skin shone golden and not one stray strand of hair found—buffed perfection!

As the victorious one, he controlled the scene using some delicacies he had delivered that morning. By the time Malcolm finished, my sweat-soaked body trembled with ecstasy while my mango-coated fingers plunged in and out of my spasming pussy. I cried out his name until my voice was hoarse.

If anything, my *no* answer spurred him to up his game with not only romantic gifts, but with intense, passionate lovemaking. Be it in person or virtual. This Labor Day weekend promises to be amazing!

"Well, I'm so glad you came early! I can update you on my Lachlan-Callum drama while we set up for tonight's sunset dinner on the beach—a traditional New England Clambake. It's my favorite part of the weekend. I cannot wait, yummy tummy!"

Haley laughs as we turn around to head back to the beach area in front of Morgan and Shelley's home. She loops her arm through mine and fills me in on the latest with her love life.

"Good of you to join us, Haley…" Harris says as he slaps his gloved hands free of sand from the wood for the bonfire. "Care to help us?"

"Do not worry, Haley. I'll help Harris," Callum responds in his sexy Scottish accent.

She grins and thanks him with a chaste kiss to his cheek.

Malcolm and Harris exchange glances. Sebastian hired his guy to conduct an extensive background check on Callum Graham, Duke of Montrose, as soon as they met him while we were in Verbier for Christmas. Nothing in it caused concern. They're happier Haley is with Callum and not with Lachlan.

We finish with the setup for the clambake, then the siblings drive to the heliport to pick up Lola, Sebastian, Blair, Leonie, Roger, The Twins, and Nanny Grace. Billie will fly in with Patrick on his helicopter later this afternoon and stay at his beachfront property. Leonie's parents and Luc should have landed by now at the private airport for the Hamptons. They flew in from Paris on Luc's jet.

The day turns into evening, and we go to the beach for a seafood feast with the backdrop of a spectacular sunset. The perfectly steamed clams, lobsters, potatoes, and corn on the cob topped with melted butter and paired with local beer and white wine make for a scrumptious meal. Dessert options include warm blueberry and apple pies with vanilla ice cream. Afterwards, we sit around the bonfire chatting.

"Don't forget beach yoga at seven tomorrow morning!" I call out to Leonie as she and Roger leave the beach with The Twins.

I lean back, huddled up with Malcolm and sigh happily.

"And don't you get too comfortable, My Angel. I have plans for you tonight," he rumbles in my ear.

"Bring it, baby," I whisper against his smirking lips, then rise to my feet and extend my hand to him.

* * *

"What a gorgeous start to the day! I'm so glad the summer weather continued into September."

"It could stay summer year-round as far as I'm concerned."

Lola, Leonie, Haley, Billie, and Blair spread their yoga mats out on the sand at the beach in front of Shelley and Morgan's house. Originally, I wanted us to gather for a sunrise meditation at six-thirty, but after the long night they convinced me to start later—if only by half an hour.

After a reflective guided meditation, I plan to take them through a vigorous flow that builds up to the challenging peak pose of Scorpion Handstand with a dharma talk during Savasana.

"Let us begin. Come to a comfortable sitting position with your palms face up on your knees, fingers in Gyan Mudra. Center your mind…"

In practicing asanas, the point isn't to twist oneself into a pretzel and the more you can bend, the better. Rather, the focus on the breath and releasing the mind to move the body.

I love to push my students' abilities to focus, and Scorpion Handstand requires lots of it.

During Savasana they settle onto their backs with their eyes closed and their minds open, I speak to the girls about surrender. My submission to Malcolm's Alpha Dom dances at the edges of my mind.

Just as we stand to take a dip in the ocean, here they come…

"Rats, did we miss the yoga?" Patrick jokes in his thick Scottish accent as he strides towards his lover.

It turns out he and Callum know each other, and it surprised them to find the other with us.

Last night at the clambake, Billie teased how she and Haley are into bangers and mash. The visual of the double entendre made her blush and Callum sputter his ale.

"Of course it's over since I left you snoring almost two hours ago!" Billie replies, her Granny Smith apple green eyes sparkling in the bright sunlight.

Patrick towers over her by eleven inches. He scoops

Billie into his arms and carries her off to the water as she giggles.

"How about we put you in that position with your pussy in the air? Then I'll come up behind you, grab your thighs, and fuck you until you see stars in the daytime."

A gasp slips past my lips as my pussy flutters and my nipples tighten beneath my orange cropped tankini.

"Namaste!" I call to the others as Malcolm flips me over his shoulder and jogs up the dune.

THE NEXT FEW days are so relaxing. We do more yoga, lounge around the pool, swim in the ocean, or hang out on the entertainment level of the primary house to bowl, play in the arcade, or watch movies.

It's good to unwind with everyone since it's the first time we've all been together in a few weeks.

Malcolm's laughter comes easily, and he jokes with his siblings. They along with Patrick and Callum played a rowdy game of touch football on the beach.

Between drooling over the gleaming muscles, the girls and I cheered them on. Morgan, Shelley, Guy, Josy, Luc, and The Twins watched from the sidelines.

Patrick and Callum told them American football sucks and isn't even football since the ball stays in the players' hands more often than not. They insisted on a round of rugby—"the real man's sport."

We couldn't care less as long as the guys remained sweaty.

.   .   .

JUST AS GOOD as they look shirtless, they look incredible dressed for social events. The STEELE Quaternity along with Patrick and Callum stand out amongst the guests gathered for the annual STEELE White Party.

The giant side lawn of Morgan and Shelley's house, aglow with thousands of fairy lights and lanterns, has two sumptuous pavilions, one for dinner and the other for dessert and dancing. Beyond it, on the beach, several bonfires burn. Waitstaff mill about with trays of champagne and wines or hors d'oeuvres. To one side a band plays lively music piped through speakers, also out on the sand.

Guests mingle, sipping drinks in the different areas, all dressed in the theme.

It's already bustling since it's the party of the season and everyone wants a ticket for a chance to see and be seen amongst the world's elite. Not to mention raising funds for STEELE Foundation.

My gaze scans the room as I stand beside Malcolm. I catch sight of Haley and Lachlan talking off to the side. It appears serious, so I'll greet her later.

The Jacksons, who also have a compound nearby, came over for the party. Laurent, the playboy, flirts shamelessly with three female guests. Lydie—Lola's former rival for Sebastian's affections—who seems to have a new boyfriend laughs with some industry titans. Lucien, whose Southampton restaurant caters the event, holds court in the dining pavilion for last-minute preparations.

"You're the most beautiful woman here, My Angel. Your eyes sparkle brighter than your earrings."

Malcolm's compliment rouses me from my musings.

My fingertips graze one of the dangling diamond drops that match the beautiful, intricate platinum lacework covered in tiny sparkly diamonds of my collar. The earrings complete the set with the bracelet he gave to me for our one-month anniversary.

"Thank you, Sir," I purr.

The gong rings to announce dinner.

We follow the guests to the dining pavilion and take our seats. The Steele clan disperses across the room, sitting at tables with guests to make everyone feel welcome and included.

Malcolm helps me into my chair. Once he's seated, he introduces me as his girlfriend to our dinner companions. Malcolm reaches into my lap to hold my hand in his and place it on is thigh.

I smile at him. As I turn my gaze to my dinner partner, I catch a snippet the hushed conversation on his other side.

"—came to meet Malcolm Steele! Only him and Harris are left, Daddy!"

I bristle. WTF?!

The twenty-something's father glances at me, then averts his gaze quickly. He whispers in her ear, and she throws a glare in my direction before she shifts her attention to the man on her other side.

A squeeze to my hand distracts me.

I put a smile on my face and turn to my man.

Malcolm brings our entwined hands to his mouth and kisses my knuckles. His dove gray eyes twinkle.

In my periphery, the wannabe huffs.

Yes honey, Malcolm Steele is mine.

After appetizers, Shelley makes her speech, and the emcee keeps the party going through dinner and on to the dessert and dancing. A DJ famous for his skills on the turntables spins popular music that gets the guests on their feet.

The fireworks display from a barge offshore lights up the inky night sky with vivid sparklers, crowns, glitter, and crosettes. We cheer with each round, delighted by the glitziness.

"I'd like to thank you properly for your lavish gifts, Sir. Do you approve of us returning to your home now?"

For the rest of the night and well into the early morning, we make our own fireworks.

* * *

"You have to get a microchip. It's not up for debate, Starr."

Malcolm decrees.

It's been two weeks since we left Southampton Village for Beverly Hills. We stayed an extra week after they kidnapped The Twins to support Leonie and Roger. Fortunately, the boys had a microchip connected to an app Harris created. The state troopers found them quickly and unharmed. It was still a terrifying ordeal.

All the Steeles have microchips for just those circumstances.

Now Malcolm insists I have one too.

I'm not partial to a foreign object implanted underneath my skin. So we've been debating me getting the tracking device.

My stubbornness kicks in at his declaration.

Who does he think he is? He can't just tell you what to do?!

My inner warrior goes off on a rant.

I'm about to voice her words when Malcolm stops me.

"Babe, I can't lose you."

His voice cracks.

Surprised at this vulnerability in my strong Alpha Dom, I shut my mouth and stare at him.

The anguish in his eyes is heart-wrenching.

Since The Twins' kidnapping and the injuries Leonie and Lola sustained, Malcolm has been fierce and super protective of them. The Steele clan with the Beaulieus closed ranks. He and Sebastian led their combined families like a force to be reckoned with.

To see a chink in *The Enforcer*'s armor makes me give in.

He only wants to protect me too. Include me in his precious nest of loved ones.

Why not allow him to take care of me in this way? I tell my inner warrior, who agrees wholeheartedly, softened by Malcolm's vulnerability.

I reach up to cup his face in my hands. When he lowers his head, I cover his mouth with mine. I pour my love into our kiss, and he responds just as ardently.

Malcolm lifts me from the ground, and I wrap my legs

around his waist. My tunic raises up my thighs to bunch at my waist. My hot bare pussy rubs on his eight-pack abs through his t-shirt.

His caveman takes over with a feral growl. One arm bands under my ass while the other reaches between us to loosen the drawstring on his lounge pants. The bulbous head of his massive dick prods at my pussy folds. A snap of his hips drives his length deep inside of my slick core.

We groan when our bodies connect as close as a man and woman can. Lips locked; groins fused.

Malcolm's need to protect me rushes to the forefront, and he pours it out with each upward thrust. We ride out his urgent desire until we're a panting, sweaty mass collapsed on the living room floor of his Sunset Strip penthouse.

Once I catch my breath, I gaze up from resting my head on his muscular chest.

Despite the release, Malcolm's eyes still burn with vehemence. He opens his mouth, but I place my fingers against his lips and shake my head. He raises an eyebrow to protest.

"Okay," I interject. "I'll get the microchip."

Malcolm beams and slants his mouth over mine.

"Thank you, My Angel," he says as he rises with me in his arms.

Once he places me on the sofa, he pulls a briefcase from beside the coffee table and opens it on top. A syringe nestled in a foam surround appears. Malcolm puts his mobile on speaker and smiles at me reassuringly.

"Hey, bro. Walk me through the process for implanting the microchip," he says.

"Hi, Starr! Our boy persuaded you to join the Steele side?" Harris' voice comes through the speaker.

Before I can answer, Malcolm grasps my chin between his thumb and idea finger, bringing my gaze to his burning one.

"Almost, bro, almost."

"What's going on in that head of yours, Steele?!"

The smirking face of Quinn Fucking Peters flies out of my head. Borya *The War Defender* Alexeyev—my personal trainer, former MMA champion, and Anton's cousin—delivers a roundhouse kick to my right flank.

Damn… that shit hurts likes a motherfucker.

When I was younger, my fighting was chaotic. Now with the proper training from Borya, I control my fighting with the MMA fights I take part in regularly to blow off steam.

Harris nicknamed me *The Enforcer* from my lethal fighting skills and for my no-nonsense, take-care-of-it attitude.

So while Baz is the leader and Roger the responsible one, I've become the guy everyone comes to get shit done… Or corrected.

Right now, I want to use my skills on Peters. The only

reason I'm holding back is because of My Angel. I refuse to allow anyone—including myself—to ruin the opening of her Starr Light Fitness & Wellness Resorts at STEELE Cabo San Lucas.

Borya, Anton, Lucien, and I arrived yesterday afternoon two days ahead of the opening celebration. The STEELE teams along with My Angel, Adrienne, and SLFW's staff have been on site this past week for the soft opening.

When My Angel posted to her Instagram account photos leading up to the event, my head spun.

Apparently that fucker Peters came with Peace and Sun on their private jet the day before. He weaseled his way into some photos My Angel posted. He positioned himself next to her for every. Single. One.

I didn't mention my irritation to her because she was already frantic over the shipment delay of some important custom items. A mix-up caused the delivery to SLFW Beverly Hills instead. Anton called in some favors and had the factory complete a rush order with expedited shipping.

Adrienne swore she provided the company with the correct delivery address and showed the confirmation email. The owner said he received a phone call to change the delivery but couldn't recall to whom he spoke. Another unexplained occurrence for them I think is Vicky, but no proof.

Haley has a person on her Cyber Security team investigating all the instances. If they even hint at a connection to Vicky, she'll answer to me.

In the meantime, I have to deal with Peters and his bullshit. He better quit sniffing around my woman. Or he'll regret it.

Last night, I kept My Angel in our villa, reminding her who she belongs to—ME!

"Get—"

Whack!

"Your—"

Bam Bam!

"Shit—"

Whack!

"Together!"

Bam Bam!

Before Borya's next series of blows can hit me, I quickly crouch low and use my leg to sweep him off of his feet. The giant Russian lands on his ass with an oomph.

"What were you saying, asshole?" I growl as I crack my neck from side to side.

"*Da, mal'chik!*"

Borya punches his fists together as he effortlessly back-flips to land on his feet.

"*Da*, that's more like it, Steele. Be here or go jerk off. No room on this mat for *zhopas* with the smell of *kiska* on their breath! Meow. Meow."

Sufficiently chastised and pissed that I'm letting Quinn Fucking Peters mess with my head, I refocus.

I fake a charge at Borya, then at the last second turn and back kick him, the momentum throwing him off balance and causing him to stumble forward. I follow the kick with a few, well-placed punches then taunt him as I bounce on my toes backwards, fists in the air, "Take that, sucker!"

Norman throws his head back and laughs.

"Neither of you are ready for me. So hurry up pussy-footing around and give way for the Champ!" He says giving the speed bag a last punch.

"Exactly!" Lucien chimes in from the weight bench.

Anton chuckles between crunches on the floor.

We're in the gym for the primary hotel getting a workout in this morning. My Angel went to her center earlier for classes, so I met my boys here.

"Norman Green! I'm a huge fan of yours!"

Our heads swivel to the glass double doors to find Peters grinning at the Champ. The fucker strides over with his hand extended for a shake.

Norman—unaware of my ire with Peters—grips his hand firmly and smiles.

"In the flesh, man," he responds.

"Starr didn't mention you'd be here. She told me some names the other night—"

His words end in a gurgle.

With a growl, I launch myself at him and slam my forearm against his throat as my elbow and palm make contact.

His back hits the wall, and I lift him the four inches to my eye level.

"Keep my woman's name out of your mouth, or I will rip your fucking face off. Be thankful I do not want to upset her, otherwise I would kick your ass all over this gym. In fact, I give you thirty minutes to pack your shit and get the fuck off of my property. Security will escort you to your room and remove you from the premises. Move.

Now."

I tell him in a deadly tone, eyes blazing molten platinum. Then remove my arm from his neck to let his body crumple to the ground in a heap.

I stride to my mobile and dial the head of hotel security while I keep my narrowed eyes locked on Peters panting on the floor. This fucker went too damn far talking too much shit.

"Forget her name and that you ever knew her. Oh, and do not think I give a damn you are an attorney. Any legal action you take, and I will bury you," I promise him as he struggles to his feet.

Security arrives within moments, and Quinn Fucking Peters exits My Angel's life for good.

"Well, I see *The Enforcer* is up to his old tricks…" Sebastian chuckles as he walks into the gym past Peters and the two security team members.

Harris slaps his forehead and adds, "Damn! I missed all the fun."

* * *

"Congratulations, Starr. Another successful center launched. Your partnership with STEELE International is a coup! Here's to an even brighter future with our family."

Morgan beams at My Angel as he lifts his crystal flute filled with mimosa in a toast.

I grin broadly at my father's not-so-subtle hint at her being a part of our family. Everyone knows I plan to make her mine in every way.

The opening celebration exceeded expectations: more guests than the St. Barth's center; a wait list three months long; extensive media hype with excellent reviews; on track to cover the center's costs within five months. It impressed Morgan and Baz as former and current CEOs, respectively.

"Yes! Hear, hear!"

"Wonderful, Starr! We're so proud of you!"

"Girl Power rules!"

A congratulatory chorus rings out.

My family—except for Roger and Leonie—My Angel's parents, Anita, Norman, Billie, Patrick, Blair, Luc, Anton, Borya, Lucien, Adrienne, and Claudia gather for brunch at the resort's beachfront restaurant. Lucien's three Michelin star eatery known for its blending of Mexican traditional dishes with contemporary cuisine. It's the perfect backdrop for our families and friends to meet for the first time.

Tonight My Angel and I will dine with our parents. Of course my mother can't wait. I'm sure she thinks I'm going to propose. I learned my lesson; I'll wait a little longer. When I'm guaranteed a yes response, I'll pop the question again...

"Thank you so much, everyone! I'm so grateful for your support!"

My Angel's effusive response brings me back to the conversation.

"I have to thank Lola for paying it forward when we met three years ago," My Angel says as she raises her flute and inclines her head to my SIL.

"You saved me and Baz. So you deserve all your success and happiness with a Steele!" Lola responds with a wink.

My Angel's cheeks sun kissed to copper blush red as she peeks at me.

I lean over and brush my lips over her temple. She smells so good. I take a deep inhale of her fragrant skin and sit back.

She sighs and rests her head against my shoulder.

Automatically my arm wraps around My Angel, and I hold her nestled against my side.

My gaze lands on her mother, who smiles back. I grin in acknowledgment of her approval and hug My Angel tighter.

Once again, my mind drifts.

"Are you satisfied with your expansion so far?" I ask My Angel as I wrap my arms around her from behind.

Her round ass presses against my upper thighs as I draw her closer to me with my palms on her lower belly.

We just returned to our villa after the party ended and stand before the open terrace doors facing the beach. The full moon shines down on the inky surface of the Pacific Ocean while multitudes of stars twinkle in the night sky above. The sounds of the waves crashing on the shore create a seductive rhythm.

My Angel raises her arms over her head to run her fingers in my hair, then twine them behind at the nape of my neck.

The movement juts her ample D-cups in her ocean blue backless maxi dress. The lustrous, fluid silk-satin skims her bodacious curves. While the hip-high slit shows off her long leg and the glittery crystal straps frame her toned back.

I slide my hands along her flanks, then slip them inside her dress to cup her tits. My thumb and index fingers pinch and tug her plump nipples into peaks. I dip my head to skim my lips down the column of her neck to nip the sensitive juncture at her shoulder.

"Oooh... Yes... So satisfied..." My Angel moans as she pulls my hair, prickling my scalp.

I chuckle wickedly. My mouth sucks on her sensitive skin, and she cries out. Once my mark raises on her neck, I kiss it softly.

"Are you satisfied with the expansion or with my mouth and hands on your sinful body, My Angel?" I ask her.

She purrs and gyrates her hips.

My cock thickens and lengthens in response to the pressure.

I step back and press my palm between her shoulder blades to bend her forward.

Knowing what's coming, My Angel widens her stance and braces her hands on her thighs. Her curly hair falls like a curtain on either side of her head.

Thwack. Thwack. Thwack. Thwack.

She yelps but holds her position.

My nostrils flare at the sight of her ass jiggling beneath the soft material of her dress. A few more spanks have her rising on her toes and a wet spot forming where her bare pussy rests against the silk-satin. Her arousal fills the surrounding air.

"Oh, Malcolm," she moans as she wiggles her hips.

A spank to her pussy has her yowling.

With a quickness, I flip her dress over her head and unzip my trousers to free my cock dripping with pre-cum.

"Hold your ankles, Little One," I command on one breath,

then thrust in the next as I mount her like a stallion taking a mare in heat.

"Oh... Ohhh!" She cries out at my forceful entry to her tight, wet pussy.

A pattern of a fast thrust followed by a slow drag with shifts in my stance to vary my angle has her panting in moments. The difficulty to hold back her orgasm causes My Angel to beg for release.

I deny her.

Again.

And again.

Until her legs tremble and her pussy walls quiver.

I pull out, spin her around, and lift her leg to place her calf on my shoulder. Gripping her hips, I bend my knees and drive up into her throbbing, soaked pussy. The balls of my Prince Albert piercing brush her engorged clit, then stroke her G-spot until they rest deep against her womb.

"Oh, my—"

My Angel's groan catches in her throat when I draw her nipple into my hot, wet mouth to suckle. Hard. I latch on to her tit as my hips continue to piston.

Her head lolls from side to side. One last plea falls from her parted lips.

"Malcolm," My Angel pants.

"Who... do... you... belong... to... Starr?" I growl with each upward thrust.

"Aaaahhhh..." She replies as her pussy pulsates around my cock.

I smack her ass to make her focus and not cum.

"Words!" I demand.

She yowls, then cries out my name over and over.

"Then cum for me. Now!"

No sooner do the words leave my mouth than My Angel explodes.

Her greedy pussy clenches hard on my dick.

White sparks flash before my eyes. I increase my tempo while my cock expands painfully. My head falls back as a roar rips from me along with copious amounts of my seed. The release is so intense, my knees buck.

I carry her up the stairs to the bathroom of our bedroom suite and settle her on the pouf. My clothes drop to the marble floor as I stride to the shower. The spray jets from the rain shower. I return to my sated, sleepy Angel and lift her in my arms.

After I bathe and dry us, I place her under the cool sheets and slide in behind her, aligning our bodies—her back to my front. My eyes drift close.

"Malcolm, what happened to Quinn?" She murmurs.

Ah, no.

I shift to my elbow and cup her chin to turn her head towards me.

"I will tolerate no one attempting to come between us. He's gone from your life, Starr. And I will not hear his name from your mouth, especially not in our bed," I tell her.

Her eyes widen, and she bites the corner of her mouth.

I prepare to argue my point, but My Angel surprises me.

She shifts to face me and wraps her arms around my neck, burying her face. She inhales deeply, then sighs.

"Thank you, my love. He was becoming too much," My Angel responds.

I stiffen. WTF?!

"Malcolm, baby, no need to do anything more. He's done. Okay?" She breathes.

My molars grind, but I give in with a roll of my eyes. This woman makes me do things I never thought I would do. Ever.

Just as now when Billie asks if I'll take My Angel's prenatal yoga class since I lost the bet Patrick would lose the drinking contest we had two nights ago. I should have known the Scott would drink me under the table.

My Angel giggles and claps her hands.

"Oh, I cannot wait for this one! The women in the class will have a proper laugh at this brawny man doing Kegels!" She says gleefully.

I zerbert her neck, and she giggles hysterically.

"The makings of a beautiful partnership!" Harris quips.

Everyone joins in our laughter.

Absolutely! I chuckle as I kiss My Angel breathless.

STARR

"Understand Starr is my only child and means everything to her mother and to me. Our family unit is inseparable. Starr shares every aspect of her life with my wife and with me. She made us aware of the situation with Vicky Reynolds and her declination of your proposal, along with the lifestyle she's chosen with you. My daughter is an intelligent, grown woman who thinks for herself. However, Starr is still mine to protect by any means necessary. I am no Quinn Peters. You were together for eight months; broke up for two; back together for ten. Now what are your intentions with my daughter, Steele?"

Peace's sharp obsidian eyes pierce me as we stand in the garden of his and Sun's Bel Air mansion.She and Starr are in the kitchen with the chef finishing our early Thanksgiving dinner.

My Angel and I want to spend time with both of our families for the holiday. I extended an invitation for Peace and Sun to join the Steele clan in Capri, then Verbier for

Christmas. But My Angel felt it's too soon for a blending of our families. I kept my disagreement to myself—no pressure, for now.

I consider my response carefully.

Of course, My Angel has a close relationship with her parents. She's made that clear many times. I value and cherish my family, so I appreciate their connection. Besides, I'd have our children do the same.

Vicky Fucking Reynolds. No words.

My Angel's no, still rubs me wrong, but I respect her decision. My actions since reinforce my love for her and desire to build a life with her.

Interesting, she revealed our D/s lifestyle, and her father hasn't killed me... But as he said, My Angel thinks for herself and chooses to be my sub.

I wouldn't expect anything less from Peace whose Alpha male protectiveness of his daughter equals mine.

Apparently Peters ran like a wuss to Peace. Fucking loser. Peace must agree with me since he's said nothing in a month. But as I said: I give zero fucks because I. Will. End. Peters.

What are my intentions?

"Peace, I respect Starr, Sun, and you—your family dynamic. I love your daughter with every fiber of my being. I value her and the life I want to build with her. Starr may have said no once. But I am a patient man determined to prove my worthiness. I ask for your permission for her hand in marriage now. So when Starr is ready, we will have your blessing."

My Angel's father scans my face as he considers my heart-felt words.

"I appreciate your candidness and your respect. Starr loves you and in time will say yes." His gaze goes beyond my shoulder and his lips curl up in a smile that makes his obsidian eyes shine like liquid ebony.

Then Peace narrows his eyes at me and extends his hand.

"You have my blessing. But… Do. Not. Fuck. Up. Steele," he says, emphasizing his words with a firm handshake.

"Daddy! Don't break Malcolm's hand!"

My Angel's exclamation returns the smile to her father's mouth.

He deadpans, "Well, if he can't handle a handshake, how will he handle me whooping his ass if he hurts you?"

My Angel and Sun gasp as their matching sorrel brown eyes widen.

Peace chuckles and slaps me on the shoulder.

"Come, let us enjoy our early Thanksgiving dinner."

"WHAT A GORGEOUS VIEW of Southern Italy and the Mediterranean Sea from up here!"

Malcolm and I ride in the Sikorsky S-92 Executive Helicopter with Morgan, Shelley, Sebastian, Lola, Harris, and Haley en route to Roger and Leonie's Villa dei Fiori in Capri for Thanksgiving.

After Malcolm and I flew from LAX on his Gulfstream

G650 to meet up with his family in New York City, we joined them on STEELE's Gulfstream G700. The $65 million expansive private jet accommodates nineteen passengers and the ten-hour flight to Naples.

"The Med is my favorite place. Morgan and I either stay at our Villa Sogno in Positano or yachting aboard *Serendipity*. I've heard great things about Roger and Leonie's villa. I can't wait to see it!" Shelley says.

Everyone agrees, and I turn to glance out of the window.

Moments later, the Sikorsky touches down on the helipad at the rear of the villa. Leonie and Roger stand holding The Twins, waving at us.

Morgan and Shelley alight from the back of the helicopter first, followed by Sebastian and Lola. Malcolm and I, then Harris and Haley disembark next. We wave and troop over.

"Hey, Little Pumpkins! Did you miss your favorite auntie?" Lola asks as Sebastian scoops Gaspard out of Roger's arms.

"And your very favorite uncle?" He adds giving Malcolm and Harris the side eye with a grin.

We make our way around to the terrace where Guy and Josy sit. They flew in this morning. Everyone exchanges greetings before Leonie and Roger show us to our sumptuous bedroom suites.

Villa dei Fiori has fast become one of their most cherished homes. It's where they had their babymoon when Leonie was nineteen weeks pregnant and they'd been back together for nine months. She fell in love with Lucien's former home the moment she set eyes on it. So, of course, Roger bought it for her.

The salmon-colored stucco exterior with white trim around the windows, columns, and roof lines blend beautifully with the lush greenery and stunning sea views from all sides. The sea-edge gardens, bountiful with camellias, magnolias, and palm trees prove as captivating as the impressive views of Mount Vesuvius, the Peninsula of Sorrento, the entire Gulf of Naples, and Anacapri. Its private swimming pool set in the side garden's grass and its exclusive sea access with a second plunge pool below makes it a unique property.

Malcolm and I, the siblings, and Guy and Josy take advantage and stay on different occasions. Since Morgan and Shelley have Villa Sogno across the Tyrrhenian Sea and their megayacht, this is their first visit.

While Roger shows them around, Malcolm and I settle in our plush suite. Then we head outside.

We find Leonie, The Twins, and Haley seated on blankets in the grass near the lunch table. They gathered here before we have lunch alfresco in the seaside garden. Just as we sit down, Roger strides over.

"How was your flight?" He asks me since Malcolm and I traveled the farthest from Beverly Hills.

I smile and my dimples pop.

"It was long and hard, but comfy on Malcolm's jet," I respond, winking at him.

He smirks and adds, "Yes, and rather palatable."

Leonie bursts out laughing, then starts to snort uncontrollably.

"What's so funny?"

We glance up to find Sebastian and Lola behind us.

"Oh, just the rigors and demands of travel," I deadpan.

Malcolm sits back on his hands, all smug with a cocky grin on his face. The Alpha Dom took his carnal tastes to the skies for fifteen hours.

Sebastian snickers and Roger snorts.

"No comment…" Haley says, rolling her eyes, disgusted as usual with hearing about her brothers' sex lives, even as innuendos.

She glances down at her mobile and smiles. Then types a response at lightning speed. When she raises her head, her cheeks flush, and her eyes shine. No longer wearing her glasses makes the dove gray orbs more expressive. Happy Haley, hmmm interesting.

"What's up, Baby Girl?" Roger asks, knowing the nickname drives her crazy.

Still in la-la land, Haley startles, then responds rushed, "Oh, uh… Callum's over in Sorrento."

When she doesn't continue, Roger prods her. He wants to take Haley to dinner. So Roger tells her he can come here if they want. He's more than welcome. They agree, and Roger arranges for the helicopter to pick him up in an hour.

Leonie and Roger's parents appear. We gather around the table for a delicious lunch of flavorful local dishes prepared by the chef and served by the staff with wines from the villa's prized cellar.

Malcolm rubs my thigh under the table while we chat with everyone.

Shortly after we finish eating, Callum touches down. Haley goes to greet him, and some time later they join us for Limoncello Gin Collins on the lawn furniture. Her lips appear swollen, and his eyes gleam.

Mmhmmm.

"How are things with you, Callum?" Morgan asks as he sips his digestif. "I read in the *Financial Times* renewable energy is on the rise for another year in a row for Scotland."

They get into a discussion on Callum's family's business, Graham Energy, Oil & Gas Company, based in Aberdeen, Scotland. His father still leads the company as CEO, but he's in the process of grooming Callum for the role in five years. His younger brother and sister hold positions, too.

The conversation flows easily with everyone's participation.

The siblings grew up discussing business to prepare for joining their family's legacy while I worked to create SLFW. All of us volunteer in some way to help others, so we're a well-rounded group. All of our perspectives add to the conversation.

As we continue to chat, Malcolm reaches over and pulls me onto his lap. Content to relax in his arms, I snuggle against him and drift off, exhausted from the travel.

"LET'S BEGIN WITH SOME BREATHWORK."

Each morning I start our day with yoga in the sunroom

facing the sea. Aside from the girls, the guys join us. My influence runs deep.

Even though we welcomed the guys to yoga, we're kicking them out so we can have some much-needed Girls' Time. We have a lot to catch up on and only two days left before we go our separate ways until Christmas.

After a peaceful Savasana and light sharing namaste, we kick Malcolm, Sebastian, Roger, Harris, and Callum out of the sunroom.

Malcolm swats my ass on his way out and growls in my ear, "Do not think you are the boss of me, Little One."

I stifle a yelp as I hop onto the balls of my feet.

Malcolm chuckles.

"So, spill with Callum and Lachlan, Haley," I say as soon as I shut the door behind them.

Haley turns scarlet and reaches to push her glasses up the bridge of her nose. It's her nervous tell she can't stop even after wearing contact lenses for the last couple of years.

"What do you mean?" She asks, not realizing we know she's bluffing.

We giggle at her gaffe.

"Oh, don't play the innocent, Ms. Kiss Me Until My Lips Swell Steele!" Leonie laughs.

On a breathy sigh, Haley fills us in on the last couple of months since she saw Lachlan at the Labor Day fundraiser. The drama of her love triangle with one man who's her brother's best friend and one man who's had his eye on her since Harvard Business School proves more intriguing than any telenovela I've seen!

"Well then, what about you, Ms. Comfy on Malcolm's Jet Knight?" Lola adds.

Now it's my turn to blush. My chestnut-colored skin adds a crimson hue to my cheeks.

Haley smirks.

"Fine! He's a monster!" I laugh as I hold my hands two feet apart in front of me.

We fall onto our mats, snorting as Haley sings at the top of her lungs with her fingers in her ears.

Once we catch our breath, I fill my girls in on how Malcolm fills me and not just with his "monster" dick. I admit he proposed, and I said no. They empathize with my need to go with the flow—especially Leonie, my fellow free spirit. Lola repeats it'll only be a matter of time before I head down the aisle. Haley agrees, crossing her fingers.

By the time I finish my tales, Shelley and Josy come in the sunroom to invite us on a shopping trip to Capri town between the Piazzetta and Via Camerelle. It's one of the most fashionable centers in the world, with high-end boutiques and jewelry stores.

Less than an hour later, we're strolling along the streets, popping in and out of the boutiques filled with designer pieces and handcrafted items by local artisans.

Most of the people in the shops and on the streets recognize Leonie. She takes it in stride when they ask for her autograph or a selfie. Our security detail keeps any overzealous fans at bay—precautions Sebastian and Roger implemented after the Labor Day situation.

My shopping spree is complete when I order two pairs of bespoke Canfora Sandals, my favorite, purchase some hand-painted silk scarves, including three ties for Malcolm, and perfume that reminds me of the island's natural scent.

"Lola, honey, the sun did you some good. You're glowing."

Lola glances up into Shelley's smiling face.

"Yes, the fresh sea air and warm sun make a tremendous difference," she grins. "Plus, your son makes sure I eat properly and rest."

Shelley throws her head back and laughs. Her brown eyes shine with mirth.

"I'm sure he does! My boys better treat their women well. Right, Starr and Leonie?" Shelley adds with a wink at the girls.

We giggle and nod our agreement.

Maman Josy cups Leonie's face and says, "And you treat those boys well, *non?*"

"*Oui, Maman, absolument!*" Leonie smiles lovingly at her mom.

I sigh and think about having children with Malcolm. But Leonie's cry stops my musings.

"*Chérie!* What's the matter?!" Leonie cries as she rubs Lola's back.

Shelley answers, "She's fine, just a bit overwhelmed. Let's head back to your villa, shall we?"

Leonie agrees and takes Lola's arm while Shelley holds the other. Josy, Haley, and I gather around them, and we make our way back to the Mercedes-Benz G-Wagens. The security detail follows, then drives us to the villa.

We'll gather for Thanksgiving dinner tonight.

.   .   .

"THIS IS FANTASTIC! I agree we should have an opulent Edwardian-themed-*Gigi* party!"

Leonie and Roger finished giving everyone a tour of the vintage steam yacht he bought for her. She named it *Gigi* after her favorite film.

Lola tells everyone how she can't wait to plan the soiree.

She and Leonie do their happy shimmy dance, then continue on to the bow where we'll have cocktails before Thanksgiving dinner begins.

The last few days have been full of swimming at the private beach or in the pool and excursions to the Blue Grotto, Monte Solaro, and Villa di Tiberio. The Blue Grotto thrilled The Twins when their laughter echoed inside of the water-filled cavern.

Leonie wanted to save *Gigi* for last as the highlight and setting for our Thanksgiving dinner as we cruise around Capri for three hours. They time it for cocktails at sunset and dinner by torchlight—electric since they don't want to risk damage to the boat.

We dress in semi-formal attire with the guys in suits and the women in dresses. The Twins wear shirt and shorts one-piece sets with socks that mimic shoes and outdo us all.

Once we're gathered at the bow with drinks in hand, Morgan leads us in expressing his thanks over the past year. Each of us takes a turn ending with Roger. It's obvious he's already emotional after Leonie's heartfelt words of gratitude for their lives together and most of all for the safety of their sons.

On the end of her touching speech and tears, he holds her close in his arms and address us.

"Thanks can never express the depth of my feelings for all of you and others who are not present. Your love and support from the start of that fiasco to the joy of our wedding with the addition of my in-laws and the wonderful holidays we shared to the return of our sons mean more than you can imagine. Mom, Dad, all of our lives you raised us to be a close-knit clan. This past year proves you succeeded. I love you all beyond measure."

Roger lifts his glass and proclaims, "Now let us enjoy this Thanksgiving dinner and here's to many, many more!"

"Hear, hear!!"

"Bravo, Roger! We love you, too!!"

"Happy Thanksgiving, everyone!!"

Malcolm nuzzles my neck and whispers, "Happy Thanksgiving, My Angel. I love you with all my heart. Next year, we'll have an early dinner with my family and spend the weekend with yours. Unless, of course, we're all together…"

I turn to Malcolm and caress his cheek with my palm, the five o'clock shadow prickles my palm.

"We should all be together, my love," I respond with a smile.

The Cheshire Grin that breaks out on his face makes my heart swell. Yeah, I can see us having babies and so much more.

"Hey, hey, hey! The gang's all here!! Merry Christmas Eve!"

Roger and Leonie laugh as Harris makes his way through the front door after Lola and Sebastian, arms laden with gifts. They tease he looks like a young Santa Claus.

He rejoins with, "A sexy AF one, no doubt! And no last-minute presents for me, Roger dear! Let's see if you get coal in your stocking this year…"

Malcolm and I enter behind him, and the girls hug while Malcolm and Roger bro hug.

"Good to see you, man!" Roger tells him.

"Still looking goofy, bro!" Malcolm teases.

Haley walks in looking glum, and Roger pulls her into a bear hug, lifting her off her feet.

As per Lola's intel, Haley was going through some relationship issues, so he tries to cheer his baby sister up posthaste. Malcolm told me *Duke* Callum will rue the day if he hurts their little sister: *I'll duke his ass.*

"You better have brought your, A game or I'm going to leave you in the powder tomorrow morning for our Christmas Day run!" Roger teases Haley. "Don't blame me when your googles get covered in snow!"

She rolls her eyes and retorts, "Even on my worse day, I can outrace you, Roger!"

Guy and Josy enter carrying The Twins. They cared for Rodolphe and Gaspard while Roger and Leonie enjoyed their first wedding anniversary.

They scoop The Twins up and hold them close. These past few days are the longest they've been apart from them. They laugh at their parents' overzealous kisses and pat their faces with their chubby hands.

I smile to myself at their cuteness. Then I wonder what it would be like to have babies with Malcolm and where they'd stay: Bel Air with my parents or New York City with Shelley and Morgan.

Come to think about it where would we live in general? I've never lived anywhere besides California other than a semester abroad in Oxford, England to study economics at Pembroke College at the University of Oxford.

The idea of living in the concrete jungle of Manhattan doesn't appeal to me. Despite Malcolm's urging to open an SLFW in the Flat Iron District. It's *the* neighborhood for fitness lovers with its many high-end gyms, sportswear stores, juice bars, and luxurious spas.

But his home in Southampton Village more than makes up for the lack of open space near water. Perhaps we could live there instead of The STEELE Tower. That's a consideration and compromise. Then I'd open a center out there—

"Where are you, My Angel?"

Malcolm's rumbling baritone rouses me from my thoughts. His lips brush against the shell of my ear, and I tremble.

Damn this man gets me every time!

I peek at him from beneath my long eyelashes.

"The Twins are so cute. I can't help but wonder what my children will be like," I murmur, baiting him.

Malcolm growls under his breath, "You mean *our* children. No other man will plant his seed inside of your womb, Starr Knight!"

I swallow my yelp when he smacks my ass.

"We'll work on them later…" he adds quietly as Morgan and Shelley pass us to greet Roger and Leonie warmly.

"This tree is even bigger than last year's," his mother says, smiling as she takes a glass of hot mulled wine. "I love the new decorations!"

After we place presents beneath the Christmas tree, everyone makes their way to their suites while Leonie and Roger tend to The Twins. Malcolm grasps my hand and tugs me towards the stairs.

"How many? I think two is good, maybe three," Malcolm says from the bathroom as he unpacks his kit.

I walk back out of the closet to slip my arms around him from behind. My hands stroke his eight-pack abs beneath his red cashmere turtleneck sweater. My man is ripped!

"How many what?" I ask peeping at his handsome reflection in the vanity mirror.

Malcolm's dove gray eyes twinkle as the corners of his mouth lift.

"Babies!" He exclaims as he spins and places his palms on my lower belly. "*My* babies inside of *my* woman!"

He nuzzles his face between the valley of my breasts and mumbles, his words muffled by the cashmere.

"What???" I ask giggling when his teeth nip through my sweater. "Hey!"

Malcolm lifts his gaze to mine while he continues to mouth my breasts now against my skin.

"Breastfeed… I want your milk, Hot Mama…" he says between licks.

I roll my eyes and cup the back of his head, then moan when he pushes my bra aside to suckle my aroused nipple.

"You'll have to share with *our* babies, Malcolm Steele!" I admonish.

He chuckles before he pulls back with a pop. My wet nipple glistens from his attentive ministrations.

"But of course. But I get first dibs!" He teases.

I adjust my breasts since we don't have much time before dinner starts.

"Well, you'll eat le *Réveillon de Noël* now!" I say as I swat his wandering hands away from the waistband of my leggings.

With a wicked chuckle, Malcolm promises later, and we head back downstairs to the dining room where Josy chats with the chef she favored last Christmas about tonight's dinner. It's like the holiday before, in honor of the French tradition of le *Réveillon de Noël* for the Christmas meal.

We relish in each other's company as we dine on fine dishes and excellent wines. The conversation flows easily.

Once we're gathered in the great room and exchanged our first gifts as our tradition for Christmas Eve, Roger stands and pulls Leonie to her feet with him. The two female Bichon Frise puppies Roger gifted Leonie and The Twins scamper around their feet, playing with a toy.

"Well everyone, Leonie and I have some news to share with you," Roger gazes from one smiling face to the other before his eyes turn to his wife's gorgeous face.

"We're twenty weeks pregnant with a baby girl!!" Leonie announces, grinning like the Cheshire Cat.

Everyone whoops and hollers.

"Congratulations!!"

"*Oh, Mon Dieu!*"

"Awesome news, Roger and Leonie!!"

"*Fantastique, Mon Trésor!*"

Malcolm nudges me and raises his eyebrow as he mouths our turn.

Before I can answer, Sebastian clears his throat and stands, too.

"Roger and Leonie, Lola and I are so thrilled for you! Once again you'll make us an aunt and an uncle—the most favorites, of course," he pauses to pull Lola into his side. "And we will make you an aunt and uncle, too. The most favorite is up to the others."

At first everyone smiles and nods. Then the room

erupts when they realize what Sebastian mean about them expecting a baby, too.

"We're twenty weeks, too!" Lola gushes as she rubs her belly covered by an oversized sweater. "Can you believe it, BFF?!"

"Oh, Lola, Sebastian! We're so happy for you, too!!" Leonie exclaims as she hugs a beaming Lola and they start to cry, overcome with hormonal emotions.

Malcolm bro hugs his brothers while I embrace Leonie and Lola. We squeal with Haley, Josy, and Shelley.

The doorbell chimes, and Shelley waves Roger off as she heads to the entryway to answer. Everyone is present, so we're not sure who it could be.

Roger glances down at Leonie, and she shrugs her shoulders.

Everyone turns to the entry, wondering who has arrived at this late hour.

Shelley returns to the great room with Lachlan behind her. She glances at Haley questioningly, then at Sebastian worriedly.

Lachlan strides right in and stops in front of Haley, clasping her hands in his. Without his emerald green eyes leaving her dove gray ones, he addresses Morgan and Baz.

"No disrespect, Uncle Morgan. We're like brothers, Sebastian. But Haley is mine, and I won't go another day without her for anyone."

Silence descends on the great room. Talk about the other shoe drops, rather the third...

"What the fuck, Lachlan?!" Sebastian growls as he

advances on his best friend. "What do you mean Haley is yours?"

Lola puts both of her hands on Sebastian's arm to hold him back.

"Baz, babe, let them be. It's Haley's decision, not yours," Lola says calmly.

"*Oui*, give them some privacy," Leonie adds, then turns to Haley and Lachlan. "Haley, go to the library. No one will disturb you, *Chérie*."

"Leonie—" Roger pins her with his intense stare.

"*Non*! Enough of the big brother meddling! Let Haley live her life," Leonie demands, her fierce feline gaze sparking golden amber.

Haley nods, and she leaves the great room with Lachlan in tow.

Malcolm, Roger, Harris, and Sebastian glare after them. I swear I hear Harris growl. He's the most easygoing of them, but he's extremely protective of his twin.

"Now, Sebastian, Lola, boy or girl?" Josy asks, clapping her hands to diffuse the situation. "We must know how to prepare, *non*?"

Lola jumps right in and tugs Sebastian to the sofa.

"We're having a... baby... BOY!!" She shouts as she shimmies in her seat beside me.

Her exuberance melts the arctic chill from the air in the room. No one can resist her joy, especially her husband.

He wraps him arm around her shoulders and leans over to kiss her temple. Then he faces their family.

"Yes, a son! A healthy baby boy! See for yourselves,"

Sebastian says as he stands to pass out color copies of the ultrasound images he had in an envelope.

"Fantastic! You're right, Josy, we have so much to prepare!" Shelley gushes. "June will be here before you know it."

"A girl and a boy at the same time! Busy, busy, busy!" Sebastian laughs.

While I chat with Lola and Leonie, I subconsciously place a hand on my lower belly. Then giggle when Leonie arches her elegant eyebrow as her feline gaze that never misses a trick shifts between my hand and Lola.

They join in my laughter, and we hug each other.

"WELL, My Angel, when will we make our announcement?"

Malcolm strokes my bare lower belly as he spoons behind me in our bed later that night.

I place my hand over his and turn my head sideways to speak.

"The em comes before the cee, you know," I respond softly.

Malcolm rises to an elbow and stares down at me.

I shift into a seated position and meet his questioning gaze. My fingers twist the sheet in my lap as I consider my next words.

"Starr and Malcolm, sitting in a tree, K-I-S-S-I-N-G. First come love, then comes marriage. Then comes Starr with a baby carriage." I whisper as I shake my head.

I'm still not quite ready to walk down the aisle. Nor do

I want a baby before I get married. I may be carefree, but I am traditional.

Malcolm opens his mouth to respond, but I silence him with my raised hand.

"I'm all for babies—in our future. So let's just leave it there for now, my love," I request.

Malcolm nods without commenting, a wistful expression marring his handsome face. He understands it's best not to push me.

Instead he makes sweet love to me, pouring all of his emotions into it. My body quivers with need and succumbs to his carnal intensity over and over again.

Other than our passionate cries and the joining of our bodies, we remain silent allowing our actions to speak for us.

Afterwards, I lie with my head resting on his heaving, sweat-slick chest. The rhythm of his heart lulls me to sleep.

My last thought before my sated slumber overtakes me: we have plenty of time.

"I know you'll be busy with your pregnancy, your work with Lola's Coterie and STEELE, and your volunteering with the girls. But... I'd love if you'd design my nurseries... Please, bestie?"

Lola, Leonie, Haley, Blair, Billie, and I sit in my chill room on the first floor of my New York City penthouse while The Twins play with their Bichon Frise puppies and toys on a blanket. The boys including Morgan, Luc, Patrick, and Lachlan went to the STEELE box at Madison Square Garden for the Knicks versus the Los Angeles Lakers basketball game.

The girls and I take advantage of some time alone. It's been a month since we left Verbs and the first time we've all been together.

As the Head of STEELE Children and Young Adults Division and since she did a fantastic job with Lola's Sutton Place penthouse, Leonie would be perfect to help her BFF.

The Twins' nurseries—nine in total, no less—are spectacular and suit each of Leonie and Roger's and their grandparents' residences. They need eight: their and Morgan and Shelley's New York City penthouses; their and their Southampton Village beach houses; our and their Paris penthouses; Josy and Guy's Paris mansion; their London mansion.

It's a Herculean task. Lola gives Leonie puppy dog eyes.

"Of course, *Chérie*! I was hoping you'd ask!" She says clapping her hands as her amber eyes twinkle in delight.

Leonie has always had an eye for design. The combination of being the world-renowned megamodel *The Lion* for almost nineteen years and as the daughter of an old, wealthy Parisian merchant family that travels seeking antiques, antiquities, and fabrics instilled in her a love for the aesthetics. Transitioning into interior design was her dream for years.

"*Merci! Merci beaucoup, mon amie!*" Lola thanks her with a huge sideways hug to avoid bumping their bellies. "We must start with the nurseries here and in Southampton Village. The ones in Paris and London can wait since we won't travel abroad until after the summer season."

Since Baby Boy is due in June, Sebastian and Lola decided to stay out in The Hamptons after they're born. Time away from the city during the sultry New York summer proves just the solution. Who wouldn't prefer to be on the beach?

The smart parents-to-be are on the same wavelength as me. The Hamptons are much better as a residence.

Shelley already told the couple she and Morgan will

stay out there and not go to Positano for the summer. So Sebastian and Lola will have plenty of support.

"Do you want to remain true to your interiors or go with unique designs? Have you decided which rooms you want to convert? Oh, and Shelley showed me some incredible heirloom pieces from their family we can incorporate like we did for The Twins. Not to mention antiques from mine and pieces from the collections of Beaulieu Enterprises. I know just the ones…"

We jump right in on ideas. Leonie sketches on a pad Lola pulls from her secretary desk as her creative juices flow from her head to her fingers. In no time at all she has several options from themed to traditional, down to the layouts and the color palettes.

We love them!

"Do you think Nanny Grace would make a blanket for Baby Boy? Rodolphe and Gaspard's are beautiful," Haley says. "They'll treasure them forever."

Nanny Grace hand-crocheted two navy blue cashmere blankets. Everyone admired the fine stitchwork of the intricate design. The center panels have entwined B and S for Beaulieu and Steele, surrounded by a twelve-inch border of swirls and whorls. She made matching beanies and booties to complete the sets.

Lola claps her hands together and lace her fingers as she bounces on the sofa.

"Ooooh! That would be phenomenal! Will you ask her for me, Leonie?" She says. "I'd love to combine Baby Boy's initials."

"Have you chosen a name, yet?" I ask.

Lola shares their decision to wait until the day he's born to pick based on which feels best once we set eyes on Baby Boy with us, and we understand.

"Being that you and Lola are due at the same time, I spoke with Anita since she's a doula now. She can help you, Leonie, while I help Lola. It's better for you both with me in the States and Anita in Paris. We can give you the attention you need without concern for distance," I say.

Lola smiles at me. She asked me to be her doula. She did not know when she asked Leonie was expecting too and would want to have me help her again.

Of course, Lola's easygoing BFF took it in stride. Leonie rarely allows situations to become problems. She figured she'd make do with a referral from Dr. Berger, her OB-GYN.

"Starr offers the perfect solution!" Leonie exclaims as she hugs me too.

Anita became Leonie's yoga instructor once she was further along in her pregnancy, and I wanted her to have hands-on attention not possible through our Skype sessions. Over the years, Anita and Leonie, then with the other girls, became close. She's now a part of our clique.

"Wonderful, *Chérie*! I remember when Anita completed her doula training. She'll be perfect, *merci*!" Leonie gushes. "I'll send a text message to her now."

"While we're on the topic of baby plans... Leonie, Sebastian and I want to meet with Nanny Grace's agency for selecting a nanny and a nurse," Lola says. "Baz and I figure you can speak with the owners since they're based in Paris before we meet with their New York City office."

Grace Hart is one of their stellar nannies who's also a trained nurse. The überwealthy and celebrities use her agency to hire their nannies, nurses, and governesses. Their training is top-notch in everything from changing a diaper to language lessons to disarming a would-be kidnapper. Even though Sebastian has a security detail for his wife, it's good for the nanny to have training.

"*Absolument!* Nanny Grace is the best! Roger and I will call them tomorrow morning Paris time. Perhaps we can video conference into the call the head of this office," Leonie responds.

The house intercom rings, and Lola answers it to Shelley on the line. The spa day with her best friend and the Jackson Matriarch Lucie ended early. Shelley asks what we're up to, and Lola tells her to come down since we're talking baby plans.

When she arrives, we fill her in on the latest. She's just as excited as we are about the developments.

"More grandchildren to spoil," she laughs, clapping her hands. "I cannot wait!"

She turns to me and beams as she winks.

My cheeks heat, and I glance down at my hands in my lap. The baby bug has bitten everyone, and they want Malcolm and me on deck.

Not just yet, I say to myself. Even if my womb begs to be filled by Malcolm's virile seed...

. . .

"Excuse me, everyone. May I have your attention? I have an announcement to make."

With a nod, Lola stands and smiles at Blair.

We're in the private East Room of Per Se, Lola's favorite restaurant in New York City.

As we walked in, my gaze went to the stunning views of the Manhattan skyline and Central Park clear across Columbus Circle to Fifth Avenue. The other side of the East Room is a glass panel that overlooks the restaurant's main dining room. But prior to our arrival, the staff closed the silk drapes for privacy.

"Years ago I thought I was Wonder Woman and could do every aspect of Lola's Coterie by myself. From the design to the marketing to the management of the Paris flagship and the London boutique. My wise mentor told me to focus on the creative design side and let an assistant handle the day-to-day tasks. In came Blair and she blew me away with her efficiency, dependability, and cleverness when balancing the activities that didn't need my constant or immediate attention."

Then she turns to Billie seated beside Patrick and smiles.

"I learned from my experience with Blair to find someone I can rely on to handle my business affairs long distance for Lola's Coterie Las Vegas. Thanks to Baz's director of STEELE's West Coast retail properties, I met Billie. I needed someone who could handle the contractors, staff, and clients who like me could charm the best of them but can turn into a spitfire when necessary."

Everyone laughs when Lola waggles her eyebrows.

"Over the years, you've proven yourselves to be incredible in your jobs, but also wonderful friends. With Baby Boy on the way, I realize once again, I cannot do it all"—she raises her glass of iced lemon ginger tea—"So this decision was a no-brainer. Blair I would like to offer you the position of my chief marketing officer and Billie my chief operating officer!"

Blair and Billie gasp while the others stand and clap, then raise their glasses in a toast.

"So deserved, *Chéries!*"

"Whoohoo! Congratulations!"

"*Félicitations!*"

"Cheers!"

After a few moments, Lola quiets everyone down and turns back to Blair and Billie.

"Do you accept?" She asks. "I mean, just don't leave a preggie lady hanging, no pressure!"

Billie jumps up and gives her a hug, and Blair does the same. They agree wholeheartedly. And the servers appear with chilled bottles of Dom Pérignon Rosé Vintage 2005—another of Lola's favorites—and a variety of desserts.

"We'll drink for you, Leonie and Lola!" Malcolm teases.

Lachlan adds, "We know it's your favorite bubbly, Lola!"

"Awww... Don't tease my sisters. Although I must say you are missing out, ladies!" Harris chuckles.

Leonie laughs, and Roger pops Harris on the back of his head good-naturedly.

We spend the rest of the time chatting and enjoying one

another. The boys rehash the basketball game, including the "incredible last second three-pointer by LeBron *King* James." Billie jokes about her date with another basketball superstar. But Patrick whispers in her ear, and her eyes widen as she turns bright pink. He sits back and smirks.

I giggle knowing Patrick being an Alpha Dom must have told her just how he feels about her date with another man. Malcolm squeezes my thigh under the table, and I can't help but snort. Then cover my mouth with my linen napkin to hide my laughter.

Malcolm silences me with words said in my ear. His warm breath tickles my neck as he leans over. His lips trail along the side of my neck, making my nipples pucker against the silk of my wrap dress and my pussy clench with need. My mind was already on lascivious thoughts. He just drove me closer to the edge.

"You had better never mention being with another man with me around—or not, Little One," My Dom warns.

It cracks me up further to realize how each of my friends—who despite being Independent Women—find themselves attracted to Alpha males, Doms or not. Sometimes when you're in control of your business, career, life... it's a relief to turn over control to your lover. No need to think, just feel as Malcolm tells me.

"Well, Sir, since you asked... A vision of my wrists bound by red silks to the corners of your bed with my ankles in the spreader bar in your private suite at LEVELS New York. My legs thrown over your shoulders as you lie between my trembling thighs, thrusting your tongue and fingers into my dripping, tight pussy. I scream your name —hoarse from my previous carnal cries—as you wring a fourth orgasm from my wrecked pussy. My pussy juices coat your mouth and chin as you rise to your knees. Your tongue darts out to lap it up, then grip your massive dick to align it with my dripping slit. With a ravenous cry, plunge into my depths and take me mercilessly until I cum again and again. Head thrown back, eyes shut, a roar rips from your throat as you blow your load deep inside my pussy. It squeezes every drop from your cock."

I lift my lowered gaze to his and smile in triumph when I see his pupils blown and his mouth slack.

Malcolm flares his nostrils and smirks, "Well Naughty Girl, let us go to LEVELS to make your vision our reality."

My grin widens, "Yes, Sir. Thank you, Sir."

"Masquerade Night at LEVELS New York, how perfect. How does a scene in the Cellar sound to you, Little One? You bound in my white silk Shibari ropes trussed up from the ceiling above the primary stage for a bit of breath play? After which—if you are a good girl—we will retire to my private suite for your aftercare before we bring your fantasy to life. The choice as always is yours, Little One."

My pussy creams and my nipples tighten against the silk of my wrap dress when My Dom gazes at me with hooded eyes as we ride in the back of his chauffeured Bentley Mulsanne. As promised, he's taking me to his club for an after-dinner treat...

And what a treat he proposes!

"The scene sounds marvelous, Sir. And I promise to be a very, very good girl deserving of my fantasy brought to life," I respond huskily as my fingertips brush against my evening collar.

"Excellent! I will have one of the staff bring masks to the car. No one gets to know it is you or see what is for my eyes only, Little One," My Dom says with a gleam in his dove gray eyes.

I have to suppress an eye roll. The possessive caveman!

"I will keep my shirt on so no one will recognize my tattoo," he adds as he types a text message on his mobile.

When we arrive, a handsome man brings masks to us a pair of flesh-tone silk thongs packaged in a tiny box. My Dom tells me to put them on. Then the staff member escorts us into the renovated warehouse in a prime spot of the Meatpacking District. The building is six stories and has a brick facade with oversized windows treated to block outsiders from seeing through the panes of glass since the interior is not visible.

Two men in custom-tailored black suits stand outside. A queue that extends around the corner of people in expensive attire patiently await admittance to the Dance Club. Not surprising given LEVELS is for the über-wealthy and influential, too refined to behave boorishly. The hopeful patrons are not rambunctious as one would ordinarily see waiting outside a Manhattan nightclub.

The flagship location has seven levels: 7th Sky Lounge that offers a stunning, 360-degree view of Manhattan and across the Hudson River to New Jersey's shoreline, a bar, restaurant by day dance club by night, a coverable pool that's open during the warmer months, and a glass-retractable roof; 6th and 5th multilevel dance club with two bars and a lounge for food and drinks; 4th Level 4 Restaurant and bar open for breakfast, lunch, and dinner; 3rd has twelve private suites for members to continue their pleasure apart from the BDSM levels; 2nd Peepshow for BDSM with seating alcoves, primary stage, mini-stages, performance rooms, and a bar that serves non-alcoholic mocktails; below ground the Cellar a BDSM dungeon with mocktails bar.

Tonight, My Dom leads me by the hand through Peepshow and down the stairs to the erotic pleasures offered by the Cellar...

I shiver in anticipation when we step through the double doors. My eyes scan the expansive, grand hall, austere in design.

A multi-beamed high ceiling; cobblestone floors; brick walls; lighting that resembles flickering torches in brackets on the walls and in metal stands scattered around the room; an assortment of what looks like Medieval torture devices placed in clusters. My gaze bounces from one area to another. An older man cuffed to one of the several St. Andrew's Crosses, his head thrown back in pure ecstasy. His engorged dick eagerly sucked by a younger man on his knees. A woman in a swing, her thighs glistening with her pussy juices and stretched wide to accommodate the large man standing between them aligning her core to his massive cock. Several men and women attached to hooks hanging from the ceiling in varied positions being whipped by Doms and Dommes with canes, floggers, and paddles extending from their hands. Still others lead naked subs by leashes while they crawl on their hands and knees to one of the partitioned rooms for a bit of privacy. Here and there voyeurs stand watching, mesmerized by the decadent, sexual activities.

The sight has my throbbing pussy so wet that I can feel my juices coating my inner thighs. The aroma of my arousal rising to fill my nose and to join with all the other scents. I shift subconsciously on my feet. I'll never get over the initial sight of the BDSM dungeon, no matter how many times My Dom brings me.

"Come along, Little One."

The warm breath of My Dom against my ear rouses me from my thoughts. With a *yes, sir*, I follow him to the primary stage. Where miraculously his kit awaits us beside a table. He did more than request masks…

"Strip while I prepare our scene," My Dom commands.

I comply then stand in my black lace balconette bra by Lola's Coterie—his favorite style.

He smirks in appreciation before he lifts me onto the table. With knowledge gained from years under the guidance of a Japanese Master, My Dom begins the complex task of binding me in his Shibari ropes.

This is one of my favorite forms of play. The sensation of the silk rope bound in an erotic pattern against my skin to hold me immobile allows me to let all stress, problems, life shit, fade away. I give in to complete submission under the trustworthy hands of My Dom. Pure bliss.

In moments, he has me hovering face down above the table, captured in his silks—arms bound behind my back; breasts jutting forward; knees spread and bent with thighs pressed to calves. Only my head and feet move freely.

"Are you fine to proceed, Little One?" My Dom asks for my permission to take our scene to the next level.

"Yes, Sir," I respond with a shudder as his lips skim the side of my neck.

He pushes the table away, and I sway in the air. A soft push to my hip, and I spin in a circle to display My Dom's beautiful art of rope play.

Murmurs of appreciation come from the members who gather around the stage.

Once the circle completes, My Dom grips my hip with one hand while his other unzips his pants to unleash his beast of a cock.

Eyes already closed from the thrall being bound has my submissive mind, I moan in anticipation.

My sopping wet pussy as illustrated by the wet patch on the thong calls to his primal need to mount his mate. He swipes it aside and slides his girth into my ready channel that begs for him to stuff it full.

"Fuck me!" My Dom grunts when he's balls deep inside of me.

My mouth hangs open as I swing on the ring rope attached to the middle of my body. Like a pendulum, My Dom keeps me coming back to impale my pussy on his erect cock.

The rippling of my inner walls precedes my climax. But

I will not give in until My Dom allows it. When I'm at the point of begging, he gives me the command.

"Cum for me, Little Pet! Cum for me. Now!" He roars as he lets loose a torrent of his seed inside of me.

My pussy implodes, and my mind floats in subspace as I hear a faint:

"Good girl. You deserve your fantasy…"

MALCOLM

"*W*ell, I must say, Lola did a good thing when she recommended you reach out to her friend Starr Knight, Malcolm. The partnership with Jackson Hole at STEELE Resorts for her fitness retreats pleases Father. And of course Lucien and me. Father says it was an excellent decision—CEO worthy!"

Lydie's emerald green eyes glow as she speaks.

As always, my cousin hyper focuses on gaining Uncle Connor's approval of her as the next head of Jackson Corporation. He prefers Lachlan as the eldest male child, despite Lydie being the *eldest* and her passion for running their family's business. Not to mention she's proven herself repeatedly over the years from internships through her current role as their overall Vice President.

While Lachlan is their Vice President of Liquor. He loves his sister too much to battle her for the role. Instead, he's a reluctant heir apparent who's happy to take a back seat and let Lydie shine.

Her and Lucien's idea of Jackson Hole beach clubs serve as a prime example. They approached Baz with it just over three years ago. Now it's another profitable STEELE-Jackson partnership. My Angel's fitness retreats add another level to the clubs' offerings. An impressive addition to the revenue over a short period. People look and feel better in their skimpy bikinis and trunks when they're in shape. Getting their summer bodies ready, Lydie says. I agree.

"We should add more retreats to the calendar or develop a theme around the location's holidays or make them a permanent feature—"

"Whoa," I cut in with my hands raised palms out in surrender. "Let's have this conversation when Starr arrives. We can discuss your ideas at dinner tonight or tomorrow as we do a construction site visit for Starr Light Fitness and Wellness Resorts at STEELE Monte Carlo."

Lydie throws her head back and laughs heartily.

Her silky, dark brown hair flows down her back to her narrow waist that flares to her curvy hips and long legs. The cut of her silk blouse accentuates her full tits as they jiggle with her laughter. She's definitely a banger, so I can understand Lola's concern when she started dating Baz.

Combine Lydie's beauty with her smarts and her confidence, and she makes most women nervous around their men. Besides the fact she was crushing secretly on Baz for years hoping to appease her father by blending our families and companies through marriage... I shake my head recalling the drama.

"Okay, okay, I'll reel in my exuberance, Malcolm!" Lydie

says as she continues to chuckle. "It'll be good to see Starr. The last time I was in Beverly Hills, I had a few sessions with her. She's phenomenal!"

I beam with pride for my woman. Everyone loves her, but not as much as me!

"I've had plenty of yoga teachers, but Starr is the best by far…" Lucien quips with his emerald eyes dancing with devilry.

His play on words makes a vicious growl rise from the depths of my chest. MINE!

Lucien snickers.

"Oh my, Malcolm. Aren't you the possessive one all of a sudden?" Lydie says joining in her brother's laughter. "I never thought I'd see the day the rebel bad boy would hand in his playboy Dom card!"

I roll my eyes and sit back on the sofa. Instead of knocking Lucien onto his arrogant ass, I jab a brass stud in the tufted leather.

Lydie and Lucien continue to crack up at my expense while they recall some of my bawdier moments through the years. I recount some of Lucien's for good measure before we get back to business.

The vibration of my mobile interrupts our discussion.

As I remove it from my trousers pocket, I notice Haley's name appear on the screen. I excuse myself from the sitting area of my office to move to my desk before I accept the call.

"Hey, Lil' Sis, what's up?" I ask as I stretch my long legs beneath the desk.

"Hey is for horses, Malcolm…" She responds dryly. "I'm

still working on the psycho sub reconnaissance, nothing concrete as of now. But I found an interesting bit of information…"

Haley fills me in after I remind her ex-psycho-sub, and I promise on our family to hold tight until she has irrefutable proof. She knows I'm about to go ballistic.

"As Starr says, 'take a deep cleansing breath' before you explode, Malcolm. Do it for Starr," Haley cajoles.

I squeeze my eyes shut on an inhalation through my nose, pause, then exhale through my mouth slowly as I envision the anger leaving my body. Another inhalation brings in fresh air with thoughts of Starr smiling at me with her sorrel brown eyes sparkling. The process calms me. For now.

"Fine. But as soon as you have solid intel, call me no matter the time," I tell Haley.

She agrees, and we end our call.

Before I rejoin Lydie and Lucien, I vow to exact revenge upon that *psycho sub* then take another deep cleansing breath to rid myself of the negativity.

"All good, cuzz?" Lucien asks, no longer gleeful when I sit down on the sofa again.

His concerned expression lets me know the breath didn't clear my face…

"Yeah, no worries," I respond. "Let's finish before Starr lands."

Lydie eyes me for a moment, then nods as she picks up her laptop. Lucien turns to his notes. We end our meeting shortly thereafter.

. . .

WHEN MY EYES land on My Angel, I relax finally. No breathwork needed.

Well, except for the air I capture as I kiss her breathless, held aloft in my embrace.

Fuck, I miss my woman!

A month is way too long a period to pass before she's in my arms. Between our businesses—my travels to Latin America and her retreat in Bali—claiming our attention and being on opposite ends of the planet, we haven't had a moment to connect in person. FaceTime goes but so far.

"Wow! You missed me that much, huh?" My Angel giggles once I put her back on her feet. "Maybe I'll host two retreats next month! Absence makes the heart grow fonder and all!"

I narrow my eyes at her and growl in her ear, "I do not think so, Naughty Girl!"

Her giggles make my heart soar. She loops her arm through mine, and we stride to the Black Badge Rolls-Royce Cullinan driven by one of STEELE Monte Carlo's drivers.

"How was your flight?" I ask as I pull My Angel onto my lap on the back seat.

She drapes her arms over my shoulders and grins.

"Wonderful! I love the new bedding. Not only was I floating in the clouds, I slept on them!" My Angel laughs.

I shake my head, "More than you love me?"

Fuck if I don't sound like a wuss. I used to tease Baz and Roger when they swooned over Lola and Leonie. Now, I'm exactly like my pussy-whipped, lovestruck brothers. Good grief.

My Angel smirks and ruffles her fingers through my hair.

"No need to worry, little boy, I love you too," she says.

I thrust my hips up to bump her lush ass with my burgeoning erection.

"Who is a 'little boy,' Naughty Girl?" I rejoin with a growl.

Her pupils dilate and her chestnut-colored cheeks flush with desire. When her the tip of her tongue swipes across her plump lips, I lose my control.

My mouth slants over hers as I claim her in a dominating, passionate kiss. My tongue sweeps the seam of her mouth, demanding admission.

Her lips part on a pleading mewl.

I enter with gusto. My tongue licks inside her warm mouth from side to side, top to bottom, before it seeks hers. It wants to prove it's in charge of our reunion kiss.

My Angel writhes on my lap. Her movements insistent. She wants me as much, if not more than I want her.

Her moans fill the enclosed section of the luxury SUV. No better music to be heard.

I pour every aching second we've spent apart into our kiss. My wicked tongue battles for dominance while dancing with hers. I grunt.

The little minx nipped my tongue!

Without missing a beat, I flip her over onto her belly, across my muscular thighs, pull her yoga pants down to bunch at her knees, and smack that ass.

THWACK. THWACK. THWACK.

She squeals and jolts with each connection my palm makes with her fast-glowing-red ass.

"Malcolm!" My Angel wails under my unrelenting blows.

But for the scent of her musky arousal and the dampness on my palm as it makes contact with her pussy, one would think the spanking displeased My Angel. Ah, no.

The more I punish her, the wetter she becomes. Her pussy juices flow below her butt crease and along her legs to puddle on my lap.

My cock weeps.

"Ooohhh fuuuck… Sir… Yes… Yes.. Yeeesss!" My Angel screams in ecstasy, her head tosses side to side and her eyes squeeze shut.

The rough pads of my fingers rub against her G-spot as the thick digits plunge in and out of her soaking wet, tight pussy.

"It appears as though you missed me and love my erotic touch, Naughty Girl," I growl in her ear.

She groans and rides my fingers as I continue to fuck her just how she likes it.

Her inner walls contract, squeezing my four fingers to the point of pain. One more stroke, and she'll explode in orgasmic bliss. Her mouth opens ahead of her climax.

THWACK. THWACK. THWACK.

My Angel screams in frustration, then shock as I withdraw my fingers from her pussy and spank the swollen folds.

"You will not cum until tonight or tomorrow

depending upon your behavior for the rest of today, Naughty Girl," I purr in her ear.

Her fists clench tighter than her empty pussy. She throws me a dirty look and grinds her molars.

"Ah, ah, ah… One word and it will be three days of edging you for hours before you cum," I warn her.

One last glare, and My Angel collapses with a sigh onto my lap dejectedly.

I pat her reddened ass before I rearrange her silk G-string and pull her pants back up. Another pat, and I sit her beside me.

Just in time since the Cullinan stops in front of STEELE Monte Carlo. The valet opens the door.

My Angel throws one last glare over her shoulder at me before she takes his proffered hand to exit the SUV.

I chuckle. Still so naughty. I love it.

"Starr, so good to see you! I adore your outfit! The mushroom color looks great against your tan. Where have you been?"

Lydie gushes as she hugs My Angel.

We arrived at the bar of the seafood restaurant run by Lucien on Avenue des Spélugues, close to the hotel. Lucien stepped into the kitchen to survey his domain while Lydie waited for My Angel and me.

I agree with Lydie, My Angel dazzles.

The fluid, semilustrous silk brings an understated elegance to her camisole and track cargo pants. The draped neckline and delicate chain straps embellished with lustrous pearls add to the luxurious appeal. While the strappy sandals and clutch won't allow one to mistake the evening outfit for the gym.

I only care she swept her long, curly hair in to a bun atop her head so my collar shows on her swan-like neck.

Perfect. And mine!

"Thank you, Lydie! So good to see you too! I was in Bali for a retreat. When will you join one? The next is in Sri Lanka," My Angel replies as she returns my cousin's hug.

They chatter on while I place our drink orders, then sip my Jackson Special Blend Scotch. My eyes rove the room, forever vigilant.

The glitterati celebrities, royals, and the überwealthy congregate as they people watch as much as they enjoy the top-shelf liquor and the fine cuisine. I nod and raise my glass in greeting to a few of them who catch my eye. Every Steele is instantly recognizable. But keep my gaze moving as I'm not here tonight for small talk—it's family time.

"Damn cuzz, you cost me a stack!" Lucien says as he claps me on the shoulder from behind. "I bet Lydie you'd cop out on us since you haven't seen your woman in a while. But here you stand with a drink in hand, as calm and cool as ever. Thanks a lot…"

He taps his crystal snifter to mine and rolls his eyes.

"You know me, Mr. In Control. As tempting as my woman is for me, I can handle my carnal urges"—I cock my head at him and smirk—"One Alpha Dom to another, you could learn a thing or two from me, cuzz…"

We laugh as he fake punches me for my audacity.

"Come on, you barbarians. Let's get to our table. I'm starved!" Lydie says, shaking her head at our less-than-adult behavior.

"*Little boys* will be *little boys*," My Angel adds referring to her earlier comment saucily.

She hops off of her bar stool and flashes her sorrel brown eyes in my direction.

The girls loop arms and saunter into the dining room without a backwards glance. My Angel's grip-worthy hips sway in the soft silk of her pants as she walks away from me. Talk about making it clap…

I growl under my breath. The minx won't cum for days, I vow.

"Man, you are whipped as fuck!"

Lucien's chuckle makes me give him the stink eye before I follow My Angel's blazing path across the room.

* * *

"This is absolutely stunning, Malcolm! Look at the sparkling waters of the atoll! I cannot wait to go scuba diving!"

My Angel's cries of delight fill my headset as we hover in a helicopter over Mnemba Island off the coast of Unguja, the largest island of the Zanzibar Archipelago.

The beautiful tropical private island of Tanzania off the coast of East Africa makes for a barefoot beach paradise. Its seclusion proves the perfect setting for my Valentine's Day surprise to celebrate a year of us being back together.

We can relax and unwind in the exclusivity of our

stretch of beachfront, where our banda peeps out onto unblemished sands from the dappled shade of the casuarina pine forest. The villa is situated to overlook the Mnemba atoll. As My Angel suspects, it's a scuba diver's delight. From snorkeling, swimming, and kayaking to massages in the beach, to doing nothing at all—plus sex on the beach—that's my plan for our holiday.

"I'm glad you like my surprise," I respond through the mic attached to my headset. "Wait until you see the villa's outdoor bath."

My Angel faces me with a breathtaking smile.

Gorgeous. And all mine!

Once we land, I jump off of the helicopter and swing My Angel into my arms to carry her to the villa. She laughs and wraps her arms around my shoulders as she cranes her neck to take in the island's splendor.

"Incredible," she whispers as she stares at the fragrant flowers, the lizards that scurry into the foliage as we pass, and the white-washed villa.

A grin spreads across my face at her happiness.

"How long can we stay? I never want to leave!" She exclaims as she kicks her legs and throws her head back in jubilation.

I laugh and hold her tighter in my arms.

"Five days, but who knows. If you're a good girl, maybe longer," I tease.

My Angel turns puppy eyes at me and pleads, "Oh, I'll be so very, very good, my love."

We barely make it to the bedroom before I ravish her.

· · ·

"This is simply amazing, my love. Thank you so much."

My Angel sighs as she leans back against my chest in the warm water of the outdoor infinity edge bath.

I agree the view is unlike any other I've seen—and I've traveled to all parts of the world.

The white powdery sand of the beach leads into the turquoise waters of the Indian Ocean as it stretches before us. We're nestled amongst the pine trees as we soak right in the heart of nature. Planks made from native trees and softened by the weather surround the bath. The staff spread flower petals on the planks and tossed some into the water to fill the air with their floral bouquet.

I kiss the side of her head, pressing my lips against her damp curls. A deep inhalation allows the fragrance of the flowers, pine trees, and My Angel to soothe my senses. Then I sigh with equal contentment.

"You're beyond welcome, My Angel," I murmur.

I hand to her a crystal flute filled with her favorite— Krug Clos d'Ambonnay Champagne—and take one for myself.

"Happy Valentine's Day and here's to gratitude for one year of togetherness," I add in a toast.

"Happy Valentine's Day and here's to many more years of togetherness," My Angel replies as she shifts in my arms to face me.

Her heart-shaped face has an open expression of such love my heart stutters in my chest.

Wuss and all, I love my woman with every fiber of my being. I capture her mouth with mine and proceed to prove

my everlasting love and devotion with my body and my
soul.

MALCOLM

"Go Baz! Go! Don't lose them, bro! No one wants to listen to them gloat!"

Harris shouts over the crashing waves of the Atlantic Ocean as he trims the jib sheet of the new sailboat we're racing against Roger's team.

We're on a Guys' Getaway before Sebastian and Roger become dads for the first and second times in just over a month. Along with Roger, Lachlan, Lucien, Laurent, Borya, and Baz's close friends Scott and Porter join us for the four-day getaway. The destination of choice is Bougainvillea Cay in the Exumas, Bahamas, Caribbean. The guys wanted to have time to try out the new toys I ordered for the private island retreat Baz bought for Lola a few months ago.

The racing yachts are on top of the list. So now it's the United States against The Others. Baz, Harris, Scott, Borya, and I make up the US. Roger, Lachlan, Lucien, Laurent, and Porter—based in Paris, Aberdeen, and Dubai—comprise our opponents.

"Scott, adjust the mainsheet! Let's go, let's go!" Baz shout as he mans the helm.

Exhilaration runs through me as we take to the open water at the top speed of fifteen knots. The balmy weather—clear of any rain—provides the best backdrop for being on the ocean. Salty spray flies back and lands on my face. I laugh as I lick it from my lips, not daring to move my hands from the wheel.

"Yeah, baby!! We're gaining on them!!" I whoop. "Let's get it, boys!"

Lucien chances a quick glance as we come abreast with their sailboat. Lachlan shouts orders for Porter and Lucien. They rush to adjust their sheets for optimum performance.

Aside from being Alpha males, we're a super competitive group. Not one of us likes to lose. So it's balls to the walls on both yachts.

We round the regatta buoy for the return stretch with The Others ahead. But we're on their asses! Damn near our bow to their stern.

As we overtake them, Porter gives us the finger and Borya yells back curses in Russian. Both crews hustle to reach the finish line. The winner's buoy beckons to us.

With a burst of wind in our sails, we pass the marker less than a minute ahead of Roger's sailboat. The US crew hollers in victory as we head for shore.

"Yeah, yeah, yeah. Whoop it up all you want. Congratulations already…" Lachlan says as he claps Baz on the back when he steps onto the dock.

"Tomorrow it's the JetSki relay, so let's see who's bragging then!" Laurent adds as he grabs Harris in a headlock.

At thirty-one, they're the two youngest boys of the Steele and Jackson clans. Laurent's bottle-green eyes sparkle with mirth as he noogies Harris in the back of his head. Evenly matched in muscle although Laurent at six feet, three inches has two inches on Harris, they wrestle as they've always done—two wolf cubs angling for dominance.

They're close, like Baz and Lachlan. Although I'm still not that keen on him and Haley, I've let it go to avoid a distance between my baby sister and me. Not to mention sparking Starr's ire. Not worth it.

However, should Lachlan misstep, I'll beat his ass senseless. And he knows it.

"Fuck off, Laurent! Sore loser," Harris retorts as he flips him off the dock and into the water.

Everyone laughs. Then Borya hauls Laurent from the water.

"*Davay rybka,*" Borya rumbles as he pulls the little fish back onto the dock. "We'll do a training tomorrow so you can learn to defend yourself!"

Again, we crack up. While Laurent rolls his eyes and shakes his head, slinging water over us.

"Time for celebratory drinks, boys!" Baz chuckles as he strides back to the villa. "The winners will even pay!"

"Aw hell, dude! Pay what? We're at your place!" Porter responds.

Baz chuckles and nod, "True!"

. . .

WE SHOWER and change into swim trunks. Then lounge on the beach drinking local favorite Kalik beers. In the outdoor kitchen, the chef grills vegetables, fresh fish, lobster, and steaks to go along with the pigeon peas and rice.

The sun dances on the waves as they lap onto the beach before us. Other yachts dot the horizon, taking advantage of the glorious weather. The Exumas live up to their name as one of the best yachting areas in the world.

"Okay, Pops, how do you feel?" Lucien asks as Baz as he lifts his bottle to his mouth.

A goofy grin spreads across my brother's face.

"Oh brother, man. He's grinning like the Cheshire Cat. Sebastian the Alpha Dom playboy turned faithful married man, soon-to-be father will complete his transition to domesticated chap," laughs Porter. "I can't bloody believe it!"

"Well, my friend, believe it. And I'm thankful for it!" Baz responds as he tips his bottle in Porter's direction. "I pray you'll find a woman who will make an honest man out of you. Although I don't know how lucky she'll be. Bless the poor lass!"

Porter throws his head back and guffaws.

"What about you, Daddy of Three? What're your thoughts on fatherhood?" Laurent asks.

Roger grins wider than Baz did. His usually intense stare softens whenever he thinks of Leonie, The Twins, and now Baby Daphne.

"Enjoy every day with your children. Cherish each moment. They grow up in the blink of an eye," he answers, leaning forward with his elbows on his knees as he glances at each of us. "Don't waste a second of your time with them. And just as important with the woman who gave them to you."

"Amen, brother," Baz says as he strides over to him and taps his bottle to Roger's beer. "And I will add, take the advice of those who have gone through it. Roger has been an invaluable resource for me. Thanks, bro."

Roger grins and inclines his head.

"You're more than welcome, brother. Based on the way you've cared for all of us from childhood to now, you'll be an incredible father," he says sincerely.

Harris and I along with Lachlan, Lucien, and Laurent nod in agreement.

Now it's Baz's turn to bow his head.

Then he takes a swig of Kalik.

We sense he has to give himself some time to control his emotions before he responds. So we give him a moment. A brief, but comfortable, silence descends on our group. The sizzle of the food on the grill amplifies. The aroma tantalizing.

With a nod, Baz rises.

"Thank you, my brother. Now, let us eat. Team The Others will need their strength for tomorrow's challenge!" He quips.

Boisterous claps, whistles, and denials fill the air.

* * *

"THE PERFECT WAY TO end our retreat: pumping music, fine liquor, and most of all hot babes! Here's to Harris for the fantastic idea!"

Laurent says with a flourish as he raises his crystal snifter of Jackson Reserve Scotch in salute.

"Hear, hear."

"*Za nashu druzjbu!*"

"Yes, Borya, to our friendship!"

After two more days of testosterone-filled macho challenges, we had a tiebreaker this afternoon for the best water jetpack acrobatics. I—the biggest daredevil of us all —won. So the US beat The Others with flying colors, literally.

To celebrate and to cap off our Guys' Getaway, we came to STEELE Exumas Hotel and Resort for dinner at the restaurant run by Lucien. Afterwards, the singles—Harris, Lucien, Laurent, Porter, Borya—wanted to party at the resort's nightclub.

Everyone agrees to go.

Harris makes out with a leggy brunette in a micro dress damn near showing her ass cheeks. Borya sandwiched between two fashion models bumps and grinds on the center platform of the dance floor. Lucien has Miss Bahamas in a corner on his lap with his hand between her legs devouring her mouth.

While they flirt with the more than interested female guests, those of us in relationships hang out in our VIP section partaking in a rum tasting. Lachlan gained cool points when he declined an offer to dance from a Bahamian beauty with long curly hair and doe-shaped eyes in her sepia-colored face. Instead, he stayed seated at one booth in our area.

"You should have seen Scott's face when—"

"Excuse me, aren't you Sebastian Steele?"

A stunning ash blonde woman interrupts our conversation to approach Baz. She stares at him with large turquoise blue eyes before she scans him from his head to his lap, her gaze lingering on his groin.

Oh brother, here we go... I tune her out and talk to Lachlan about his new blend of Scotch.

After a bit of banter, a member of the security team strides to our section and asks the woman to return to her table. She takes the hint and throws a nasty glare at Baz before she leaves with no further comments.

"Good grief. That was the worse pickup line ever," Scott laughs.

"And equally ridiculous reaction," Lachlan adds with an eye roll as he sips his rum.

Roger and I agree and return to our tasting.

These women are thirsty as fuck! My mind drifts to Starr. I cannot wait to get to Beverly Hills to her, my soul mate love.

* * *

"Babe, what's the matter?!"

My urgent demand results from seeing My Angel sitting in her bed crying.

I just flew in from Bougainvillea Cay, not wanting to miss the chance to see her before I have to fly tomorrow night to New York City for meetings the next day. I thank the time difference for getting a few hours with my woman.

I used my access code to enter her Benedict Canyon Drive mansion, then made my way to her bedroom. She looks distraught. Red-rimmed eyes and a puffy face greet me.

What the fuck?!?!?!

"Talk to me or I'll lose it," I say as I close the distance between us and cradle her on my lap.

The warmth of her body through her silk camisole and sleep shorts coupled with her alluring scent of coconut and frangipani tempt my cock.

Down, boy. Not now.

Between hiccups and more tears, My Angel tells me a third of her clients canceled their memberships after a breach in SLFW's database exposed their personal information to the dark web.

I growl and reach into my jeans pocket for my mobile. Angrily, I jam the screen to call Haley.

"Starr tells me—"

"We're on it! She called me a couple of hours ago—"

"Why didn't anyone think to call ME?!?!?!" I roar.

My Angel jumps, and Haley gasps.

Fuck! Now I've upset them. I'm just so fucking pissed because I just know it's that scheming bitch Vicky Reynolds! I'm going to—

"Listen, Malcolm, I do not have time for your Alpha Dom bullshit right now. I have work to do. Tell Starr I will have an update shortly," Haley retorts then ends the call.

I drop my head, ashamed of yelling at her and My Angel. Then type a quick apology text message to which Haley responds with an eye roll emoji. Typical little sister.

"Angel, I apologize for yelling. It pisses me off—"

She places her fingertips against my lips and shakes her head. She shifts on my lap to straddle my thighs, then leans back to the mattress to bring my body over hers.

"I need you, Malcolm," she whispers. "Make it all go away. All the craziness: the blackout, the delivery mix-up, the schedule confusion…"

My Angel rattles off a string of odd occurrences, but I cut her off with a searing kiss.

Eager to meld our bodies together, I strip us of our garments. Then slip between My Angel's welcoming thighs, notching my ready cock to her warm, wet pussy. I nuzzle her neck to inhale her sweet scent and palm one of her D-cup breasts with my sizable hand.

"Oh, Malcolm!" Starr groans asks in a voice husky from her tears as I drive my cock balls deep in one brutal thrust.

"Yes, babe, give it to me. Give me all of your pain. I'll make you feel so much better," I respond, as possessive of my mate as ever.

No one gets to make My Angel cry. No. One.

I lower my mouth to latch onto a plump brown nipple and suckle. My hips continue to piston with long, fast strokes to get her over the edge quickly. She needs me to ride her hard, and I oblige.

Rolling my hips, I deepen my thrusts. The Prince Albert twin balls stroke her G-spot and her cervix.

She tosses her head and digs her fingernails into my

back. My Angel meets each of my thrusts with one of hers as we rock as one.

I flex the muscles of my back and make the tattoo wings beat. The mantle is heavy with the weight of protecting My Angel. I will do whatever it takes to remove the pain from her. Until she slumbers peacefully in my arms, I give My Angel just what she needs.

While I watch her rest, I consider my options to deal with Vicky Fucking Reynolds one last time. Haley better get me that solid intel pronto. Or I'll take matters into my own hands.

"These onesies are just too cute! Look at the little giraffes doing cartwheels!"

I giggle as I hold the tiny outfit up. It's just so nice to be away from Beverly Hills for a while and not having to deal with the drama. Thank goodness for Lola's pregnancy and my doula duties!

"I love it!" Shelley exclaims. "And get a load of this one with teddy bears!"

At forty weeks pregnant, Lola wants to complete the finishing touches before Baby Boy's arrival. We're in nursery one at her and Sebastian's duplex penthouse at The STEELE Tower. They kept one close to their bedroom, so it's two doors down.

After the summer, Baby Boy will move into his suite of rooms that includes nursery two, a bathroom, sitting room, playroom, and a room for Nanny Janice Smart when she's at the penthouse. They moved her into an apartment on the thirtieth floor so she can be always near.

The parents-to-be chose Nanny Janice since she's trained appropriately as a nurse and has a master's degree in early childhood education. She can dress a scrape, teach early academics and social, motor, and adaptive skills, and disarm assailants. She's a total Wonder Woman!

Nanny Janice never married and is a mature woman in her late forties. Equally important, she has zero interest in Sebastian. I laughed when Lola told me that benefit—not that I blame her. I'd have a major problem with a nanny-gate situation. Vicky was enough of a problem...

Also checked off her list is the completion of the nurseries here, Southampton Village, and Paris in our and Morgan and Shelley's and Guy and Josy's residences. Surprisingly, the London nursery only needs the furniture delivered. Leonie worked her magic and finished ahead of schedule.

Each nursery reflects Lola and Sebastian's homes: the color palettes, and whether traditional, Parisian elegance, or beach chic interior design style. She told me her favorite is the Southampton Village with its calming greens, blues, and tans. The bleached wood and hand-painted tiles keep with the nautical theme.

The girls and I surprised Lola and Leonie with a dual virtual baby shower a week ago. It was so much fun to play the games and to open the many presents while we interacted on the giant screens in our respective media rooms.

Blair, Billie, Shelley, and I decorated Lola's while Josy, Haley, Anita and Hettie Bailey—a friend of Leonie's from Paris married to Roger's good friend Joel—did Leonie's room. They decorated hers in shades of pink and cream and mine in blues and grays.

Lucien had their favorite dishes from his restaurants in both cities for their lunches. The only downside for Lola was not having *Maman* Josy's delectable desserts! Instead, Sylvia Weinstock the Cake Queen who made her wedding confectionery delight crafted a gorgeous and delicious cake in the shape of a cradle. It was an edible piece of art.

Instead of the baby showers being limited to women, we included the guys. Anita and Norman's daughter Antonia and Joel and Hettie's toddler son came, too. Rodolphe and Gaspard, almost two years old, helped to hand presents to Leonie.

The whole affair turned into a fun fete we enjoyed for hours.

Since that time, Lola has had the urge to nest. Hence reorganizing the gifts they received from the shower along with others delivered in the last few days from her friends, fashion colleagues, and business associates. She even reordered Baby Boy's supplies in his bathroom!

I agree with Dr. Rice: it's instinct to use the burst of energy she's gotten to prepare for the baby's arrival. It's no different from mama birds, cats, and other humans—male included.

Lola straightens up to glance at the onsies Shelley and I hold.

"Oh, those came from Anna Wintour. A baby boutique in Londo—"

Her words get cut off as she doubles over with a cry. She whimpers and clutches her belly as she collapses.

But instead of hitting the floor, two sets of hands hold her up.

"We have you, Lola, sweetheart!" Shelley exclaims.

"Deep breaths, Lola," I tell her in a calm manner. "Focus on your breath."

We maneuver her to the glider, and she sits gingerly. The bracelet on her wrist beeps, and my mobile vibrates. A second later, her mobile rings.

Sebastian.

Harris—the tech wiz—created a monitor to track vitals, particularly for erratic or elevated heart rates that deviate from the norm. Plus, it has a fall detection and a GPS tracker for location of the wearer. He gave one to Lola and one to Leonie. The app connects to the monitor, then alerts Sebastian, Roger, Harris, Anita, the OB-GYNs, and me.

Shelley answers Lola's mobile while I check her vitals.

"Lola! What's happening?!" Sebastian asks over the speakerphone.

A pitiful moan spills from her lips as she grimaces.

I rub her back and murmur for her to breathe.

"I'm on my way up!!" Sebastian shouts and disconnects the call.

"Where do you feel pain, Lola?" I ask, followed by more questions about her pre-labor.

Meanwhile, Shelley answers a call from Dr. Rice's nurse. Shelley and I relay Lola's answers to the nurse, and she advises we come to the hospital even though Lola's water hasn't broken since her due date is tomorrow. Dr. Rice will meet us there.

"Okay, Lola, sweetheart. We'll help you to stand," Shelley says.

I clasp her arm and brace to lift her.

Just as we stand Lola on her feet, Malcolm and Sebastian rush in the nursery room's door. Sebastian takes one glimpse at Lola and barks for his mother to call their driver Eddie to bring the car around. He and Malcolm carry Lola between them.

I grab her hospital bag and follow them out the door.

"Hold on, babe, we got you!" Sebastian says as we hurry down the hallway to their private elevator. "Just breath like Starr taught you."

"Yeah, Little Sis. Don't worry, just focus!" Malcolm adds with a nod. "You and Baby Boy are all good!"

I smile at his words, so like mine. I've rubbed off on him.

Shelley talks to Harris, who called because of the alert on his mobile. Lola grimaces, then glances around, embarrassed.

I raise my eyebrows and cock my head to the side at Lola. My silent question hangs between us.

She glances down at her lap, then at me with wide eyes as we descend in the elevator. She's wearing a white off the shoulder loose tunic and black leggings.

Ah, her water must have broken. I nod in understanding and turn to Malcolm.

"Honey, before you put Lola on the car's seat, let me place a towel down," I say as I rub his back.

Malcolm nods, and Sebastian's gaze shifts from Lola to me to Malcolm.

"Did your water break?" Sebastian asks softly.

Lola flushes bright red and nods.

"It's okay, babe. That's good! Baby Boy is on his way!" Sebastian says with a smile full of love.

WHEN WE FIRST ARRIVED AT the hospital, the nurses settled Lola in her suite at New York's best hospital, renowned for its OB-GYN department, of which Dr. Rice is the head. Moments later, he arrived with his team. An anesthesiologist, a pediatrician, labor and delivery nurses, an OB tech, and a nursery nurse followed him into her suite.

I reviewed my role as Lola's doula and her expectations before they went to work in prepping her for the first stage of pregnancy, pre-labor.

Dr. Rice explained in first-time pregnancies, it can take six to eight hours for my body to be ready for the actual delivery. Once her cervix dilates to ten centimeters, he expected the second stage to be as short as 20 minutes or as long as a few hours.

Seven hours later and Lola screams at Sebastian so badly, he's struck speechless. Poor man.

"Let's have the labor nurse check your cervix. Since the contractions are coming closer together and occur for ninety seconds, you may be ready," I suggest as I massage Lola's calves.

Shelley agrees, and I step out.

"Oh! Babe, how's she doing?"

"Is everything all right, Starr?"

Malcolm and Morgan wait in the anteroom of Lola's suite. They ask about her as the door shuts.

Since she and Leonie are due around the same day, the family split between New York City and Paris. Haley and Harris flew to Leonie as support for her and Roger three days ago.

I give them a brief update as I head to the nurses' station. The labor nurse and I return to the suite.

"Let's have a peek, Mrs. Steele," she says.

Lola nods, and I help her lean back against the pillows while the nurse peeks under the sheet.

"Well, well, well, Mrs. Steele, your cervix dilated to ten centimeters. I'll get Dr. Rice now," she says with a warm smile and a gentle pat to her knee.

"Oh, thank you, Lord!!!" Lola cries.

Sebastian takes her hand in his and smiles as he says, "Babe, you're doing so well. Soon it'll be over, and we'll have our Baby Bo—"

He yowls.

"FUUUCK!!!!!" Lola bellows, followed by a string of curses.

The labor nurse chuckles as she leaves for Dr. Rice and the rest of the obstetrics team.

"Mr. Steele, would you like me to have a look at your hand?" She asks over her shoulder.

"No, thank you. That's all right," he grunts as he rubs his hand.

Shelley rises from the sofa and reaches for Sebastian's hand.

"Sweetheart, it's not the best idea to hold a woman's hand when she's in labor," she laughs as she massages his hand with her fingertips. "Ask your father and brother. I'm sure I broke one or two of your father's fingers over the years!"

Sebastian groans, "Lesson learned, Mom, thanks."

"Sounds as though you're ready for me, Mrs. Steele!" Dr. Rice booms as he enters the suite. "Let's have a look."

He takes a seat on the stool at Lola's feet and lifts the sheet.

"All right, Mrs. Steele, we're in the second stage of labor. The time to push is now," he says with a fatherly smile.

"Thank the good Lord!!!" Lola cries.

Shelley places a kiss on Lola's sweat-soaked, flushed forehead and murmurs words that bring a smile to Lola's face. Shelley gives the rest of us a nod before she leaves the suite.

My attention stays on Lola as I dab her face with a cool cloth. For a moment, my thoughts drift to me being the one on the delivery bed. My mouth curls up in a smile, and a wistful sigh escapes my lips. I'll leave it to the Universe.

"He's crowning. Get ready to push, Mrs. Steele," Dr. Rice raises his eyes to mine and nods. "All right, now! Push!"

"AAARRGGGHHH!!!" Lola growls as she bears down.

"Breathe with it, Lola. Breathe," I say as I stand to Lola's right, just in her line of sight. "Focus on your breath."

"That's it, my love. You're doing well," Sebastian murmurs as he strokes Lola's hair that I put into one long braid down her back.

"SHUT UP STEEEELE!!!" Lola growls as she slaps his hand away from her with a kyber crystal-powered super laser stare from the Death Star. It's strong enough to destroy an entire planet. Or a Steele.

Sebastian opens his mouth, then thinks better of it speaking and closes it. He glances at me.

I shake my head, biting my lip as I suppress a giggle. Poor man.

More contractions, more choice words, more killer looks, more pushing, and their Baby Boy makes his debut.

"Mr. Steele, you may cut the umbilical cord now."

Dr. Rice hands a pair of sterile scissors to Sebastian with a broad smile and a nod of encouragement.

I have to avert my gaze from Lola and Sebastian's private moment as their love-filled gazes meet after nine hours of intense labor.

Once Sebastian does the honor, the pediatrician, Dr. Samantha Woods, takes the newborn off to the side in order to care for him.

I comfort Lola.

"You did it, Hot Mama," I whisper as the team works on her.

She nods, resting her head against the pillows. A tired smile appears on her face.

"Thank you so much, Starr," Lola murmurs as her eyelids close.

The labor and deliver may have tired her, but she's radiant. I'm so happy for my friend.

Then Lola reopens her eyes as if just remembering something.

"Baz? What's taking so long? Is he okay?" She asks in a soft voice filled with concern.

"He's perfect, my love. See for yourself," he responds as he strides over to her and places their son on her chest.

Lola's face lights up with such love and joy when she stares at their Baby Boy. Tears stream down her cheeks. Her fingers tentatively touch his soft jet-black hair, and his eyes open slowly.

Gray eyes and black hair. The Steele family traits continue.

Lola peers up at Sebastian and smiles angelically.

"Your son, my love," she whispers. "He looks like you, like a true Steele. Are you pleased, Baz?"

Sebastian nods, overwhelmed, and buries his face in her damp hair.

Discretely, I take a few more photos for their album, then leave the new family to bond.

"Well???"

"Are we grandparents again?"

"How's Baby Boy?"

A grin threatens to split my face in two as I clap happily at Malcolm, Shelley, and Morgan.

"Baby Boy is in excellent health! All ten fingers and toes! He weighs 7.8 pounds. An acceptable size for a male newborn. Congratulations!" I exclaim, bouncing on my feet.

Malcolm swoops me in his arms and spins in a circle as he shouts with joy.

Morgan grabs Shelley in a bear hug and kisses her.

"Lola is doing well, and Sebastian survived!" I say with a

laugh once Malcolm sets me on my feet, still tucked into his side.

Shelley walks over and hugs me.

"You're so very good, Starr sweetheart! First Leonie, now Lola. I want you next!" Shelley declares as she arches an elegant eyebrow at Malcolm.

"Shelley, honey," Morgan says sternly.

She purses her lips, then squeezes me again.

"You're good for my son, too," Shelley whispers before she releases me.

My gaze goes to Malcolm, and he smirks.

A vibration from my pocket draws my attention to my mobile. Anita.

"Hey! How's Leonie?" I ask when I accept the call.

I put it on speaker as Anita tells us Leonie gave birth to Daphne Beaulieu Steele right on time.

More cheers fill the anteroom of Lola's suite.

We spend the next hour chatting while we wait for Sebastian to give us the all clear to join them.

Shelley can't contain her eagerness and calls.

Sebastian and Lola have been so focused on enjoying these first few moments with Baby Boy they forgot to communicate with us. They ask for a minute before we enter the room.

As soon as we walk in, Shelley makes a beeline for Lola and Baby Boy. She coos softly as she strokes his little leg.

"How are you, Lola, sweetie?" Shelley asks. "You look so happy. But you need to rest. We won't stay for long."

Morgan agrees, "No, we won't keep you, dear. Only a quick peek. You need your rest."

"Congratulations, Little Sis, bro! You did it," Malcolm says as he fist bumps with Sebastian. "Now, what do we call Baby Boy officially?"

Sebastian grins like the Cheshire Cat as he wraps his arm around Lola's shoulders while he pats their son's back. Lola turns him around to rest against her big boobs so he can face everyone. Sebastian hands his mobile to Malcolm for him to take the video.

"Dad, Mom, Malcolm, Starr, Roger, Leonie, Harris, Haley, meet Slade Steele!" Sebastian announces, beaming.

"Slade! I love his name!" I exclaim as I clap my hands. "It means valley."

"It sounds badass!" Malcolm grins, his eyes twinkle with mischief.

Morgan grips Sebastian's shoulder and smiles. "Well done, son, daughter! A strong name for the next generation of Steeles. Your brother- and sister-in-law had Daphne, a beautiful baby girl. Today is a great day for our family!"

"Four and counting!" Shelley says pointedly.

Everyone turns to me, and I feel my cheeks heat.

But my womb tingles.

MALCOLM

"I have irrefutable proof Vicky Reynolds sabotaged Starr and Starr Light Fitness & Wellness Beverly Hills, Resorts, and SLFW's international retreats at Jackson Hole at STEELE Resorts. That psycho sub cannot writhe her way out of this intel!"

Haley's triumphant declaration settles on us gathered around the conference table.

We're in Sebastian's office at STEELE International Inc. along with Starr, Morgan, Roger, Harris, Anton, Adrienne, and my attorney Engelbert. Haley called me to schedule this early morning meeting and insisted Starr and Adrienne attend. I flew them to New York City on a STEELE jet, and they came straight to the office.

The room erupts.

"What the fuck?!?!?!"

"That bitch!!!"

"Are you fucking kidding me right now?!?!?!"

"Gotcha!!!"

"Shady AF!!!"

I swivel my chair to face My Angel.

She sits speechless. Her eyes shine with unshed tears as a myriad of expressions cross her flushed face. Then she closes her eyes and breathes deeply. Her lips move in silent words—undoubtedly one of her prayers of gratitude.

"Let's get that hoe!" She exclaims as her eyes pop open and flash with anger. "What do we do next?"

I grab her heart-shaped face and level our eyes.

"Finish that bitch," I respond.

My father coughs.

All heads turn to him at the head of the table opposite Baz.

"Haley, run through the details," he says, then adds. "In language we understand."

She nods and presses the button to lower the big screen to project a presentation from her laptop. In four-color, bold as day, she outlines every move Vicky made over the last year. Photos, itineraries, emails, phone records, text messages, names and details on associates, and more. She used software Harris developed to track Vicky. Then Haley compiled a complete dossier.

I sit back in shock, completely clueless Haley started her surveillance before I asked her. Damn, my little sister beats the FBI, CIA, Interpol, and any other espionage organization. Case in point as to us nicknaming her and Harris the Dynamic Duo.

"Well, all righty then, smarty pants. I'm so glad you're on our side!" Sebastian quips.

Roger nods and adds, "Absolutely! Look how she saved the cases with Delia Shaw."

"Haley, Harris, thank you so very much. I am ever so grateful for you and your work. We had an inkling it was Vicky, but now you've cemented it as fact. I want her to pay. What are the next steps?" My Angel says.

Anton gives me the look, and I nod subtly. He excuses himself, but winks at Adrienne as he stands. She stiffens and purses her lips. With a chuckle, Anton leaves the office.

Engelbert leans forward and thanks the Dynamic Duo before he goes into his recommendations. He reminds everyone the civil harassment orders still hold, so Vicky has them as a strike against her. The best course of action involves a meeting with Judge Susan Dixon, who presided over the case. Engelbert will meet with her at her earliest availability.

I make it clear civil harassment orders will not suffice. Vicky inflicted monetary and psychological harm. Like My Angel, I agree Vicky must pay.

An incoming text message from Anton lets me know my version of her paying is in play as we speak. No more pussyfooting around with Vicky anymore. Time to deep-six the bitch.

"Make sure you handle the situation completely, we don't want another slim opening like Delia Shaw took advantage of."

Roger's comment draws me back from my response to Anton. My brother continues as he speaks on his experience with a nutty bird and the legal system—albeit in Paris, then New York City.

As Steele's we're used to frivolous lawsuits sprouting from disgruntled exes, vindictive employees, and randoms. From my father to Haley, we've had our fair share of legal situations. The most absurd being a former assistant of my mother accusing her of throwing a hot cup of tea in her face. The woman had an adverse reaction to Botox and didn't want to admit it. Everyone wants a piece of the Steele billions…

"Not a crack will we leave for that weasel to slip through," I assure everyone while I squeeze My Angel's hand.

She nods and covers her mouth to hide a yawn.

"Malcolm, take Starr upstairs. A red-eye flight is never restful, even on a private jet," my father says. "Adrienne, are you staying in one of the guest apartments?"

Her buttery pecan-colored cheeks flush. Then she lifts her gaze to respond, "No, I'm staying at Anton's apartment."

My Angel stifles a giggle.

I maintain a blank expression. I'm no snitch.

We part ways with a promise for dinner later with Harris and Haley. My father, Baz, and Roger will return to STEELE Southampton Village. They're still out on the Island with my mother, Lola, Slade, Leonie, The Twins, and Daphne.

I thank my father and brothers for coming into the city for the meeting. They brush it off with a reminder: Steeles stick together.

My father pulls me aside as we head to the elevator.

"I taught you and your brothers better. Take care of

your woman. Let no one harm her, Malcolm," he says with a raised eyebrow.

He's an Alpha Dom and knows my past with subs and Vicky being one of them. So he doesn't judge me. Instead, he reminds me of the importance to keep every aspect in check.

Vicky became a loose cannon despite an ironclad nondisclosure agreement, warnings, civil harassment orders, and her ruined career. My father expects this shit to end right here, right now.

I agree.

* * *

"When will you learn, *narushitel' spokoystviya*? You fail to heed warnings. Why?"

The thickly accented, giant Russian paces in front of the *troublemaker* firing off questions.

"What will it take to make you stop your nonsense?" He asks, then pauses before a table covered with a selection of implements. "You enjoy pain. But not the kind I enjoy, *narushitel' spokoystviya.*"

Vicky's cries increase tenfold behind her gag as he lifts a long, serrated blade in the air. The dim light from the single bulb in the ceiling casts an ominous shadow across the dank, underground bunker. Dirt floors, rough-hewn stone walls, timbered ceiling.

He puts the knife down in favor of a medical-grade bone cutter.

The whirring sound fills the air as Vicky's garbled pleas

intensify, and she rocks the wooden straight-back chair she's bound to by her wrists and her ankles. Her bare tits bobble with her useless efforts. She's going nowhere.

"Such a pretty little girl you are, *narushitel' spokoystviya*. A pity you chose to ruin an innocent woman and her business. All for your selfish vendetta against a man who treated you well and ended things with you nicely."

He pivots to face Vicky with a pair of pliers held aloft.

"You were given chances he so graciously afforded you. I am not that kind of man. No chances, only lessons. Very. Precise. Lessons."

The pliers snap together with each word spoken.

"Let us see if we can change your mind and end your quest. Shall we, *narushitel' spokoystviya*?"

Vicky screams past her gag, and liquid gushes to puddle beneath her chair.

The six-foot-nine-inch Russian towers over her. With the tips of the pliers, he swipes a sweat-soaked strand of blonde hair from her eyes, displaced by Vicky's thrashing to break free.

A menacing growl erupts from him.

"*Dostatochno!*" He roars.

The situation proves *enough* for Vicky. She faints.

I stride into the bunker from the outer room, where I watched the scene unfold on the monitor. Not a scene my ex-psycho-sub's pussy weeps for; but she did weep.

Good.

It was easy to lure Vicky here under the pretense of making up with her. She's still so focused on being the next Mrs. Steele, she didn't hesitate when I asked her to meet me. She just didn't figure I'd tie her to a chair after she stripped and leave her with a scary as fuck mountain of a Russian...

The malodorous scent of sweat, piss, and fear hit me as I cross the threshold. I inhale deeply. Ambrosia.

The giant Russian nods at me, and we converse in his native language fluently. We agree Vicky may be ready to sign the new agreement at this stage. If not, he'll continue to terrify her with the threat of pain until she complies.

It's not a raw deal. Vicky must agree to move to South Africa—far from any STEELE or SLFW property—immediately; end her acting career—already in shambles from Operation Nightingale—officially; never contact Starr, myself, or any of our connections directly or indirectly. Hell, it could be worse.

I grab the smelling salts and pop them open under Vicky's nose. The pungent odor wakes her posthaste.

Her red-rimmed eyes widen in her puffy face when she sees me standing in front of her. Then she starts to beg me through the gag.

The glare I shoot her makes Vicky flinch.

"You have two choices: sign this agreement and leave or stay here with him. What say you?" I snarl as I yank the gag from her cracked lips.

The Enforcer in me brokers no empathy for this psycho sub.

Vicky sobs and blubbers on about being sorry and never hurting me again.

Only me.

Well, damn.

After this scare tactic, she still disregards My Angel.

"You do realize you're sitting in that chair because you fucked with Starr—my girlfriend?" I growl in frustration.

Vicky stares at me wide-eyed.

When I cock my eyebrow, and the Russian snaps the pliers, she nods emphatically.

"Words!" I thunder.

She jolts and responds, "Y-y-yesss, Sir!"

I swipe my hand through the air.

"I am not your 'Sir,' and you know that!" I growl. "Sign it or stay!"

Vicky's mouth gapes at the face of my unprecedented anger. Then she agrees to sign. After she reads the document and confirms she understands every detail, she signs.

"Get dressed in the clothing in the corner. He will escort you to your home and to a jet. You leave now," I tell her, then stride to the door.

"Or I will ship you off my motherland. I have friends who will find good use for you there or wherever they deem fit for a *narushitel' spokoystviya*," the Russian threatens as he cuts her ankles loose with a hunting knife.

Vicky jumps from the chair with a whimper and rushes to the darkened corner like a frightened rabbit.

Good, I smirk as I leave the bunker.

I'll have to pay the Russian actor a bonus.

MALCOLM

"Hey, guys. I hate to bother you during your baby leaves. If we could have avoided it, we would have done so. But Dad said it's best to run the situation by you."

I say over videoconference from my office at STEELE International's Asian headquarters in Tokyo to those gathered at Sebastian's beach house office at Steele Southampton Village. The trip is my latest to oversee our most recent division combined project.

The plan requires Retail, Entertainment, Residential, and Children and Young Adults. Even Lola's input matters since her lingerie boutique will serve as an anchor for the mall—her largest location to date because of the popularity of her lingerie in Japan. Harris and Haley join for their take on technology and cyber security. So the gang's all here, as Harris loves to say.

"Fine, tell us the net net of the situation," Baz responds as he sits back in his chair at the conference table. The shift from beach bum to multibillion-dollar global company billionaire seamless.

Lola sits across from him with her tablet at the ready. She has a determined expression on her face. Her shift was as seamless as his.

"We can also incorporate the children's clubhouse within the adults' and require a form of recognition to enter the section. The added security would ease my worries for The Twins and Daphne. Don't you agree, *Chérie?*" Leonie suggests as she turns to Lola.

She nods and leans forward, "I most certainly do agree, Leonie. Now, with the mind of a mother, I understand their concerns. The security wouldn't have to be imposing and scare the children. But obvious enough for those who shouldn't be there and warn them off."

Roger and Baz glance at each other over the screen and grin. Their wives—the mothers of their children—have become not only an integral part of their personal lives, but of STEELE. They prove their worthiness of heading a division, as with Leonie, and holding seats on the board, as with both of them.

I beam and sit back in my chair as I clap my hands and chuckle.

"Well, ladies, your points provide another perspective and solutions we can use to solve that part of the problem. Do you agree, Haley and Harris?" I ask.

The Dynamic Duo nod and go into tech lingo that's above my pay grade! Their knowledge of their industry astounds all of us each time we listen to them. They expound upon Lola and Leonie's recommendations.

After another hour, we call it a wrap.

I take a moment before I start my next task.

This has been a peaceful month since the final phase of Operation Nightingale. Vicky left that night for Johannesburg on a chartered jet accompanied by a member of my security team. No disturbances reported during the flight or when he escorted her to the apartment I paid for two months in cash. She has the funds to build a new life for herself far the fuck away from My Angel and me.

No drama means my full focus on business.

First, I'll finish my business in Tokyo, then make stops in Singapore, Hong Kong, Beijing, and Kuala Lumpur. I plan to make the most of the Tokyo trip with visits to cities in the area before I return to the United States. Afterwards, I'll stop by Beverly Hills for business and pleasure. My Angel will return with me to Southampton Village for Labor Day.

Harris leaves for site visits in South America. Several of our retail and hotel properties require a review of their infrastructure. He and his team will meet with the leadership and the staff for concerns and feedback before Harris makes changes. Afterwards, he'll fly here.

Haley is over the Pond in the United Kingdom. She's working on a project out of our London headquarters. Some new idea she has for cyber security. Although I believe Lachlan the bigger factor in the choice of her location. Haley can work anywhere in the world with her gadgets. However, London is closer to Aberdeen, Scotland than her base in New York City. How convenient? As though she can fool her big brother…

Roger and Leonie won't leave Monte Carlo until it's time for them, along with Guy, Josy, and Luc to fly here. Roger doesn't want Daphne to fly such a long distance now. She and Slade will celebrate their three-month birthdays when everyone arrives.

So, I bid everyone safe travels and end the video call.

To witness how well my brothers fare with their wives and their children makes me want the same. My mind drifts to My Angel.

We're at a good place, but I still want more. It's been a year since I proposed, and my patience is waning on putting my ring on her finger. I'll let her have the next month with our planned Labor Day festivities and all. But after I return from my Guys' Getaway, it's on.

Mine!

* * *

"WELL, well, well, My Angel, don't you look stunning this evening."

A wolfish glint to fills gray eyes as I walk down the stairs of my beach house at Steele Southampton Village.

We're headed to the village for Date Night with Sebastian, Lola, Roger, Leonie, Anita, and Norman. We arrived earlier for Labor Day next week.

It's the first time we've been together since Lola and Leonie gave birth almost three months ago. They wanted to take My Angel and Anita out to thank them for being their doulas. However, Baz overheard their conversation and invited himself and the boys saying he and Roger are just as grateful.

Anita and Norman will stay through the Labor Day festivities and STEELE Foundation fundraiser. They're offering great silent auction items with custom VIP fitness training sessions with them for a year. The way they whipped Leonie into shape postnatal every person at the event will want to win the bid.

My Angel and Borya put Lola on a mommy makeover regimen—My Angel and her names for things. She says the intense kickboxing, strength training, and conditioning workouts with Borya trim the extra pounds and tighten muscles. Meanwhile, the vigorous yoga and Pilates sessions with her increase mind-body connection, flexibility, and core strengthening.

Hell, she's even put me on her client list. It went from occasional sessions to regular ones in person or via Skype when we're apart. I don't mind it since my fighting improved from the added flexibility and use of my muscles at a deeper level with Pilates. Even better are My Angel's hands-on adjustments. Nothing beats her delicate hands on my flexing biceps and her tits at my mouth level in Trikonasana.

"Why are you leering at me, Mr. Steele?"

My Angel's question brings me back from my lust-filled thoughts to realize I'm licking my lips.

I chuckle and wrap my arms around her, then bury my face in her neck. Damn she smells good, like a tropical vacation all coconuts and frangipani. My cock tents my trousers to poke against her lower belly.

She shimmies her hips in her seashell and starfish printed dress. The thin-pleated jersey material skims her curves with a scoop neckline showing the tops of her ample D-cups. A ruffle hem mimics the ocean's waves dancing around her calves that lead to fuck-me mules.

I smirk down at her.

"Playing with fire are you, Naughty Girl?" I ask as I finger my collar around her neck.

My Angel sub smirks back and purrs, "Is it a punishable offense, Sir?"

My palm taps that ass, and she yelps.

"Does that answer your question, Naughty Girl?" I rejoin.

She licks her plump lower lip, then bites it.

My nostrils flare.

Mine, all mine. Hot damn!

We kiss until my mobile pings with a text message. My Angel growls at the disruption, and I smack her ass before I respond to Baz. Roger and Leonie picked him and Lola up, so we need to get going.

We take my Mercedes-Benz G-Wagen and head to the village.

When we arrive at the restaurant, everyone waits for us at the bar. Anita and Norman are staying at STEELE's version of a bed-and-breakfast just outside of town. It's a luxury property with excellent amenities similar to the offerings found at our large resorts.

We move to banquets at the bar for cocktails while we catch up before we move to our table in the dining room. The Champ tells us about some of his encounters with celebrity clients—without divulging names—that crack us up. Then Leonie adds her handsy times with some of the fashion industries most prominent designers and CEOS of conglomerates. Roger however will hear none of it and growls his dissatisfaction.

Laughter ensues, and we decide it's time to move to our table. As we make our way through the bar and dining room, other patrons follow our progress. Some greet us and others—particularly the women—ogle the guys.

I lift My Angel's hand to my lips and kiss it. Make no mistake, my heart belongs to Starr Knight. We may be the only couple of our group unwed, but not for long. I'll wear a platinum band on my left ring finger that *should* deter women like the ones here who can't seem to control their desire for a Steele man.

With a chuckle at their boldness, I help My Angel into her chair.

Once we're settled at the table, we order our dinner and wine.

Lola turns to Leonie and nods. They raise their glasses to My Angel and Anita.

"Starr and Anita, thank you for helping me through our pregnancies, from the breathing exercises to the Kegels to the last push. Without your support and friendship, our pregnancies would have been a lot more complicated," Lola says.

"Oh, so what we're chopped liver?" Sebastian asks as he nods at Roger.

Leonie laughs and responds, "Of course you and Roger are invaluable, Sebastian! *Merci beaucoup, mon frère!*"

Everyone laughs.

"Well, you're more than welcome," Anita says. "You have a beautiful, loving family, and I'm glad to have had a part in it."

"Absolutely!" My Angel replies. "Bringing a baby into this world is a blessing and a joy. Here's to your health!"

We raise our glasses in a toast.

"Hear, hear!"

"Thank you so much!"

"Well said!"

"Here's to family and friends who are as close as our blood relatives!"

The rest of dinner we relish each other's company and delicious dishes. We end the evening with promises to meet in the morning for beach yoga and breakfast. The guys plan for golf and lunch. Then we'll meet for dinner at Shelley and Morgan's residence.

We say our farewells until the morning and hop into our SUVs. Anita and Norman decide to stroll back to the bed-and-breakfast to work off some crème brûlée dessert.

Once we arrive back at the compound, Roger drops Baz and Lola off while My Angel and I continue to my beach-front home.

"Sweet dreams!" Leonie calls out as they drive away.

My Angel and I wave.

"I know something sweeter than dreams, My Angel," I growl hungrily. "And I'm going to eat it up all night long."

"Oh... Ohhh... Malcolm!!!"

My knees knock against my lover's ears as my back arcs off of the bed and my eyes roll with shudders from my colossal, toe-curling climax. I pull on the red silk cords binding me to the headboard.

I want to touch him. Push on the back of his just as silky head of ebony hair to engulf his face within my pussy.

"FUUUCK!!!" I scream hoarsely as another orgasm overtakes me.

Malcolm Steele is an extraordinary lover...

His tongue continues to lick at my pussy as he laps up my abundant juices with feral growls and grunts. My swollen folds prove no barrier for his carnal invasion. The erotic sounds of his feasting and the heady scent of my arousal surrounds us as we lie in his bed at Steele Southampton Village.

Malcolm shifts my thighs to his wide shoulders and

parts my pussy lips with his thumbs to dive in deeper. His nose presses into my core.

It's a wonder he can breathe.

I stare down my torso to the top of his head. His hair—tousled from my thighs—moves as Malcolm bobs with the rhythm of his talented mouth.

He must sense my heated stare as he lifts his eyes—pupils blown with lust—to mine.

"You taste like manna, a goddess," Malcolm groans between laps, smacking his lips.

I tug at the silk cords and raise my eyebrows.

He shakes his head with a smirk and returns to his meal ardently.

With a frustrated growl, I collapse onto the soft sheets, damp with our sweat commingled from hours of hedonistic delight.

Malcolm chuckles wickedly, blowing warm air into my pussy. When he pinches my engorged clit, I explode into a million pieces. Bright lights flash behind my eyelids, and my hearing fades.

"Oh... My... Go—"

A slick, thick finger once plunging into my depths makes its way to my back passage. The calloused pad rims my puckered hole in lazy circles, then presses against its center.

Even after all our ass play, my cheeks clench to bar Malcolm's naughty entry. Momentarily distracted from the pleasure of him gorging on my pussy, I squirm.

Thwack. Thwack. Thwack.

I yelp and lift my hips off of the mattress. Only to be held down firmly by his hand on my lower belly.

"Do not deny me access to my holes. Your mouth, pussy, and ass are mine, Naughty Girl," My Dom chastises me.

The indignation in his voice would make me laugh, but the stinging pain from him spanking my sensitive pussy stops me.

"Open!" My Dom commands.

Like the obedient sub I am, my butt cheeks relax and my ass muscles loosen as he pushes his finger past my rim —correction, *his* rim.

The burning sensation gives way to intense erotic pleasure with each inch My Dom takes. My bottom hole stretches to accommodate two, then three of his thick digits. He's prepping me for his massive ten inches.

Ten inches in my little hole.

Fuck. Me.

I close my eyes and smile, relishing the taboo act.

"Ready for me, Little Girl?" Malcolm asks as he sits back on his haunches with a smirk. "It appears you look forward to my giant cock in *my* tiny hole."

With hooded eyes I nod, overwhelmed by the multitude of orgasms. I need My Dom inside of me, filling me completely.

In one swift move, he flips me onto my knees by the spreader bar at my ankles. The silk cords on my wrists shift into the new position easily. My forehead drops to my forearms. I sigh, ready for more.

A few well-placed swats to my ass and to the backs of my thighs remind me I didn't vocalize my response.

"Y-yes, Sir!" I squeak.

My Dom grunts.

He squats behind me with his inner thighs bracketing my hips.

I visualize him gripping the base of his big, beautiful dick with a bead of pre-cum shining at its flared tip. A shudder races down my spine so hard my ass jiggles.

My Dom chuckles.

We groan as one when he plunges his massive girth to the root in my sopping-wet pussy. The natural lubrication will ease his passage into my bottom—now top—hole.

"Always so tight and so wet for me, Little One," he groans between rapid, controlled strokes.

Primed, My Dom grips my butt cheeks and parts them to give him an unobstructed entry. The platinum balls of his piercing stroke my inner walls as he breaches the rings of muscle.

The burn returns.

His skill follows it with bliss as he reaches around my hip to tug on my distended clit.

"Tell me. What do you want, Little One?" He asks in a voice gruff with desire.

My Dom's damp torso presses against my back as he murmurs in my ear. Melded as one, he rides me while I buck beneath him, caught up in his carnal embrace.

"You, Sir!" I mewl. "Deep… Hard… Please!"

His wicked chuckle serves as the only warning before his hips let loose.

The muscles in his thighs flex against my hips as he pumps in and out of my ass. My fingers grip the sheets as I pant with each thrust.

"Feel every ridge, every vein and inch of my cock, Little One. It is all yours, as you are mine!" My Dom rumbles as he strokes my ass covetously.

Suddenly my pussy is no longer empty. An impressive dildo slips between my folds, filling my greedy core.

"Yessss!" I hiss as my hips match his pumps eagerly.

With each glide of his dick and the dildo, my body notches up from my impending climax. I squeeze my ass and pussy muscles.

"Cum for me. Cum on my enormous cock and your toy, Greedy Girl. Now!" My Dom commands.

Accustomed to respond on his demand, my back bows and my toes curl as I slap the bed with my palms. The orgasm that rips through me makes my skin tingle and my nipples harden to points on my heaving breasts.

An incoherent string of words ending in a wail pours from my parted lips as my climax peaks. But for My Dom's steel grip on my hips, I would collapse to the bed, spent and sated.

He drives on, chasing his release with savage grunts and growls.

Once again, my body responds to his caveman call. I cum. Explosive.

My Dom roars as his dick expands and jerks while copious amounts of his seed fill my back hole. He strokes through his release as my muscles milk every drop.

With a sigh, he wraps his arm around my waist and lowers us to the mattress spooned together.

"Aren't you glad you skipped beach yoga this morning?" Malcolm murmurs in my ear huskily.

I think I nod then float in a state of sheer euphoria.

Ah… subspace….

* * *

"Happy Birthday, Daphne and Slade!"

"*Joyeux Anniversaire!*"

The Steeles and Beaulieu, Luc and Blair, Billie and Patrick, Anita and Norman along with Borya, Anton, Lachlan, Lucien and the other Jacksons gather on the deck of Morgan and Shelley's beachfront mansion. Today we celebrate the babies' three-month birthdays.

Their party will kick off the Labor Day festivities with the family beach bonfire and seafood feast tomorrow night and the STEELE Foundation fundraiser the next evening. Malcolm and I will stay out here through the rest of the week, then return to New York City and Beverly Hills, respectively.

My parents fly in tomorrow morning to attend the festivities and to spend the week. It's the first time they'll meet everyone officially. Almost a year passed since Malcolm extended an invitation to my family to join us I Verbier for Christmas and I told him it was too soon to blend families. Now here we are and I'm so nervous!

I shake off the negativity and say a prayer of gratitude before I turn my attention back to Daphne and Slade.

I cannot believe how quickly time passed, and they grew so big. They're absolutely adorable in their matching sailor onesies. Daphne with the French flag and Slade with the Stars and Stripes on their caps. I cannot with Leonie and Lola!

One table has a scrumptious buffet from Lucien's restaurant and delicious birthday cakes made by Leonie's mother. The other table overflows with presents.

"Nanny Janice and I spoke about the developmental stage Daphne and Slade are in now. So I ordered a few things," their grandmother says as she bites her lower lip and raises her eyebrows above twinkling brown eyes.

Shelley is about to burst with excitement.

Everyone busts out laughing. She just can't help herself when it comes to her grandchildren.

"Well, if I'm fully honest, Nanny Janice, Nanny Grace, and I spoke about The Twins' stage, too. So they have some goodies too," Shelley continues with a giggle as she claps her hands.

Josy's amber eyes shine so like Leonie's as she admits she's done the same thing for all four grandchildren.

We discuss the merits of brightly hued toys that captivate babies because of the high-contrast patterns and bright colors, infant play gyms, mobiles, and anything else three-month-old babies can swipe at. Along with the benefits of pretend play for two-year-old toddlers' learning and development.

By the end of the evening, my womb—hell, even my inner warrior—beg to grow a baby of my own. Like Shelley said after Slade was born, it's time for me to be next. My womb more than tingles at the thought.

A smile plays on my lips as I recall my dream after The Twins were born. Images of mini Malcolms played on repeat: swaddled in blankets held in my arms; smiling up at me as I breastfeed them; coos as I talk to them. All the while, his magnetic presence hovered on my periphery. Watching his sons, me.

"What has you grinning, Starr?"

Billie's Southern accent rouses me from my daydream. Her Granny Smith apple green eyes search my face as we sit on the chairs by the firepit sipping mojitos.

My gaze shifts to Malcolm talking with the boys across the deck. He's breathtakingly handsome. I wonder if our children would take after him.

He must sense my stare and raises his head to look in my direction. When our eyes connect, he beams and winks at me.

My heart flutters in my chest. My man.

I grin and blow a kiss to him.

He catches it and brings it to his lips before returning the kiss.

The guys must rib him because he shrugs and smirks. They return to their conversation, and I face Billie.

"Ah, I get it. All the baby hoopla. Girl, I know how you feel," she says wistfully as her gaze drifts to Patrick standing next to Norman.

Her man senses her too and mimics Malcolm's kiss with a wink of his own. More ribbing followed by wolf whistles, and they troop over.

Malcolm scoops me up from my chair and sits down on it with me placed on his lap. Patrick does the same to Billie, who squeaks when he nips her neck.

"Miss me, babe?" Malcolm murmurs in my ear as he trials open-mouthed kisses down to my collarbone.

I shimmy on his burgeoning dick wishing it were inside of me pumping his seed into my womb.

He growls and swats my butt cheek.

"Antsy there, Starr?" Patrick rumbles with a Scottish lilt.

He and Billie make a pair with their strong accents, I giggle.

Malcolm however, growls at Patrick who lifts his hands palms forward in the surrender as he throws his head back to laugh heartily.

"No worries, mate. I have enough to handle with my Billie!" He quips.

"You know it!" She giggles.

The boys talk about their preference for the most thrilling of extreme sports while Billie and I shoot the breeze.

Haley and Lachlan join us, and we enjoy each other's company until Patrick carts Billie away to his beachfront mansion. Her laughter floats through the night air.

"Ready to make our exit, My Angel?" Malcolm asks.

I nod, and we bid the others a good night.

Malcolm growls at Haley's suggestion of beach yoga, and everyone laughs. Instead, we promise to meet up for breakfast around ten—no sooner, Malcolm adds with a smirk.

Lachlan agrees, which gets him a glare from Malcolm.

No need to remind him of his baby sister's love life…

"On that note, good night!" Malcolm says as he grabs my hand and tugs me along behind him.

We give his and Leonie's parents hugs as we head to the side path leading to the driveway.

"I cannot wait to meet your parents tomorrow, Starr!" Shelley says before she pulls me into her embrace. Then she whispers in my ear, "Now, don't forget what I told you about your turn when Slade was born, Starr honey…"

My throat catches with emotion. So I nod and attempt a smile.

Shelley gives me an extra squeeze, then hugs Malcolm.

He too nods when she says something in his ear and grins.

They turn to me resembling Cheshire Cats.

I can't help but laugh. Then grab Malcolm's arm and wave.

When we arrive back at his residence, he dips to put me over his shoulder in a fireman's carry. I squeal and clutch his ass. Each cheek a solid muscle flexes beneath my palms as he takes the stairs two at a time.

"Come on, My Angel. I have plans for you!" Malcolm says as he swats my ass playfully.

My pussy clenches as juices flood my core. The thin cotton of my halter neck maxi dress does nothing to stop my nipples from puckering and rubbing against his linen button-front shirt.

I moan from the contact and the ache escalating within me.

"I've got you, My Angel. I know exactly what you need," my lover promises.

All tension drains from me as I give him control. I trust him implicitly. Let go and let Malcolm is my mantra.

Once inside his bedroom, he places me on my feet beside the king-size bed. The maid turned down the bedding so only fresh linens greet us. Just in time for Malcolm's 'plan.'

He reaches around to tug the string of my halter.

The soft fabric ghosts down my body exposing my heavy breasts, flat belly, and curvy hips as my maxi dress flutters to the floor to pool at my feet. I take his proffered hand to step out of the fabric and my flip-flops.

A sexy rumble comes from Malcolm's chest as he gazes at me from head to toe. His hands reach out to smooth along my skin from my shoulders to my flanks then to my hips. He tilts his head to the side and captures my mouth with his.

We moan in unison.

My hands lift to run my fingers through his wavy hair as I mold my naked body to his fully clothed one. No longer does my maxi dress pose as a barrier. My sensitive nipples scrape against the raw linen of his shirt, causing an erotic frisson to run through me.

I mewl.

Malcolm growls.

Without breaking our passionate kiss, he rips his shirt off. Buttons fly in every direction to clatter to the hardwood floor. The sound of his zipper is music to my ears.

His erect cock springs free to bob against my belly as his pants fall past his hips—commando all the way.

Yes!!!

He scoops me up and tosses me onto the bed.

I bounce and my breasts wobble from the impact. My legs spread wide, and my arms stretch out in welcome. I crook my finger at him.

Malcolm throws his head back and howls.

Then he pounces.

I purr and scratch at his back as he strokes my wet folds with the mushroom head of his dick, coating it with my essence.

He plunges deep within my needy pussy.

YESSS!!!

I match his thrusts with frantic ones of my own as our lovemaking reaches a crescendo. His dominance overtakes me.

"I'll put my baby in your belly, My Angel. I'll mark you from the inside with my seed and out with my rings and collars. You. Are. Mine!"

Malcolm Steele forces my body into total surrender. But it is now I can no longer deny he's taken my heart too.

MALCOLM

"*I* appreciate you making the introduction, Peace. We're always on the lookout for well-respected, global, luxury real estate developers who align with our core values. Few care about the environment. Their sole focus on the bottom line blinds them to their impact on our planet. STEELE International impresses my board. We'd like to schedule a sit-down to discuss our forthcoming ventures."

The head of an international consortium that owns vast tracts of land worldwide says to me once we place our lunch orders at the Bel Air country club's restaurant.

Peace invited me to join him and his clients for a golf foursome at his club.

The only foursomes I used to enjoy were the kind I partook in at one of my LEVELS clubs. Now those days are more than over since Starr captured my heart—and cock...

Her father told me they are interested in developing

some of their land in Northwest Canada for a high-end, green hotel, resort, and casino. Peace thought STEELE would make an excellent partner for them because of our recent addition of an environmentally focused development team within my division.

After over three years of being with My Angel—almost two as a couple—she's rubbed off on me in more ways than one. Her environmental beliefs and causes spurred me to review STEELE's initiatives a year and a half ago. The study found we could implement new processes in our development or existing properties not only in my Entertainment Division, but across Retail, Residential, and Children and Young Adults.

Baz gave the green light—no pun intended—to make the necessary changes nine months ago. Since then, our division-combined project in Tokyo won global acclaim for its level achieved in green building. Two additional projects received positive reviews while they're in the early stages of development. As a result, STEELE has received more requests for proposals from property owners interested in our development and management services.

Peace's client may think other developers only focus on the net net, but STEELE still appreciates a profitable revenue stream. And adding a green team to our company added lots of green to our coffers! Cha-ching!

So I put on an empathetic expression and nod in agreement with the consortium's head.

"I absolutely agree. We dedicate STEELE to lessening our impact on the Earth for generations to come. We only have one planet, and STEELE values it," I respond about the Earth sincerely.

From my periphery, Peace sits back in his chair and nods, impressed by my answer.

My Angel taught me well.

Lunch continues with more business discussions followed by sports and the upcoming holidays. Before we leave, I exchange business cards with the consortium representatives. Our administrative assistants will schedule a meeting for next week. Peace and I walk with them to the club's front entrance.

When they head to their cars, I turn to him.

"Labor Day went well with our families meeting for the first time officially. So I'm glad you and Sun will join us in the Exumas on Bougainvillea Cay for Thanksgiving," I say as we walk towards our cars. "Especially since I plan to propose to Starr."

I stop to gauge his reaction.

Peace gave me The Talk almost a year ago, asking my intentions for his daughter and his only child.

As I told him then, I am a patient man determined to prove my worthiness to his daughter. The ensuing period was a courtship filled with romantic gestures, support, and most of all love. Now I'm certain I fulfilled my goal and will propose again. This time My Angel will say yes.

Her father—an inch taller than me and just as fit as I am —pierces me with his intense obsidian gaze.

Fuck! He's worse than Roger *The Responsible*!

But I don't blame Peace. I will treat a man dating my daughter the very same way—if I allow her to date at all...

Peace nods, then claps me on the shoulder. He smiles as brightly as My Angel.

"Excellent, Malcolm! Exactly what I expected to hear from you. I believe you'll get your yes this time," he says. "Sun and I look forward to spending Thanksgiving with family."

Hell, yeah!!!

My heart bursts with happiness. I offer a silent prayer of gratitude and shake my future father-in-law's hand.

"Oh and remind Starr we'll see the two of you for Sunday brunch as per the norm," Peace adds before he strides to his BMW i8 convertible. "Her mother and I also believe in family traditions."

I confirm our attendance as I hold back a chuckle.

The hippie in him calls for his career as an environmental law attorney while his love of luxury calls for a two-hundred-thousand-dollar electric car.

Here's to saving our planet and to living well on it!

"I'm going to turn in early tonight. I have a private yoga session to teach at six tomorrow morning. So no hanky-panky, Mr. Steele!"

My Angel shimmies out of my embrace as we lie on the sofa in her media room. Some romantic comedy movie she insisted we watch just ended—thank fuck!

"What if I say I can get you off in under five min—"

The ding of a text message disrupts my lascivious counteroffer.

My Angel giggles and sashays towards the door, wiggling her fingers as a good night wave.

A glance at my mobile's screen shows Anton's name.

Great, thanks a billion, man...

Hate to bother you this late... But I just remembered a part of the deal and had to go in to the office. Meet me there???

With a grumble I respond yes and an eyeball emoji—so Haley right now.

I roll off the sofa and stalk to the foot of the stairs.

"Babe! I have to go in to the office. I'll be back later. Get your rest. For now!" I yell up towards the second floor.

As I head to the mudroom to access the garage, I think about where we should live once we're engaged. I finally convinced My Angel to open a Star Light Fitness & Wellness Resorts at STEELE Southampton Village. She didn't want to enter the oversaturated Manhattan fitness scene. Her preference for incorporating her center with the bed-and-breakfast-style resort suits a more intimate setting.

So my bet is on us based in New York City with my penthouse at The STEELE Tower and with my beach house at the compound. Rather ours, not mine, I think gleefully.

I even whistle as I put my helmet on my head and swing my leg over my Ducati Desmosedici. The two-hundred-plus-thousand-dollar engine purrs as I start it up. Much like my woman when she stretches, sated from a multitude of climaxes.

My cock twitches.

Later, I scold my unquenchable libido.

It's after eleven, so the night is quiet as I ride my motorcycle along Benedict Canyon Drive in Beverly Hills. The secluded residential enclave has some of the most magnificent sprawling estates in Los Angeles. Celebrities, moguls, and royalty own properties nestled in the natural habitat of the canyon.

Between the gates and walls, nature thrives. Trees and the underbrush make homes for birds, snakes, coyotes, mule deer, bobcats, and the kings—mountain lions. The switch from people populated to animal ruled is seamless.

My Angel loves the area because of its closeness to nature yet offers a superb setting for her environmentally friendly mansion. Like Dad, like daughter, I chuckle.

"You fool! You think you can get away with what you did?!"

An irate voice cuts through the tranquil night.

What the fuck?!?!?!

I turn my head to the right but see nothing.

"No! No, you cannot!"

A glance to the left reveals nothing.

"Now, how do you feel trapped?!?!?!"

The disembodied voice screeches.

A bright spotlight hits me face on.

Blinded, I throw my left hand up to block the light.

My front wheel jerks to the left. I pull it to what I assume is center again but overcompensate. The tire hits gravel on the side of the road. Pebbles and dirt fly up.

Fuck!

I correct the wheel and stop, then swivel my head to find the source of the voice and the spotlight.

There!

A fucking drone hovers beside me.

Hysterical laughter emanates from it.

What the everlasting fuck?!?!?!

The drone bobs and weaves around me.

I will not freak out anymore. Instead, I straighten on my seat and center my mind. Whomever it is will cut this shit out at some point. Then I'll get the fuck out of here.

The drone flies away.

Now!

I rev the motorcycle's engine and U-turn; the gravel sprays up behind my back wheel. A metallic sound suggests some of the debris hit the drone.

The fucker isn't gone after all.

And it has no problem keeping up with me speeding back towards My Angel's mansion.

The drone swoops in low and out fast as I continue to ride and duck my head. All the while the crazed voice goes on about me being an asshole.

"You don't get to ruin me, Malcolm Steele!"

Now, I know.

It's Vicky Fucking Reynolds.

And she's trying to drive me off of the road and into the brush off the side.

Not happening!

I change gears and race ahead.

The drone appears to my right.

I take my glove off and sling it at the drone. It crashes to the asphalt.

Yes!!!

"Direct hit, you fucker," I yell over my shoulder as I watch it bounce.

With a relieved chuckle, I face forward.

A different spotlight hits me, and I lose control of my motorcycle at this speed. My brakes squeal in protest as my back tire fishtails. More gravel spews around the road as my Ducati and I careen off of the side.

Everything slows.

Then I tumble to the Earth—the planet we must protect. It offers me no comfort as immense pain wracks my broken and twisted body. I roll to a stop, face up, unable to move.

How much time passes, I have no clue. Only coughs as blood fills my lungs break the silence of the canyon floor that surrounds me.

As I lie on my back and the cold seeps through my body, I am grateful the clear night sky—so full of twinkling stars—fills my vision. My Starr, My Angel, is with me to the end.

I try to raise my hand to touch her beautiful, smiling face floating before me, but my arm feels like lead. A tear trickles past my temple and collects in my ear. I'll never touch my love again.

A low growl of a mountain lion comes from my left. Its feral stench wafts to my nose. The king is near.

Fuck. Me.

As the soft crunch of dry grass under its pads increases, my last thought is of her, Starr Knight—My Angel.

I love you, My Angel, whispers my failing mind.

With a shudder, I give in to the incredible pain.

My world fades to black…

* * *

Malcolm & Starr's Story Continues: *Cherish My Desires*

Turn the page for the Steele Family, Author's Note, and a Preview of *Cherish My Desires Malcolm & Starr Part III*

THE STEELE FAMILY

STEELE INTERNATIONAL, INC

Multigenerational, multibillion-dollar business luxury real estate development and management corporation

Headquarters & Family's Primary Residences:

The STEELE Tower, New York City

A modern, gray-tinted glass fifty-seven story mixed-use skyscraper on southwest corner of Fifty-Seventh Street and Fifth Avenue within Billionaires' Row

Global Offices:

- The United States of America (New York City, New Jersey, Chicago, California, Miami, Las Vegas)
- The Caribbean (St. Maarten, St. Barth's, St. Lucia)
- The French & Italian Rivieras (Nice, Cannes, Positano, Capri)
- Monaco (Monte Carlo)
- The United Arab Emirates (Abu Dhabi, Dubai)

STEELE FOUNDATION: A STRONG AND SUPPORTIVE HOUSE

Builds and manages attractive, affordable housing for urban, lower-income families

Available for download at **bit.ly/STEELEFamily**

Author's Note

Thank you for reading Part II of Malcolm and Starr's sexy, sizzling romance! I hope that you enjoyed the continuation of their passionate love affair. If so, I'd love to hear your thoughts, please share a review at **bit.ly/ CLBooksSI8Review** and tell your friends.

Click below for what's up next for this darling duo:

Cherish My Desires Malcolm & Starr Part III

At **CharmaineLouise.com** take the *Four types of lovers. Which are you?* **Quiz** to match your Sexy Fantasy: sub, Voyeur, Dominatrix, or Dominatrix sub Switch.

Follow me on social media including my CLBooks Coterie Fan Club below or on your favorite channels below and subscribe to my newsletter at **bit.ly/ CLBooksNewsletter** for a **Free Book**.

Fulfill Your Desires.
xoxo
Charmaine Louise

bookbub.com/authors/charmaine-louise-shelton
facebook.com/CharmaineLouiseBooks
instagram.com/charmainelouisebooks
goodreads.com/charmainelouisebooks

**STEELE International, Inc.
A Billionaires Romance Series Book 9**

Cherish My Desires Malcolm & Starr Part III

Click on the link below or visit books2read.com/u/
4ELgOO to get your copy.

Cherish My Desires Malcolm & Starr Part III

Books in the Series:

Discover My Desires Sebastian & Lola Prequel
(Available Exclusively to Subscribers)

Fulfill My Desires Sebastian & Lola Part I

Heighten My Desires Sebastian & Lola Part II

Ignite My Desires Roger & Leonie Part I

Stoke My Desires Roger & Leonie Part II

Justify My Desires Roger & Leonie Part III

Deepen My Desires Sebastian & Lola Part III

Capture My Desires Malcolm & Starr Part I

Embrace My Desires Malcolm & Starr Part II

Cherish My Desires Malcolm & Starr Part III

A Trilogy of Desires Sebastian & Lola Parts I-III

A Trilogy of Desires Roger & Leonie Parts I-III

A Trilogy of Desires Malcolm & Starr Parts I-III

Series Extras

Series Playlist

COMING NEXT: CHERISH MY DESIRES MALCOLM & STARR PART III

"**I**'m going to turn in early tonight. I have a private yoga session to teach at six tomorrow morning. So no hanky-panky, Mr. Steele!"

I shimmy out of my lover's embrace as we lie on the sofa in the media room of my Benedict Canyon Drive mansion. We just finished watching the rom-com movie my girls were raving about. It lived up to the hype, even if the male lead isn't as sexy as my man. Well, then again few men can compare to Malcolm Sexy AF Steele!

His gray eyes zing me, set my nether regions afire with carnal lust. The full lips and angular jaw coupled with his thick, tousled ebony hair I love to run my fingers through then pull the silky strands. All six feet, four inches of pure muscle developed from years of MMA fighting and extreme sports. Either clean shaven or a 5 o'clock shadow covers his firm jaw. The dominating sex god with wings tattooed across his powerful back and a Prince Albert's

301

piercing on his ten-inch dick captured my heart despite our crazy love triangle start.

Vicky Reynolds Malcolm's ex-psycho-sub who happened to be my client unbeknownst to me. The same client who sought to ruin my company Starr Light Fitness & Wellness Beverly Hills in her zealous desire to reclaim her Dom—now my Dom—and get that ring. Vicky the Hollywood royalty actress who tends to name-drop her great-grandfather the founder of a movie studio, her father a major producer, and her mother a screen siren. Crazy woman!

"What if I say I can get you off in under five min—"

The ding of a text message from my lover's mobile disrupts his lascivious counteroffer and pulls me from my musings.

Not tonight, Vicky. You won't get in the middle of me and my man! I giggle to myself then sashay toward the door, wiggling my fingers to wave good night to Malcolm. But to be sure I escape his amorous demands, I rush through the house and up to my bedroom. The way we go at it, I'd never sleep and my client would not appreciate me yawning throughout her session.

"Babe! I have to go into the office. I'll be back later. Get your rest. For now!" Malcolm yells up from the foot of the stairs to me on the second floor.

Momentarily saved by the proverbial bell!

Minutes later I hear Malcolm's Ducati Desmosedici motorcycle rev its way out of the garage and down the driveway. Yeah, a two-hundred-plus-thousand-dollar motorcycle. My man is a badass rebel multibillionaire—and an Alpha Dom to boot!

Malcolm *The Enforcer* Steele.

The second son; the rebel; the bad boy multibillionaire playboy of the Steele family, as in STEELE International, Inc. His family's multigenerational, multibillion-dollar luxury real estate development and management company based out of The STEELE Tower in New York City. Malcolm is the President of STEELE's Entertainment Properties Division and the First VP of the Board. He oversees their casinos, hotels, and resorts and generates the most revenue of all divisions.

That's how we met, through our partnership negotiations for SLFW Beverly Hills to expand to a location in the Caribbean and in to international fitness retreats at luxury resorts.

I followed my hippies turned into super successful environmental law attorneys parents'—Peace and Sun Knight, aka Jordan and Belinda—footsteps to their alma mater, Stanford University. Undergrad I received a degree in economics, then continued on to the B-School. Not exactly the Law School, so I couldn't join their law firm Knight & Knight LLP with eight offices around the country. I wanted to forge my path.

Health and wellness became my focus after my first trip to Rishikesh as a teenager. It helped me to regroup from the taunts of the It Girls of Beverly Hills Junior High School. Then stayed with me through adulthood.

I wanted to combine my love of wellness with helping others. So I opened my center nine years ago at 25 as my initial goal with Adrienne Anthony my CMO and General Manager of my SLFW Beverly Hills.

We met at Stanford Graduate School of Business. Everyone referred to us as Night & Day since we contrasted in our appearances and attitudes. From our long, curly hair with Adrienne's light brown and mine dark brown to her green feline eyes and my sorrel brown angelic eyes to her buttery pecan-colored skin and mine the color of warm chestnuts. I have dimples to her sharp cheekbones. But we're both five feet, six inches with curvy fit bodies from our years of yoga, Pilates, and strength training as certified teachers and students.

Again alike with our hippie vibes, independent nature, and outgoing bubbly personalities. We're loyal and open to a fault. Resourceful and trustworthy round out our traits. Where Adrienne has a tattoo of a peacock wrapped around her foot up her ankle to symbolize success, I have shooting stars on the back of my neck for wishes.

My close friend Lola Lewis when we met then Steele, paid it forward when she made the connection for me to STEELE through Malcolm since my center falls under his Entertainment Division's purview. Lola attended my first international retreat on the private Laucala Island in Fiji and loved it. Especially since the yoga and meditation recalibrated the petite spitfire and owner of Lola's Coterie —the luxury lingerie and evening wear brand—after she broke up with her then boyfriend, Alpha Dom Sebastian Steele, the eldest of the five siblings. Malcolm is Baz's doppelgänger. At thirty-six and only two years younger than Sebastian, people often confuse the brothers or think they're twins.

Each sibling shares the same Steele genetic traits and works at STEELE International and has a board position: Sebastian took over the helm from their father Morgan as CEO and Chairman of the Board while Sebastian remains president of the Retail Properties Division; Roger, president of the Residential Properties Division and Second VP; Harris and Haley, fraternal twins, co-founders of the subsidiary STEELE Technology and Cyber Security and Members. Each of them head divisions best suited to their knowledge and interests. While their mother Shelley runs their STEELE Foundation, their family's philanthropic foundation that builds and manages attractive, affordable housing for urban, lower-income families. The name is a play on the house foundation, being strong and supportive like steel.

Malcolm and I have known each other for over three years and been together for twenty-one months after we broke up because of a misunderstanding with Vicky. Seeing your boyfriend fucking another woman after he invites you over to his penthouse would end any relationship. But of course it was a ploy by Vicky. The man she was fucking on Malcolm's Sunset Strip penthouse roof deck was the concierge and not my man... It cost us time together, but we're back together. Thank God and every deity in every religion's pantheon!

For whatever reason Vicky moved to Johannesburg and has disappeared from our lives since Haley found out Vicky was behind the mysterious occurrences at SLFW that disrupted my business. Again, thank God and every deity in every religion's pantheon! Although I believe in my heart of hearts, her abrupt relocation is Malcolm's doing—not that I care, since Vicky is outta here!

I laugh out loud as I take a shower.

Since Malcolm had to go into the office unexpectedly, I settle in bed and read my book to wait up for him. Undoubtedly he'll be back soon. Nothing could be that time-consuming at this late hour.

"Hey, My Angel. Wake up, babe. I'm back. Did you get your rest? I have plans for you…"

Malcolm murmurs as he strokes my soft cheek with his calloused pad of his thumb.

My open book slides from where it slipped to my chest to land on the bed as I roll towards Malcolm's warm embrace. I sigh and stretch languorously, certain his mouth will land on my peaked brown nipples. A throaty moan slips from my parted lips. Back bows and arms reach overhead. I spread my thighs wantonly.

Fingertips skim along the insides of my bare arms from my crossed wrists to the outer curve of my D-cup breasts. A thumb flicks over my silk-covered nipple, then with an index finger pinches the bud hard like a clamp.

I tremble in erotic delight.

Malcolm's tousled ebony hair tickles the sensitive skin of my inner arm as he leans over to take my other nipple into his warm, wet mouth. A hand and a mouth tease me.

A mewl escapes from my lips.

"Wake up, babe," Malcolm murmurs against my skin as his mouth slides down my belly to cover my mons.

My hips raise from the mattress when his lips close on my swollen clit.

He slips his arms beneath and around my legs, then places his palms against my inner thighs to spread me wider. His broad shoulders keep my legs separated as he settles in to feast upon my sweet nectar. Lips, tongue, and teeth partake ravenously.

Unable to move my legs and trained to keep my arms above my head in a submissive position, I toss my head side to side as the carnal pleasure and pain rolls through me.

"Wake up, babe," Malcolm murmurs as he slides his cold body over my heated one.

His ten-inch dick rests limp at the entrance to my welcoming core.

Caught up in the echoing sensations of his mouth on my breasts and pussy, I writhe beneath him, lips parted in a silent plea for more.

An icy chill blasts through my bedroom.

My writhing changes to a shiver.

"Wake up, babe," Malcolm murmurs, his cool breath hangs between our faces. "I need you."

I open my eyes, a seductive purr at the back of my throat.

Malcolm's once handsome face floats above me.

His skin no longer olive toned, but gray, like his soulless eyes sunken in their sockets; his mouth agape in agony. Blood drips from the back of his head to land in droplets on my cheek.

His face contorts in pain.

On a stuttering breath he murmurs, "I love you, My Angel…"

"MALCOLM!!!" I gasp.

***

Click the Link Below or Visit books2read.com/u/ 4ELgOO For Your Copy

Cherish My Desires Malcolm & Starr Part III

I dedicate this novel to lovers who shoot for the sky and reach the stars. Follow your heart.

Fulfill Your Desires.

xoxo
Charmaine Louise

WELCOME TO CHARMAINELOUISE — THE SENSUAL LIFESTYLE

GLITZY. GLAMOROUS. STEAMY.

CharmaineLouise New York, Inc. invites you to indulge in *The Sensual Lifestyle* through **CharmaineLouise Books** and **CharmaineLouise Intimates**. CLBrands immerse you in *Sexy Fantasies* with CLBooks contemporary romance novels and give you *Sexy Under Things & Loungewear* with CLIntimates.

Charmaine Louise Shelton the Founder, CEO & Author of CLNY loves all things classic, elegant, feminine, and of course with an erotic edge! Favorite outfit of choice is a cashmere cardigan, leather pencil skirt, and seamed silk stockings with stiletto heels. Sexy Fantasy Type: sub with a dash of Voyeur. When not writing and designing, Charmaine Louise travels and spends time with her Maltese buddies, ZIGGY and Jynger.

CharmaineLouise — *The Sensual Lifestyle*

~ Visit online at **CharmaineLouise.com**

~ Subscribe to **CharmaineLouise Newsletter**

~ Find us on Facebook **@CharmaineLouiseNewYork**

~ Instagram **@CharLouNY**

CharmaineLouise Books *Sexy Fantasies* launched summer 2020. Sizzling, contemporary romance with your soon-to-be favorite Alpha Doms, Powerful Billionaires, and the women they lust after and love for second chances, insta-love, enemies-to-lovers, and more.

Want to chat it up and share your thoughts with other CLBooks Lovers? Read our blog, join our Charmaine-Louise Books Coterie Fan Club and follow us on my author pages and social media to be in the know about the book release dates, exclusive content, giveaways, contests, and more!

~ **Purchase your eBook and paperback novels from my Author Page by clicking here!**

~ Read and subscribe to our blog ***The World of Sex***

~ Connect on **Amazon Author Page**

~ Goodreads Author Profile

~ <u>BookBub Author Profile</u>

CharmaineLouise Intimates *Sexy Under Things &* *Loungewear* debuted in 2003. Inspired by the sensuous sirens and sylph swans of the past and present, the hand crochet cashmere and silk collections are for the sexy: hence, the line names Ginger — Bombshell; Diana — Showstopper; Jackie — Timeless; Lena — Classic. Also known as The Movie-Star from Gilligan's Island; Ms. Ross The Boss; Mrs. Kennedy Onassis; Ms. Horne.

Do you thrive on seduction and being sexy lounging at home? Read our blog and follow us on social media to receive the tips, the latest additions to the collections, private sales, and more!

~ Read and subscribe to our blog *The Art of Seduction*

~ Find us on Facebook **@CharmaineLousieIntimates**

~ Instagram **@CharmaineLouiseIntimates**

Fulfill Your Desires.